SKY DANCER

A Shoshoni Story
by
F.Jos. Diaz de Leon

Edited
by
Kathryn T. Guidero

This is a work of fiction. Any similarity between names And characters in this book and any real persons, living or dead, is entirely coincidental. FIRST EDITION

Published by Tribes Thirteen Publishing 1201 Quing-ah Ln., Lone Pine, CA 93545-1063

Manufactured in the United States of America.

ISBN 13: 978-0-615-66277-0

ISBN Converted: 0615662773

"Shoshoni Warrior" book cover artwork: Garret Spoonhunter Copyright 1997. Prints available write to: P.O. Box 493, Bishop, CA. 93514

DEDICATION

This book is dedicated to the First Nations of the Owens Valley Band of Paiute and Shoshone Indians, The Benton Paiute Nation, The Mono Paiute Tribe, Bishop Paiute Tribe, The Big Pine Paiute Tribe, The Fort Independence Northern Paiute Nation, The Lone Pine Paiute/Shoshone Tribe, The Death Valley Timbisha Tribe, The Kawaiisu Shoshoni Tribe.

ACKNOWLEDGEMENTS

Acknowledgements for Sky Dancer go to the countless individuals who contributed their undocumented stories about the history of the Owens Valley.

The Tribes of the Owens Valley, for their continuing effort to survive as nations within the greatest nation of all, the United States of America.

Garrett Spoonhunter, for his permission to use the ©"Shoshoni Warrior" print for the "Sky Dancer" book Cover.

INTRODUCTION

As far back as 1912 the Los Angeles aqueduct project and the means of its construction financiers had experienced numerous setbacks. The elements of nature seemed to hamper the project at every turn, windstorms destroying vital excavators, flooding tunnels, unbearable heat in the day, and freezing temperatures at night. Financial backers became weary of propping up the project whenever costs would spike unexpectedly, demanding more under the table money. Illicit as it was, the money continued to flow in from scheming real estate speculators. The 'L.A. Syndicate' was the tag attached to the project backers by newspaper reporters who uncovered the scheme.

However, the project continued to chug along, much like a broken down merry-go-round; warped music and all. Disgruntled by questionable covert land acquisition, women's social clubs, and church organizations joined with local power companies, and together they stepped up their newspaper bombardment on the aqueduct project. Public pressure forced a formal investigation into dealings concerning San Fernando Valley, and the Syndicate.

The investigation breathed new life into previous charges of fraud, subsequently exposing the aqueduct project as a creature born of the L.A. elite. Short of a decade later, the Los Angeles Water Department continued its assault in the Owens Valley, obtaining land with specific water rights. The 1920 Federal Census gave evidence as to the number of ranchers and farmers who were still turning fertile soil and raising cattle herds in the Owens Valley. They were prospering, continuing to grow award winning crops year after year, despite Mulholland's efforts to destroy their livelihood. The growers banded together, making known their protest and grievances through public meetings in each of the four towns in the Owens Valley. Some of the ranchers pressed on seemingly unaffected, refusing to sell their land at $1.25 an acre; the offer made by the city. In the oncoming conflict the valley residents would find themselves pitted against a city whose inhabitants knew little or nothing about their plight.

And yet, for other residents in the Owens Valley, it was hard to grasp the onslaught. Year after year they enjoyed bumper crops of new mown hay, lush alfalfa fields, vineyards, and orchards. One thing was certain; the naked aggression perpetrated by the LA Syndicate and the Los Angeles Water Board assumed the mission to procure as much land as possible. In the coming years, ranchers and farmers would stand helplessly in witness to an intentional destabilization of Inyo County. As farms and alfalfa fields dried up, and cattle ranches made insolvent, land purchases by Los Angeles soared. Most major newsprint pointed to poor management and drought, but those who were forced into the sale of their land saw the actual cause of the financial collapse. By the time the alarm bells were heard in the Owens Valley it was too late.

PREFACE

Inside the King Edward Lounge, downtown Los Angeles continues into the day at its usual bustling pace. James Fink, a reporter for the Times-Review, drops a parchment copy down onto the table. The thin papered page floats down onto the table. He takes his wire-rimmed bifocals from his nose, and rubs his weary eyes.

"I can't believe I missed that," says Fink.

Sitting across from him is a longtime friend, and fellow journalist, Bernard Smith. The San Francisco Chronicle, is where Bernard hangs his hat when reporting.

"I can believe it - the Chronicle has done everything but come down here and bite you guys on the ass to get you to run a story on a nonexistent draught," says Bernard in disappointment.

"I've been working on an angle to expose the water department, it hasn't been easy Bernie," replies Fink.

"And the St. Francis Dam?" Bernard says with appalling tone.

"We go back a long way Jim, and it's always been my opinion that nothing gets passed you," adds Bernard.

"Believe me, the crap that's been going on here in L.A. is like some nightmarish movie script that spun out of Europe," says Fink as he takes the document that Bernard nudges towards him.

"You have my full permission to use it, but get it into print soon, these nappy southlanders need something to wake them back into reality," insists Bernard.

"The Editor in Chief has already made it clear to me that he will stand by the acquisition of water, no matter what," says Fink. His take on this article will be 'drought is   drought', you can't argue with Mother nature," says Fink.

"See there? That's a perfect example of what I'm talking about. The people down here; they read something presented in newsprint, even suggesting a drought, and you cry out thirst. Next thing you know, Angelenos are drying up on the vine," says Bernard

"The rest of the state is fine. Jimmy, there is no drought. Get this article into print," he insists. Without another word, a brief handshake is offered, and he points to Fink with a delegating finger, as he leaves.

Now alone at the table, Fink begins to realize that leaving the Owens Valley for his home in Los Angeles was not so easy, his story has followed him home. The thought of the St. Francis Dam filling with water, leaves him deeply concerned.

The ominous words of his old Shoshoni friend begin to echo in his thoughts;

"the river will strike out like a snake that's been grabbed by its tail."

Fink reels from the aspect of the St. Francis Dam failing, filled with stored water from the Owens Valley. His only hope lies on the desk of his Editor in Chief; his article exposing the politics of the water war in the Owens Valley.

The consequences of a failure were too horrific to imagine. The unending water supply, transported via the aqueduct, silently flows day and night, destined to be stored behind a structurally compromised St. Francis dam. Will the article come out in time to warn the residents of several towns below the dam? With only a single word from the principle architect of the dam, the flow could be shut off, averting the catastrophe.

CHAPTER ONE
The Assignment

Eastern California desert, a bearded prospector, cups his ear as he looks off into the distance. The old man pulls a watch from his pocket, then turns to his pack animal.

"She's right on time girl," he says. The old timer hobbles over to "Suzy," a donkey with one flop ear, and a haired out head. He lifts a canvas feed bag from her nose. The prospector shakes the bag and peers downward, seeing only a few grains of feed, he becomes discouraged.

"Well, that's the last of the oats Suzy girl, you'll have to wait until we reach the springs, there's plenty of green grass there," he says to the animal. Suzy's long donkey-ears perk up and her head turns toward the direction of the valley floor down below.

There, in the distance, over a multitude of time worn banks of dry gulches, he sees a single pillar of billowy vapor, and then a well orchestrated din of iron and steel begins to fill the morning air. The old timer squints to get a better view of the northward bound steam engine. The prospector takes a moment to watch the locomotive steam into the valley below.

The *Slim Princess*, a Nevada and California Railway engine, is on schedule and is rolling towards the Mt. Whitney Train Depot, one of several destination stops in the Owens Valley. Today the Slim Princess is pulling a full line of freight cars, hauling everything from mining machinery, lumber, and mercantile goods.

Through a window of the barreling train, is a rail traveler by the name of James Fink, a reporter for the Los Angeles Times-Tribune. Inside the only passenger coach on the train are twelve passengers, seated randomly among each other. James Fink seems preoccupied, looking down at a photo, and staring out of the window intermittently. After a deep sigh while recalling a farewell kiss, shared with his fiancee at Grand Central Train Station in Los Angeles, he wishes the assignment had been delegated to another.

To compound matters, his disposition has placed him in an irrational state of mind. Fink begins to yearn for the simple ambiances. The searing heat brings to mind the cool ocean surf rolling onto the beaches at Santa Monica bay, palm trees, plush lawns, and swimming pools.

For now, Fink must deal with the fact that it is his first time in a desert region. Except for extensive research pertaining to the desert highlands, he has not experienced a single day in any California desert.

"I write for a living, so I may as well get to work, there may be some sort of storyline that I can salvage from this experience," he thinks to himself. A pencil point is touched to his tongue, and he begins to write…

"A spectacular sunrise has once again laid claim to another inhospitable California wilderness… here in the desert, nature's recital is continuous, and unrelenting. A dry wind pushes sand across the desert floor, spiraling up to form wandering dust devils…"

A slight notion of accomplishment satisfies the sudden whim, and the pencil is placed back into the fold of his tablet. Through the window and up ahead, he can see that the train has come to a long sweeping turn. He sees the sun's reflection glistening through a tall grove of tall Joshua trees. He continues to observe the surroundings as two lines of shinning steel rails disappear into an arid horizon.

At ground level, a diamond back Rattlesnake, slithers over the warming steel of the rail track. The 'gentleman of the desert', as called by some, pauses to absorb the vibration caused by the oncoming train. In a wavering apparition; a curtain of sun warped images rise into the air. A deafening steam whistle breaks the calmness of this northern desert plain. The snake coils and prepares to strike as the railway cars roar past. Fink's destination point is an exclusive part of California, other than an automobile or horse drawn wagon, railway is the most popular mode of transportation in and out of the mountain region of the Eastern Sierra.

The current year is 1924, and newspapers around the world have headlined the death of Vladimir Lenin; The first Winter Olympics is held in Chamonix, France; Charles Lindbergh is ordered to report and serve in the United States Army Air Corps; and the American Indian Citizenship Act is enacted by the United States Congress. Covering such stories is James Fink, as an investigative reporter, his exploits have led him into some very lucrative stories involving politicians and city officials. Having just celebrated his 28th birthday two weeks prior, he feels that if he submits one more expose' he may land a position as an assistant Editor in Chief. But on this particular day he finds himself feeling much older, but not much wiser, for he is on a news assignment that continues to cloud his thoughts with doubt.

Inside the only passenger coach on the entire train, Fink is seated among twelve passengers. William Mulholland, the Chief Architect of the Los Angeles aqueduct, and the subject of Fink's story, is riding in the same coach. By some accounts, it was reported that Mulholland insisted on the journey to personally assess damage caused by bombings to the aquaduct. The Los Angeles Water Board had arranged that a reporter accompany his entourage to cover the journey, but mainly to cast in a positive light, a storyline of Mulholland's return to the Owens Valley.

As with all news worthy stories, his work requires hours of tedious fact finding, part of the territory he reluctantly accepts. It is for this reason Fink was chosen for the assignment, his level of instinct combined with background knowledge of the bombings, placed him at the top of staff reporters at Time-Tribune. When the chief editor received a tip that Mulholland was heading to the Owens Valley, he called on Fink to cover the journey. In doing so, he knew the situation could turn deadly; entering into a land of turmoil. If the chief engineer of the aqueduct were to meet with an untimely tragedy, the chief editor wanted Fink to be there when it happened.

Research had shown that the Water Department's endless export of water, brought protest and claims of fraud. Intentional or not, the destabilization of the entire economy could not stop the Owens Valley citizens from shouting out allegations of corruption.

Fink could sense deep resentment, so much, that the valley locals referred to Los Angeles as the "City" and the aqueduct as the "Ditch", monikers that were created to refrain from saying the actual names. It is a plan of aggressive approach, and Fink will have to apply his best journalism techniques in seeking out the truth behind the upheaval in a once peaceful valley.

The blaring sound of a steam whistle startles Fink back into reality as he twists and turns in his seat, trying to get comfortable on the hard oak seat. He glances toward Mulholland, seated several seats back, he seems to be writing, or drawing something onto a note book. Hearing from different sources that Mulholland did not know how to read or write, he wonders what he is doing with a pad and pencil. It looks to Fink that he may be writing.

"He's an engineer; probably sketching something," Fink thinks to himself.

The constant clang of the tracks, has become annoying. The racket takes on cadence, a noise that strangely causes him to recall the equally annoying words of his boss:

"Get to the bottom of it, Jimmy. Get as much information as you can on those hooligans. We'll send them a clear message; terrorist acts of aggression against Los Angeles and its water system, cannot and will not be tolerated, not by this paper," barked his editor. Even though his request was steeped with political overtone,

Fink understood the tinge of vengeance his boss vented in his rant, Knowing that the Times-Tribune Building had been bombed several years earlier. In his research, he found that it was a matter of record that the egregious acts and methods used by Los Angeles to acquire land and water rights in the Owens Valley seemed abhorrent to everyone except those who lived in the Los Angeles basin. Further findings revealed that the Water Board failed to negotiate timely reparation claims, those claims arising out of damages from loss of profit, and undue decline of property value.

Now it is Fink's job to find an angle from which a story could be used to minimize the fallout from the fraud perpetrated upon the farmers in the Owens Valley. At this point, his assessment of the conflict was that when reparations from the City were denied, the gloves came off. The arrogant denial from the Los Angeles City Attorney Office is what triggered the aqueduct bombings.

In Fink's way of thinking, he had reason to believe that LA had a deeper, more sinister plan for the Owens Valley. Digging back into the past, he found that the valley had great potential for being an agricultural boon. The long growing season gave farmers a huge advantage over most producing farms in California. Real estate developers in Los Angeles plotted to undermine the economy in the Owens Valley to bring about a valley wide economical crash, preventing expanded agricultural production. Aqueduct export levels would drop if existing agriculture were not curtailed. By losing half of the water to the OV farmers, the loss would cut into profits of the Los Angeles WaterBoard and developers who needed the water for track homes. Fink caught on to the covert plan, and the facts implicated a huge story, once circulated, would cast Los Angeles in a very bad light.

When Los Angeles disagreed with the US Department of the Interior, whose representatives stated that if water would be denied to the farmers in the Owens Valley; why then would the Owens River water be used to irrigate crops in the San Fernando Valley?" The question went unanswered.

A few days before Fink's arrival in Lone Pine, aqueduct engineers deemed the damage done by the dynamite, as moderate. Even though, the destruction had no real effect on the Los Angeles Water Board, but, the event had them deeply concerned about an ongoing shortage of water delivery to the city.

The conflict left the reporter with doubts about the journey, careful considerations to back out left him hesitant, but he determined an assignment of this magnitude may prove to be beneficial. Other concerns were the job requirements for reporting a story in a rough and ready cow town like Lone Pine.

His instincts tell him that his abilities may fall short from his journalistic call to duty. The cowboys and mine workers will demand a certain amount of respect from strangers, especially those from the city.

"Note to self: Must learn to duck and run fast." Even though, being the youngest of five brothers, had it's advantages, Fink was not about to be dismissed as a tenderfoot. A serious decision was made to apply his skills to the best of his ability, or fall beneath trampling hoofs of a stampede in the streets of Lone Pine.

A preliminary background check on the small destination town revealed its beginnings as a cattle town surrounded by nearby silver, lead, and gold mines. The town is also suspect of collusion, harboring secrets and information of the aqueduct bombings. The numerous investigators hired by LA to gather and report information pertinent to the bombings, this activity made Lone Pine the epicenter of the chaos brought by the water conflict. The research further revealed that investigations brought by the LA City Attorney Office, concluded that Lone Pine was a staging ground for the acquisition of dynamite, blasting caps, and vigilant activists. These ingredients were readily accessible in Lone Pine. An assumption that the city attorney could not back up with evidence or witnesses.

Although miners had no dog in the fight, they were sympathetic to the ranchers and farmers struggling for their rights in the Owens Valley. As it happened, when the accusations surfaced, mine workers up and down the valley were proud to learn that they were included in such an important struggle for rights. Word of mouth spread to miners in communities of Darwin and Keeler and Independence. Weekend activity increased among miners enjoying time off in town, spending their earnings in the local saloons, and stay with locals, or relatives. Few miners and their cohorts provided explosives which were stored until needed. Lone Pine continued to be a topic spoke in whipper only.

Fink, as an investigative reporter, has to resort to base instinct, only because realizing that he will be working and living within what seemed to be a micro melting pot, much like Los Angeles. One thing for sure, his confidence is high when it comes to dishing out a serious ration of BS from time to time. With a few small town peculiarities he salvaged from his adolescence, when living in Pasadena, he hopes to at least hide in plain sight as a pariah seeking a story for a not so popular newspaper.

A thought stops him cold, he has reminded himself that in the big city, his mild mannerisms and his astute stature usually gets him by. But Lone Pine may put him to the test. Fink rubs his hand over his smooth face, and removes his round wire-rimmed glasses.

"Well, maybe I should grow a beard" he thought;

"On the other hand, these boyish looks, and muscular build may get me by on the woman's vote," he says to himself.

This is Fink's first experience at traveling an extended railway by way of narrow gauge. A quote comes to mind, one he came across previously in his research. In 1883 The Carson & Colorado Railway, came to completion. An Inaugural run was celebrated with a 300 mile railway trip, which stated in the Virginia City, Nevada area, and ended in Keeler, California. One of the officials was quoted as saying; "Gentlemen, either we built this line 300 miles too long, or 300 years too soon," the quote brings a chuckle to Fink.

On this particular trip, after having her freight cars loaded in the railway town of Mojave, the Slim Princess pulls out of Mojave with an extra heavy load of supplies bound for the Owens Valley. The main cargo consists of mining equipment, to include a rock crushing machine, ore cars and heavy timber.

The Slim Princess, on an average round trip maintains a speed of 45 to 55 miles per hour. but she begins to slow as it begins to climb a grade at the north end of Rose Valley. The windows are opened to catch the outside air, but due to the desert sun, the coach is continually heating up with every passing mile. The rising heat, and a slow moving train, combined with the hard oak seats, has Fink dreading the rest of his journey. In an effort to read through one of his files, the constant rocking of the rail coach has him wondering if car sickness is about to add to his mounting misery.

The realization that even the peculiar sounds of the train are beginning to affect him. Bare metal on metal and the creaking of sun parched wood, vibrate into Fink's skull.

"If I had to write about this journey, I wouldn't mention my cowardly intentions in wanting to jump ship at the next stop," he thinks to himself.

Looking outward, the coach window reflects his image against the desolate landscape. Fink begins to wonder if he is in the early stages of heat stroke "Next stop?" he wonders. Visions of a pale, and dehydrated cartoon man, with X's over both eyes flood his thoughts.

"They may find me dead in my seat, clutching my notes on Mulholland," he says to himself in thought.

"I hope there'll be something inspiring for me in Lone Pine," he says under his breath. As for now, fifty miles of endless sagebrush is not doing anything for his creative juices.

The dire daydream comes to abrupt end hearing a sharp 'snap' of a briskly opened newspaper. His attention is grabbed by a passenger seated in the next seat up. Fink realizes it is a copy of the Owens Valley Herald, not the Times-Tribune. As the paper is opened wider, Fink strains to catch the headline date. It shows Friday, November 14, 1924, below the headline: 'THE VALLEY OF BROKEN HEARTS'. Fink gooseneck's closer to read into the article, but the man holding the newspaper becomes annoyed. The burly looking, man in bad need of a shave, turns in his seat, and while chewing on a stubbed cigar, speaks without taking the cigar from his clenched teeth.

"Why not just slide on over? You can sit on my lap, and we can both read it together," says the passenger in perfect alpha male character. A gruff, cough-like laugh is heard from a few seats back. Fink sits back, his instincts tells him that it is an amused Mulholland; letting go with a hardy whiskey cackled laugh.

Embarrassed, Fink accepts the humiliation and brings himself to re-focus on the assignment. After the brief interlude from the monotonous train ride. Up until now, laugher seems to be the high light of the journey. Mulholland clears his throat and resumes toiling with paperwork.

"Well, I know now that he has a sense of humor," says Fink under his breath. He turns slightly in his seat, looking in Mulholland's general direction, being very careful not to look directly at him.

"I made him laugh, the man who brought water to Los Angeles; I did something that made him laugh," Fink thinks to himself, hoping that he will not have to work it into part of a byline. Fink notices that the clamor has slowed, he peers out the window of the now slow moving train is pulling and incline. The smoke from the steam engine thickens and invades the cabin. Fink chooses the scent of Oleander to smokestack coal. The pleasant thought ends with the gruff voice of Mulholland, who is heard over the slow clack of the rail, as begins to amuse himself by fielding questions from the passengers.

"Desolation was the word used when the first civilized people ever set eyes on these wastelands," says Mulholland confidently.

"In fact, the very word has been applied to many parts of this country. A few mountain ranges over lay Death Valley, but none have been critical of the descriptively dire designation, joined now by he Owens Valley," says Mulholland. Another question is asked about the tyrannous occupation imposed by City agents in the Owens Valley, by the City of Los Angeles. "What's it going to take to get the City agents out of the Owens Valley?" A passenger asks with disdain. Mulholland pauses, then dismisses the question, by not answering.

"The press maintains that our reputation in Los Angeles is under fire. Our water department has taken a great deal of bad press for any number of decent arrangements we have made throughout the county of Inyo." He looks up as if listening for a divine answer.

"In my opinion, it was a brilliant move to annexation for modernization, joining a modern City, with the distant and primitive beauty of the Owens Valley," he says.

"If that's wrong, then we need to look at the fact that never, in its history, has the Owens Valley prospered and increased in wealth as it has in the last 20 years," says Mulholland, as Fink interjects.

"Mr. Mulholland, it was reported that the San Francisco Chronicle has printed a series of sympathetic articles leaning towards the Owens Valley ranchers, and have banded with them in their plight on the water issues," asks Fink.

"Yes, I am aware of that," replies Mulholland.

"Do you think this will turn public opinion against the Water Department?" He asks. Mulholland tips his bifocals to look at Fink.

"Well, if the San Francisco Chronicle and its opinion are anywhere near the articles that the Los Angeles Record has printed, you can bet the City will return to selling water by the bucket full by end of the decade," says Mulholland vengefully. The sound of laughter erupts from his bodyguards. He then leans over a seat to peer out of a coach window. A slight smile comes over his face as he catches the view of the Sierra Mountain Range, burdened with heavy snowfall, he then continues to spin another tale.

"Our interest lies in prosperity, and most of all, the considerations of actual producers, that is the dirt farmers," he says, cleaning his bifocals. Fink smiles and shakes his head slightly, impressed at Mulholland's ability to conjure up a plausible, if not off handed statement. Fink continues to jot down notes as he returns to his seat, he notices that the Slim Princess has gained speed on a slight downhill grade. The clamor of the tracks become louder as the train reaches an incredible speed of 60 miles per hour.

Later, after a brief stop at the Keeler Train Station, Fink studies the diverse landscape. The shores of Owens Lake have receded inward, and the lake seems to be fighting for its life, not willing to dry up completely.

"Where there was water once, there will be water again," Fink thinks himself. Several miles down track, conductor enters the coach.

"Next stop, Mount Whitney Station, Lone Pine, Ten minutes," he announces. Fink seizes the moment to ask Mulholland his thoughts on the violence in the Owens Valley. "Mr. Mulholland, a question off the record? Fink asks.

"With all the conflict in the valley, are you not concerned for your safety? The farmers have already proved that they're capable of doing great harm," he asks. Mulholland pulls small bag from the rack, then faces Fink.

"I see it this way; the test of any man is his knowledge of humanity and his comprehension of the things that move humankind. In time, it will be for all to see; the L.A. aqueduct is an absolute necessity, and not at all an evil. It will prove to be a great achievement, flawed as it may seem. It should be obvious that the project will last far into the future, and benefit many," he adds, contemplating another spin.

"And yes, I am very concerned about any derivation of hostility. As you can see I have come prepared," he turns and nods toward his three bodyguards. Fink tucks his note pad into his jacket as a bodyguard intervenes by placing an arm between he and Mulholland. Returning to his seat, Fink begins to jot down a title for a potential piece. 'A modern city with modern needs,' a moment of clarity, as the sight of the snow capped Sierras come into his line of sight. It is not just the snow that grabs his interest, but the water it yields for Los Angeles. as the train begins climbing a grade at north of Searles Valley. The windows are opened to catch the outside air, but the coach continues to heat up with every passing mile. The combination of rising temperature, a slow moving train and hard oak wood seats has Fink dreading the remaining length of his journey. In an effort to read through one of his files, presents a problem. The constant rocking of the coach has him wondering if car sickness is about to add to his mounting misery. Even the peculiar sounds of the train are beginning to get on his nerves. Bare metal on metal and the creaking of sun parched wood, vibrate into Fink's skull, causing him further discomfort.

"Funny thing," he thinks to himself. "If I had to write about this journey, I wouldn't mention my cowardly intentions of wanting to get off at the next stop," he contemplates. Looking out the window at the desolate landscape, he wonders how a next stop could even be possible. Fink begins to hope that there will be something to inspire his writing once he gets to Lone Pine. As for now, fifty miles of endless sagebrush is not doing anything for his creative juices.

Fink's attention is drawn by a passenger who is seated in the next seat up. The newspaper he is holding is opened with a sharp snap. Fink notices that it is not the Times-Tribune, but a copy of the Owens Valley Herald. As it is opened wider, Fink strains to see the date. It shows Friday, November 14, 1924. Below, a headline reads: "The Valley of Broken Hearts." He gooseneck's closer to read the article, but the man holding the newspaper senses an intrusion. The burly looking character, in bad need of a shave, turns in his seat, and while chewing on a stubbed cigar, speaks without taking it from his lips.

"Why don't you slide on over? You can sit on my lap, and we'll both read it together," says the passenger in perfect Alfa character.

A gruff, cough-like laugh is heard from a few seats back. Fink sits back in his seat, slightly embarrassed. The remark suggests that he is effeminate, and the subject of his assignment, Mulholland, finds the crass assumption amusing, he clears his throat after the hearty laugh.

"Well, I now know he has a sense of humor," says Fink under his breath. He turns slightly in his seat, looking in Mulholland's general direction, being very careful not to look directly at him.

"I made him laugh, the man who brought water to Los Angeles laughed at something I did," Fink thinks to himself, hoping that it's not going to be the highlight of his assignment.

A few minutes later, it now seems to Fink that Mulholland may be looking at him. Maybe expecting him to respond to the insult. Fink opts out. Instead, he takes out a pad and pencil, and tries to appear preoccupied with his writing.

There is a certain silence that comes over a person when their senses become acute with a heart felt longings. Fink has now lost interest in his writing for the moment. He peers out the window of the now slow crawling train, and lets visions of palm trees and manicured lawns, with a thick, humid scent of Oleander fill his imagination. Fink fondly recalls the long kiss that he and his bride-to-be shared before leaving Los Angeles.

The day dream is broken, along with the kiss. The gruff voice of Mulholland is heard over the loud clangor of the train and its tracks.

"Desolation' is the word used when the first civilized people ever set eyes on this wasteland," says Mulholland to a passenger. A question was asked about the Los Angeles occupation of the Owens Valley. Mulholland pauses, for clarity then continues.

"The press maintains that our reputation in Los Angeles is under fire. Our water department has taken a great deal of bad press for any number of decent arrangements we have made throughout the county of Inyo. It is an annex for modernization, for a modern City. If that is wrong, then we need to look at the fact that never, in its history, has the Owens Valley prospered and increased in wealth as it has in the last 20 years," says Mulholland Fink interjects.

"Mr. Mulholland, it was reported that the San Francisco Chronicle has printed a series of sympathetic articles leaning towards the Owens Valley ranchers, and has banded with them and their cause by printing a string of editorials on the water problem. Do you think this will turn public opinion against the water department?" Mulholland looks over his glasses at Fink.

"Well, if the Chronicle and its opinion are anywhere near the articles that the Los Angeles Record has printed, you can bet the City will return to selling water by the bucket full by end of the year," says Mulholland, enjoying the sound of laughter coming from his bodyguards. He then leans over a seat to peer out of a coach window. A slight smile comes over his face as he catches the view of the Sierra Mountain Range, burdened with snowfall, he then continues to spin another statement.

"Our interest lies in prosperity and the considerations of actual producers, that is the dirt farmers," Mulholland says, cleaning his bifocals. Fink smiles and shakes his head slightly, impressed at Mulholland's ability to conjure up a believable response.

Later, the Slim Princess has gained speed on a slight down hill grade, a conductor enters the coach. "Next stop, Mount Whitney Station, Lone Pine, fifteen minutes," he announces. Fink seizes the moment to ask Mulholland his thoughts on the violence in the Owens Valley. "Mr. Mulholland, a question off the record?" he asks. Mulholland rises to his feet to retrieve a bag from an over head rack, he gives Fink a slight nod.

"With all the conflict in the valley, are you not concerned for your safety? The farmers have already proved that they're capable of doing great harm," he asks. Mulholland pulls another bag from the rack then faces Fink.

"I see it this way; the test of any man is his knowledge of humanity and his comprehension of the things that move humankind. In time, it will be for all to see, that the LA aqueduct is an absolute necessity, and not at all an evil. It will prove to be a great achievement, flawed as it may seem. It should be obvious that the project will last far into the future, and benefit many," he adds, as he contemplates his next statement.

"And yes, I am very concerned about any potential source of hostility. As you can see I have come prepared." He turns and nods toward his three bodyguards. Fink tucks his note pad into his jacket as a bodyguard intervenes by placing an arm between he and Mulholland. Returning to his seat, Fink begins to write a byline. "A modern city with modern needs." He then has a moment of clarity as the sight of the snow capped mountains comes into his view. It is not just the snow that grabs his interest, but the water it yields for Los Angeles.

On the South side of railway building a sign reads: 'MT. WHITNEY TRAIN STATION.' The train begins a slow lumbering approach into the loading dock. The engine steam fades, then vanishes, as the train comes to a stop. Mulholland's three suited bodyguards step down onto the loading dock, and visually secure the dock. Mulholland is then given a nod to step from the train. In unison they fall into place, and encircle their client with heightened awareness. He is whisked off toward an awaiting vehicle outside of the ticket office.

A dusty, desert wind suddenly whirls around the dock. Fink steps down from the coach and continues to catch up with Mulholland and his entourage. Then, unexpectedly, the wind sends Fink's hat flying through the air, down onto the planked dock. The last bodyguard through the door turns to see Fink scampering up the dock from one side to the other, trying to snatch his tumbling hat. Mulholland's entourage slips from view as Fink dusts off his hat. He then realizes that he is standing alone on the dock. Snugging his hat down, he hurries toward the ticket office. The door bursts open, and Fink hurries through the lobby with his luggage and camera gear awkwardly balanced.

Outside the station ticket office, Mulholland and his bodyguards have boarded the vehicle. Fink exits the building just as the car pulls away. Mulholland can be seen through the rear window talking to the driver.

It appears that the cigar chewing alpha type has taken Fink's seat in the vehicle. Mulholland is not the least bit concerned about leaving the reporter behind.

Snugging the hat down on his head, he looks up and down an empty parking lot, in his frustration, he slams his bags down onto the dusty boardwalk. Fink trudges back inside to the ticket counter.

With controlled emotion Fink asks: "Is there any chance of getting a cab or any kind of ride into Lone Pine?"

The ticket clerk answers without looking up from his desk work.

"Nope, not around here. No taxi cabs around here. Probably won't be able to catch another ride for at least an hour or two."

Fink's frustration begins to enter into the red zone. "You've got to be kidding, I'm traveling with the party that just left. There must be someone you can call who can get me into town," he pleads.

"Nope," says the clerk. "Almost impossible to get a ride anywhere nowadays. Anyone with a car is afraid to get on the road, not with all those deputized City agents stopping everyone, and searching for dynamite," says the clerk, seemingly unconcerned with Fink's dilemma.

"Now, that's just great, what am I supposed to do? You must have a vehicle! Listen, I'm a reporter for the Times-Tribune and..."

Hearing the derogatory comment, the clerk shuts the ticket window without warning, and a CLOSED sign is left dangling in Fink's face.

"I guess you don't read the 'Times'," says Fink.

"Hick," mutters Fink as he turns toward the door. The contemptuous dig is heard by the clerk, who responds sharply from behind the ticket counter;

"Flatlander!" he says as Fink exits the station.

CHAPTER TWO
The Long Ride

On the south end of railway building, Fink can see a sign: MT. WHITNEY TRAIN STATION, he gathers his bags as the train slowly lumbers along side of the loading dock. As the *Slim Princess* comes to a stop, the pressurized engine steam releases into the loading dock. The three smartly dressed bodyguards step down from the train and quickly secure the unloading dock. A guard gives Mulholland a nod, and he steps from the train. On heightened alert, the bodyguards all fall into place, encircling their client. Mulholland is whisked off toward an awaiting vehicle on the opposite side of the train depot.

After wresting his luggage from the rack, Fink makes his way to the boarding platform. When stepping down from the coach he can see that Mulholland and his entourage have already entered the ticket office lobby.

A dusty, desert wind suddenly whirls around the dock, and sends Fink's hat tumbling down onto the planked dock. The last bodyguard into the lobby, turns to see the reporter scampering up the loading dock, trying to catch his tumbling hat. With hat in hand, Fink looks up, and sees that the entourage has slipped from view.

When Fink can see that he is standing alone on the dock, he snugs his hat against the wind, and retrieves his baggage.

The clerk startles as the lobby doors burst open. Looking up, the clerk sees Fink rushing through the lobby with luggage and camera bags tossing . The clerk pushes his chair back and stands to watch as Fink desperately squeezes his bulky luggage through the narrow doorway.

Once outside, Mulholland and his bodyguards have boarded a vehicle. Fink steps off the porch landing and raises his hand to wave them down; just as the car pulls away. Mulholland can be seen through the rear window talking to the driver. It appears that the cigar chewing train passenger is sitting in the car, and riding off with the entourage. By the looks of it, Mulholland is not the least bit concerned about leaving him at the train station.

Once again, Fink snugs his hat tightly onto his head, he looks up and down an empty parking lot. In his frustration, he slams his bags down onto the dusty boardwalk. Trudging back into the lobby, Fink approaches the ticket counter, and breathlessly he begins to plead his situation to the clerk.

"Is there any chance of getting a cab or anything that resembles a ride? I have to get to Lone Pine," says Fink. The ticket clerk answers without looking up from his desk.

"Nope, no rides around here, not today. No taxi or horse drawn buggies," says the clerk. Fink drops his bags onto the wood floor.

"Probably won't be able to catch a ride for at least an hour or two," says the clerk.

"You're sure of that? How can you be so sure," Fink asks.

The Clerk continues with his work, then looks up and through the barred counter window.

"Well, there's big doing's just north of Lone Pine, emptied the whole darn town," says the clerk.

"There must be someone you can call…? Fink says. When the Clerk does not respond, Fink's frustration gets the best of him.

"Unbelievable! I'm traveling with the party that just left, and it's very important that I meet up with them in Lone Pine," explains Fink.

"That's too bad, but to be honest with you mister, it's almost impossible to hitch a ride anywhere around here," says the clerk.

"Is that so? Fink asks, in a challenging tone.

"Yup, for one thing, anyone with a car is afraid to get out on the road," says the clerk.

"You don't say," responds Fink.

"Yup, ever since the Owens Valley was invaded by deputized "City" agents, they've been rousting everyone for little or nothing at all," says the Clerk.

"City?" As in Los Angeles? L.A. cops? Fink asks.

"That's what everyone's been saying. They've been stopping most everyone, and searching for dynamite, and any other reason they can arrest you for," explains the clerk, unconcerned.

"Now, that's just dandy, what am I supposed to do? You must have a vehicle! I'm a reporter for the Los Angeles Times-Tribune and..."

Upon hearing the words 'Los Angeles' and 'Times,' the clerk becomes suspicious and shuts the ticket window. A sign is left dangling in Fink's face, reading CLOSED.

"I guess you don't read...the Times," says Fink as he turns toward the door.

"Hayseed," mutters Fink as he continues to the door. The contemptuous dig is heard by the clerk, who responds sharply from behind the ticket counter;

"Flatlander," he calls out, as Fink exits the station. The screen door slams as Fink steps outside, he scans the parking area again, now hoping to find even a truck, hauling cargo.

Through the waves of sun drenched heat and the blowing dust, two figures are barely visible from Fink's point of view. Suddenly, there is a lull, and the wind dies down. From across the parking area, Fink can see two upright silhouettes on a bench beneath a Mulberry tree. Unknown to Fink, his curious actions are being observed by more than just the ticket clerk. With no alternative, he starts walking toward the Mulberry tree and the two individuals sitting underneath the tree.

With baggage in hand, Fink trudges toward the bench beneath the Mulberry tree. Through the settling dust, he can see an elderly man, and seated immediately to his left is a small boy. As he wipes the dust laden tears from his eyes, he can see an old man, his long white hair tied in braids, hanging perfectly next to a silver ear ring.

Fink puts his bags down and looks at the elderly Indian, who seems to be looking off in the distance. The boy asks in a familiar tone;

"What happened to you?" The boy asks.

"What happened to me? Fink responds in an equally familiar tone.

"I'm stranded, that's what happened," he adds.

"What happened to you?" Fink asks trying to convey concern in local cultural consideration.

"We're just sitting here," replies the boy.

"No kidding, are you waiting for someone? Fink asks. The boy look to the old man.

"Maybe someone with a car?" Fink asks.

Again, the boy looks to the old man, who continues to distance himself from the conversation.

"We re waiting for my uncle, he was supposed to be
here by now," says the boy.

"Probably missed his ride," Fink responds in irony.

"No," replies the boy, questionably.

"Uncle usually jumps off the train before it gets here, then walks the rest of the way," says the boy. He rises from the bench and walks away for no reason, his behavior fuels Fink's curiosity.

"What did I say? Did I say something wrong?" Fink asks. His question goes unanswered. The boy, now a short distance from the bench, disappears behind a stack of cargo boxes. Fink is amused at the peculiar action. He attempts conversation with the old man.

"I don't suppose you would know where I might be able to find a ride into town, would you?" Fink asks in a dry tone. The old man continues to look straight ahead.

"Would you mind if I have a seat, it's this heat, very unusual for this time of year, it's a much drier heat than..." says Fink, stopping in mid sentence. Suddenly, the sound of an automobile engine is heard, sputtering at first, then backfiring. Fink quickly stands to determine the direction of the car engine. He faces the direction in which the sound originated, the cargo dock.

An Ooga horn cuts through the air, Fink turns his attention towards a small cloud of dust. Out from behind stacks of cargo, a dust laden Model T Ford comes rolling into view. Watching as the vehicle comes barreling toward the Mulberry tree, Fink rubs his eyes at what appears to be a driverless car, now swerving directly at him. Nervously, he steps behind the tree, hoping it will shield him from an oncoming crash.

The oncoming vehicle continues with a rolling bounce, its folded convertible top flops forward, and old Ford comes to a sliding stop.

There is an alleviated gasp. Fink is dumbstruck when seeing the little boy in the drivers seat. The vehicle has stopped, with the passenger door directly in front of the old man, who slowly rises to board.

"My grandpa can't drive because of his eyes. Get in we'll give you a ride!" The boy hollers out over the sputtering engine, his head barely clearing the height of the driver side door.

"This assignment is going be the death of me," says Fink, thinking aloud. He hesitates for a split second, then tosses his luggage into the backseat, and jumps in next to his bags.

"Oh please, let his legs reach the brake pedal," he says under his breath. Overhearing the impromptu prayer, the little boy shouts proudly.

"Don't need to, I use the hand brake to stop and the choke to go," says Solomon with accomplishment. Fink turns to see the old man snugging his hat down onto his head, much like a bull rider just before the gate opens. Fink follows his lead, and snugs his hat in the same manner; anticipating a rough ride.

The boy pulls the choke linkage, then scoots down in the seat to pop the clutch. The car lunges forward, and starts speeding down a dirt road. A child's laughter is heard as the Model T disappears in a cloud of dust.

Over the sound of the puttering engine, Fink leans forward to again attempt conversation with the old man.

"I really do appreciate this, my name is James Fink, I'm a reporter, I write news articles," explains Fink. The old man acknowledges with a nod.

"I'm writing a story about the water war that is going on between the valley farmers and L.A.," says Fink.

After a moment, the old man scoffs and says, "How can you write a story no one knows nothing about?"

"Why do you say that?" Fink asks. "This story has been well covered by newspapers around the world," he explains.

The old man turns his head in Fink's direction. "A story is only good as the truth behind it. If it's been written all over the world, why don't the people in Los Angeles know about it?" Asks the old man. Fink contemplates his words, and agrees with a half cocked nod.

"Well, there are some things that are known. It is known that L.A. is taking good drinkable water that would have otherwise been flowing into a dead lake," says Fink.

"Dead lake is right, sure is dead now after LA got through with it, nothing but sand and dust," says the old man. The old man then turns his attention to the boy's driving. Fink sits back and pulls out his pad and pencil.

The vehicle hits a hard bump. The old man turns to Fink.

"That there is my grandson, Solomon, and I am Nikani," he says. A hand is extended, and hand shake is gladly accepted by Fink.

"I don't know what I would have done if you hadn't offered me a ride. How long till we reach Lone Pine?" Fink asks.

"Oh probably an hour," Nikani replies. "An hour?" Fink says with discouragement.

"We have to make a stop at the parts place," says Nikani. Fink throws his hands in the air and sits back in the seat. "'Parts place,'" he mutters in frustration.

"I've heard that there's a dirt road leading from Los Angeles all the way to Chicago. Now there's a story," says Nikani with confidence. "Um-hmm, I heard that too," says Fink.

About ten minutes later, Fink sees a sign in passing, it reads: LONE PINE DUMP.

Shortly after they enter the trash dump, Fink continues to monitor the sun's position in the sky as it draws closer to the crest of the Sierras. He patiently watches as Nikani instructs his grandson. "Elbow grease grandson!" says Nikani, as Solomon struggles to remove a part from a wrecked automobile.

Fink keeps looking over his shoulder in the direction of town, which he can see in the distance. Thoughts flow through his head on how to remedy the situation. Should he say thank you and good-bye, and strike out on his own across the desert? A headline appears in his mind's eye:

"Reporter Disappears In Desert Never To Be Seen Again." With that, the road back to the Mt. Whitney train depot suddenly became another bad alternative. At the risk of sounding ungrateful, Fink addresses Nikani.

"Nikani, this little project, do you think we might be able speed it up a little? You see, I really have to get into Lone Pine," he says pleadingly.

"Just a while longer James Fink," assures Nikani, as Solomon continues to struggle with the stubborn bolt. Fink extends and open hand, and the wrench is surrendered by Solomon.

As he applies pressure to the stubborn bolt, Fink finally asks, "Nikani, where in the world did you get that old rattle trap?" Solomon quietly offers Fink some advice; "My grampa doesn't like anyone making fun of his car." Fink looks to Nikani apologetically.

"He's right grandson, my car is old, but it was hard earned. You see, long ago, I broke about fifty horses for a rancher. That rancher never got to pay me, because it was not a good year for him. Anyway, a few years ago, he just parked it in my yard, and it's been mine ever since. You have a car Fink?" Nikani asks.

"Studebaker," Fink says. The old man seems impressed at the mention of a luxury car.

"Studebaker," says Nikani nodding with approval. Just then the bolt breaks loose. Fink holds up the car part as if it were a trophy.

Once back on the road, Fink can see the town of Lone Pine getting closer. He begins to imagine, in a photo journalistic frame of mind, a view of an oncoming Model T Ford against the massive Inyo Mountains. Not daring to go any further into the town, Solomon pulls off to one side of the road.

"This is where I let you off Fink, Sheriff Collins told us, next time he catches me driving, he's going to throw me and grandpa in the Hoosegow," says Solomon.

Taking his bags from the back seat, Fink offers thanks by palming Nikani several dollars. The money is accepted with humbled dignity.

"I want to thank both of you for the help. Solomon, take care of your grandfather, you're a good little driver. So long buddy," says Fink.

Nikani stops Fink for a moment by holding on to the handshake tightly.

"James Fink, reporter for the Times-Tribune, your story lies in that dry lake out there. Seek the truth, leave all that fancy tongue wagging to those who can't tell the truth from a post hole. In the end, all stories about the water in this valley will return to that lake," says Nikani.

Fink looks into the knowing eyes of the old man. In an instant he is overwhelmed by Nikani's sense of truth and honesty.

Nikani keeps him in sight for a few seconds as Fink starts on his way towards the town's main street. With the towering granite mountains in the background, Nikani smiles, seeing Fink rendered almost insignificant. Fink's story lay before him, but he can't seem to see it.

"Let's go home grandson, and get some supper in us," says Nikani.

CHAPTER THREE
The Spillway, The Occupation, and The Movies

Within the deepest inhabited valley, the evening sun light can quickly fade before the steep granite peaks. Daylight continues to burn as Fink walks to the hotel, hoping to secure his reservation. He is reminded of the hard packed oiled dirt roads much like some of the backstreets in Los Angeles The county dump experience left him with sand in his shoes, and an odor of burned garbage in his clothing. But for now, he feels if things had worked out differently, he would have missed the pleasure of meeting his new found friends.

Main street can be seen a hundred yards up ahead, and as he gets closer, he can see the locals driving past. The open top vehicles pass slowly, and Fink can hear the passengers conversing whooping it up. Riders on horse back pass, one rider twirling a rope behind a horse drawn buggy.

After a few zigzags through the back streets, he reaches the main part of town. Standing on the corner of Lone Pine high school and main street, Fink can see the newly built Dow Hotel a block away. With bags in hand he continues towards the hotel, anticipating a room where clean sheets and hot water await. Looking up, he sees a "No Vacancy" sign as he reaches the main entrance.

"I'm sorry Mr. Fink, but there is nothing in the front desk files that suggests a reservation was ever made," says the front desk clerk.

"There must be some kind of mistake, I understood that the room had been reserved for a three days, and now this?" Fink exclaims.

"You might try down the street, the Lone Pine Hotel may have a room available," suggests the clerk.

Thwarted, Fink leaves the Dow, and continues toward the Lone Pine Hotel just a few blocks away.

With focus on the Lone Pine Hotel, and the need for a place to stay for the duration of his assignment, Fink finds it hard to believe the setbacks he is experiencing. Once again he becomes aware of the activity on main street, surprised at the number of pedestrians and motorists. The small town seems to be alive with festivity, but there are no banners, flags, or fireworks that indicate an event. He wonders if he has missed some sort holiday, or national event. Music of all sorts can be heard coming from inside the many patio's and saloons. Musicians taking part in the low keyed event are playing instruments that range from piano, fiddle, guitars, and horns. The air is filled with wafting aroma of rich and savory foods from near by restaurants. Just before reaching the hotel, he looks towards the West, and witnesses a sunset unlike any he has seen before. The majestic mountains now have the sun setting behind their peaks. It is subtle at first, then with a burst. A brilliant display of sunlight juts out across the powdery blue sky. So awesome is the spectacle that it stuns Fink in mid step. He turns to face the Sierras.

"God showed up...again," a smiling passerby says with a little skip in her step. Fink smiles back, acknowledging with envy.

As he comes to the middle of the block, he finds the diminutive Lone Pine Hotel. As he steps inside the arched entrance to the courtyard, he feels he has come upon a little haven just off the beaten path. The small, but elegant Spanish style courtyard draws him further in as he walks past the lobby area. He turns to see grape vines clinging to the adobe style arch. Fink imagines the quaintness of a summer evening with ripened grapes hanging in the foreground of Mt. Whitney. The festive music and ambient sounds subside, and it becomes amazingly peaceful.

Once inside the lobby, a tired and dusty Fink walks up to the front desk where a clerk greets him.

"Welcome to the Lone Pine Hotel. Would you like a room?"

"Yes, one with a soft bed, plenty of pillows," says Fink, entering information in a register book. The clerk reads the register.

"The Times-Tribune, and you're James Fink. We have a couple of messages here for you," says the clerk as he hands over the message envelopes.

"The messages were received by phone early this morning by the night clerk," adds the clerk, sensing Fink's frustration, he places a telephone onto the counter.

"Thank you," says Fink as he takes the receiver from its cradle.

"Operator, this is a collect, person-to-person call to Walt McIntee in Los Angeles, Madison 8-5421," says Fink, waiting patiently.

"Walt, will you please tell me what's going on...I have no transportation, hotel reservations are all screwed-up...yes, I was supposed to be in the same hotel, and now this! Hell, at this pace, by the time I get to Bishop Mulholland will be back in LA......," explains Fink, now waiting for McIntee's opinion. Fink hangs up the phone. Weary, he leans against the front desk and becomes preoccupied with finding a solution. A room key is handed over.

"Room 10 will be your room tonight. You can find that it is right next door to the bath room. Extra towels will be provided upon request. Have a wonderful stay," says the clerk, as Fink turns towards a door leading into the courtyard, the clerk poses a question.

"I couldn't help but overhear, did you say Mulholland is in Bishop?" The clerk asks. Fink realizes that in his exhausted state of mind, he inadvertently leaked confidential information.

"Oh, no I was referring to...a Mrs.... Moll Landers, my boss, she's on vacation and will be spending the night in Bishop," explains Fink, on the fly. "I can certainly understand your curiosity, I hear that Mulholland certainly has somewhat of a bad name around here," adds Fink as he walks to the door. The desk clerk follows him with a suspicious eye. Fink is pleased with himself, thinking that the improvisational comeback seemed to have worked.

"Where's the best place in town to grab a bite ?" Fink asks.

"Just up the street, Rossi's Cantina," replies the clerk.

Later, in his room, a quick bird bath and a clean shirt, has Fink feeling better about his assignment. He is ready to quell his appetite with a hardy meal. He decides to walk to the restaurant suggested by the desk clerk. With a folded copy of the Times-Tribune tucked under his arm, he sets off to take in the sights of the small town.

Fink does not get very far before he hears what sounds to him like gun shots.

"A gun fight," he thinks to himself.

"That would make an interesting piece for the article; 'A small town, beautiful setting, restless cow pokes, dueling over a beautiful senorita,' he says in thought. He can see the face of his chief editor, grimacing as the piece floats down onto a round-file. Just then, he looks down a side street, where he can see several young boys setting of firecrackers.

"Well, so much for the gun fight," he says to himself. A short distance away, Fink comes upon one of the town saloon's, the sound of a player piano can be heard ringing out through the swinging doors. He hears loud and uproarious laughter over the cracking of billiard balls.

As Fink continues to the cantina, he passes a sheriffs patrol car parked outside yet another saloon. It appears to Fink that there was a brawl on the sidewalk, and a sheriff's deputy was dispatched to keep the peace. After passing the last saloon on the block, a hanging sign catches his eye. The sign; "Cantina" gently swings in a soft evening breeze.

As Fink enters the restaurant, he is greeted with a warmth that could only come from a very busy cook stove. To his stomach it can only mean that it is a popular eatery, and there is a good meal to be had. His appetite grows as he looks upon a glass case, filled with freshly baked pies. A waitress shows with a pleasant greeting, and Fink requests a table with a view. He is led to an unoccupied table by the window. While waiting for his order, he scans the restaurant, trying to acquire a sense of atmosphere in which the townsfolk prefer. Fink's initial impression of Lone Pine left has him reserved, it is hard for him to believe that the town has been deemed a harbor for villains. Realizing that the Times-Tribune had portrayed the town as a less than savory destination. One article went as far to depict shadowy figures laying in wait, ready to pounce with another aqueduct bombing. He figures that if he is going to write about its people, he had better get acquainted with the unique little community.

Reaching into his coat pocket, he pulls out a note pad. He notices that the towns main thoroughfare has dwindled down considerably. "Is there a correlation between the sudden decrease of townspeople and the aqueduct events," he writes. After jotting down a few notes, he unfolds his favorite newspaper; the Times-Tribune. A cup of coffee and a glass of water is placed before him by the waitress. It is then that Fink finally begins to relax.

It isn't long before she returns with his order of steak, mash potato and gravy, and corn on the cob. Fink wastes no time in catching up to a much needed meal. An hour before boarding the train in Los Angeles, he enjoyed a breakfast at Phillipi's Restaurant, his only meal of the day.

Out of the corner of his eye, he catches movement on main street, As he looks up from his plate, he sees a sheriffs patrol car has parked directly across from the restaurant. Fink takes a long drink from his water glass, he sits back in his chair, thinking of the restaurant review he will give to the hotel clerk. He adjusts his round, wire-rimmed glasses to focus in on the pie display, but his view becomes obstructed by the torso's two men.

"Howdy Mr. Fink, I'm Sheriff Collins, this is my deputy, Jack Wright. My apologies for interrupting your supper, but it's important that we talk," says Collins, as they seat themselves at his table, uninvited.

"Have a seat, gentlemen," says Fink with some sarcasm.

"What can I do for Inyo County's finest?" he asks.

"I'll get right to the point Mr. Fink," he says, looking down at the news banner of the Los Angeles Times-Tribune.

"Up here, we have a certain way of doing things, and one of those things is being hospitable to the people who come into our little valley of milk and honey. Lately, with all that's happened, well, I feel you should be warned," says Collins.

"I've already been warned, and I know about the bombings, but please, feel free. I'm a reporter, not a tourist or an insurgent," justifies Fink.

"Then you should understand that it's no longer safe for reporters to come and go as they please," says Collins. Fink sits back and contemplates the sheriff's attempt at mediation.

"As long as the Owens Valley is not under Marshall law, I intend to do just that; come and go as I please," replies Fink.

"You being a lawman and all, I'm sure you've heard of Freedom of the Press. I assume it also applies to this neck of the woods," says Fink.

"I'm not saying that you can't report on what's been happening around here. We are in an elected position to provide everyone with the service of protection, that includes you Mr. Fink. Considering our situation, this undue protection can be somewhat demanding on my men. As for now, there is no immediate danger. But I suppose that if a certain faction knew that a Times-Tribune reporter were in town, that bunch might not look too kindly on it," says Collins.

"I see where you're going with this sheriff, but go on, this is beginning to sound a little like Alabama, and I don't mean Alabama Hills. Still, it's good information," says Fink lowering his coffee cup.

"Put some caution in your tone Mr. Fink, I'm trying to help you," says Collins.

"That's very kind of you sheriff, but I know the climate of animosity the valley citizens hold against the City of Los Angeles, and I can say this with certainty; around here it's felt the City and the Times-Tribune are one-in-the same. The last thing I want to do is to give this nice, little town more bad publicity," says Fink.

"Just be careful of the things you say and do while in our Little Town...," begins Collins. Jack Wright pulls his coat back and inadvertently reveals a holstered pistol.

"With Lots Of Charm," Wright concludes.

"Thank you for your time, now get back to your dinner... the hot apple pie is the best in town," adds Sheriff Collins as he excuses himself with a nod. Jack Wright allows the sheriff to take the lead out the door. He turns to Fink and tips his hat with a short intimidating stare.

Later, Fink makes his way back to the hotel room, and settles in for a good nights rest. But, sleep eludes the weary reporter. Outside his room, a flickering light from a court yard lantern shines through the curtains. The sounds of a nearby saloon have grown faint as the clock nears midnight. As Fink lay on the bed, his eyes remain wide open, staring up at the ceiling. Although exhausted, his thoughts return to one problem, his news assignment. He reflects on the day's events. A faded image of Nikani resounding his parting words;

"In the end, all stories about the water in this valley will return to that lake."

Fink sits up, turns on the table lamp, and fumbles on the night stand for a pencil and pad. Another angle to his story has come to him by way of Nikani's words, an angle not covered by other newspapers. There on his hotel bed, he begins to pen his story.

Early the next morning, Fink is at the front desk in the hotel lobby, standing over the telephone waiting for a return call. The morning clerk is sorting room messages when the telephone begins to ring. An overanxious Fink snatches the receiver. "Sorry," apologizes Fink..

"Walt, what took you so long? Yes, I've come up with an angle," he says, turning his back, with a lowered voice.

"When this story breaks, our detractors will see that the Owens Valley has been abused with unrestrained exploitation ever since the white man showed up in California. The land and its watershed was being exploited way before Los Angeles became involved," insists Fink. In his enthusiasm, he forgets that the desk clerk is standing near by and can overhear much of his conversation.

"That's right, along those lines...say...we just happened to end up in a long line of the able and willing. You got it. LA Was just waiting in a long line of investors, waiting to take our turn," says Fink in a low secretive voice. He then listens as his boss gives a briefing on what has transpired while he has been away. Among the subjects of interest is the San Francisco Call newspaper.

A long series of articles have been set to print, concerning the Owens Valley and it's water war with the City of Los Angeles. The series will be ongoing for the next two months. The first of the articles will be forwarded within a couple of days. Walt asks him if there is anything that he needs; other than a story.

"Other than a story? Very funny," says Fink.

"On a more serious point, as you know, most essential to any investigation is a vehicle. Good, I'll see you then boss man," says Fink ending the call. Fink hangs up the phone and turns to the desk clerk.

"Is there anywhere in town I might to obtain an edition of the San Francisco Call?" Fink asks.

"Sorry, closest we have to a newspaper is our local paper, the *Owens Valley Herald*," says the desk clerk, dropping a copy onto the desk. Fink looks down at the headline: "Aqueduct Bombing Investigated." He continues to quickly read through the article. "The site of this bombing, is it accessible? I mean, can I make it by car, or do I need a horse?" Fink asks.

"Well, if I were you I'd drive north until you find a place where there is heavy construction, and muddy road side water - you've found the place," suggests the clerk.

"Now why didn't I think of that?" Fink says, putting on his hat. He takes the copy of the Owens Valley Herald and starts for the door.

Just as Fink steps out onto the sidewalk, a brand new Columbia Touring Car pulls up and parks in front of the hotel. Fink does a double take when he sees that the car is stuffed with Hollywood types.

"Jimmy! Jimmy Fink," shouts someone from inside the vehicle. He approaches the car and bends down to look through the passenger side window. Inside is a friend from Los Angeles.

Under a broad brim Stetson, smiling with shining eyes, it is Tom Mix, star of western movie fame.

"What in the hell? Tommy Mix?" says Fink with surprise.

"In the flesh. I thought that was you, looking lost as usual. What are you doing in Lone Pine?" Mix asks.

"I'd ask you the same thing, but I know you can't find a date in L.A., had to come someplace you aren't known," laughs Fink.

"I'm covering a story," he adds.

"Here I am Jimmy. Start writing," he laughs.

"What are you doing here? No, wait, let me guess," says Fink with a foolish expression on his face.

"You got it. Up here with the crew shooting 'Riders of the Purple Sage,' we'll be wrapping in a few weeks, and I'll be home for Christmas," explains Mix.

"Christmas in L.A., that'll be the day. You better get back to the set, your horse is probably worried sick," says Fink.

"I have your horse Jimmy. Hop in, were scouting a new location at the river," says Mix.

"The Owens River? I thought Los Angeles diverted all the water," says Fink, his mind spinning out a story.

"They should have told the river, because there's still flowing water, but I understand its just run-off water. The cameras can't tell the difference. We can visit the set afterwards, maybe put you to work as an extra," says Mix with a laugh.

"I've got business today, but I'll look you up tomorrow, we'll shoot the breeze and catch up on old times," says Fink.

"The set's been located in the Alabama Hills, off to the right, you can see the camera trucks from the road. Come on up," says Mix.

With a tip of his hat, Mix and his entourage are off to scout a new movie set location.

"Adios amigos!" Fink hollers as they drive off.

To Fink, being the stranger in town, it is always good to see a familiar face from home. Continuing his walk down main street, a sign comes into view that reads: "Calloway Motors." The automobile dealership is the southernmost used car business in the Owens Valley. It is where his boss, Walt, had arranged to rent a car for the duration of his stay. Fink walks past the newly built Dow Hotel, he scoffs, knowing that he should have been sleeping there had things not changed at the train station.

Inside the Calloway show room, he is greeted by a salesman who helps him with the rental. "It's the first time we've ever rented to the Los Angeles Times-Tribune ," says the salesman as a 1922 Model T Ford coupe is brought from the lot and parked in front of Fink.

"You wouldn't happen to have something with a little more style to it, would you?" Fink asks.

"You're a day late," says the salesman. "Why's that?" Fink asks. "The movies are in town. Tom

Mix came in yesterday and rented a Columbia at top dollar, right off the showroom floor," he says.

"Well, that figures, the car's going to be worth twice as much now," says Fink.

"That's exactly what Mr. Mix said before I rented it to him. I take it you're here in Lone Pine reporting on the bombings," he says.

"That's right, it's just a job. If it were left up to me, I'd have left the valley to the Indians," says Fink. The salesman scoffs at the remark and hands Fink the keys.

"It seems I can't say anything around here without getting someone all riled up," Fink says. Turning left as he pulls out onto the Sierra Highway, he heads north to find the location of the last aqueduct bombing.

CHAPTER FOUR
The Lone Pine Indian Camp

In Independence, Fink continues to piece together a back story on the bombers, their mission and their cause. The rebellion has pushed Inyo County into a land of intense scrutiny enveloping anyone who ventures into its boundaries. Climbing the courthouse steps he visualizes the angry mob that protested the injustices that were being perpetrated upon them by the deputized LA City agents.

Once inside, he walks down the marbled hallway and soon finds himself in the supervisor's chambers. Supervisor Clayton Smith walks up and greets him with a handshake. Fink wastes no time digging for something newsworthy. Not unlike the towns people who have banded together to protect the militant activist against prosecution, he finds that the county supervisors are closing ranks in order to protect their interests and constituents as well.

"Truly Mr. Fink, I wish I could help you with your story, but the Times-Tribune has earned a bad reputation for twisting the unfortunate events in such a way it ends up tarnishing the names of our valley citizens," says Smith.

An aid enters the chambers and hands Smith some papers to sign. "I can say this about the political climate that exists today in the Owens Valley; the feelings of betrayal are deep. The ranchers and farmers claim they have been swindled, and the City attorneys counter with groundless accusations of being money grubbing and greedy," says Smith.

"With all due respect, Mr. Smith, the Times-Tribune only reports events as they happen. We published a great article on the riparian water rights that were held in the valley. It's why I'm here, I want to write an objective story. I feel that if the readers are educated about the history of who had the water rights first, how they got them, and from whom, there wouldn't be so much resentment. I need something that will give me some insight on the valley's early history from a local political point of view," says Fink.

"You mean a suicidal point of view, which is what it would be if just one of my words is taken out of context. My advice to you Mr. Fink, if you want early history go interview the Indians. They're about the only people who could give an unbiased opinion. That is, if you can get them to talk," says Smith. "That may not be such a bad idea," says Fink, thanking the supervisor with a hand shake.

Back in Lone Pine, a slight rain starts to fall as Fink enters onto main street. The oiled road becomes slippery, and he decides to go to the hotel. Pulling his vehicle into the alley behind the hotel, Fink He grabs his briefcase and runs for a back alley entrance.

Inside the hotel lobby, he goes to the front desk and begins to read his messages.

"If a person were to go looking for Indians, where would he find them?" Fink asks. "An Indian reservation?" The clerk replies, as if he were answering a test question.

"I hear there's one north of Bishop," says the clerk.

"Are the majority of Owens Valley Indians living there?" Fink asks.

"You won't find any Indians there, the government placed them on land so desolate, even Indians didn't want it," says the clerk.

"But, you do have an Indian tribe here?" Fink asks.

"Well, yeah, there's Indians, but they live in camps all up and down the valley. Why do you ask?" The clerk asks.

"I need some first hand accounts for this story I'm about to write," says Fink.

"You're not thinking about going out there, are you?" The clerk asks. A blank look from Fink gives the clerk his answer.

"It's your damn funeral," says the clerk as he begins to draw a makeshift map showing where the Indian camp is located. Fink takes the map and starts to leave, but before he can open the door the clerk calls to him.

"Don't go telling anyone where you got that map. I don't want anything to do with whatever it is you're up to," says the clerk. A thumbs up is given by Fink as he walks out of the lobby.

"Crazy city folks," grumbles the clerk as the door closes.

The rain has slowed to a light drizzle, and the sun is coming out from behind the clouds. "The Land of Little Rain," Fink says, thinking aloud. "Not today," he adds.

After a stop at the general store, Fink's vehicle can be seen rolling west on an oiled road leading towards the Alabama Hills. The map is unfolded and held up over the steering wheel.

"Go past the Lone Pine Brewery, go up a quarter mile to a dip in the road, north fork of Lone Pine Creek, cross the creek, don't get stuck," reads Fink aloud.

The road becomes more rugged as he reaches the designated dip in the road. The vehicle comes to a stop just before crossing the broad, but shallow creek.

He now sees the risk of getting stuck. After a quick assessment, Fink cautiously continues across the swift creek water. The tires pull the steering wheel from side to side as the vehicle crawls over several large, submerged boulders. Fink opens his door and looks down, the running board has become washed over with water. The rear wheels begin to spin, and the vehicle quickly bogs down. The engine races, but only bogs down further, past it's axles.

In his frustration, Fink pounds on the steering wheel. Opening the drivers side door, he takes a step onto the running board. The ice cold snow water sends a shiver up his spine. "Darn it to hell," he curses. Now standing in the middle of the creek, in almost knee deep in water, he looses his footing as he slips on a boulder and begins to stumble. Pulling off his sports coat, he throws it into the rear seat. A closer look reveals that his tires are buried in the creek sand.

From the other side of the creek, behind a clump of sage brush, Solomon the Indian boy from the train station stands quietly observing Fink's unfortunate situation. After getting back into the vehicle, Fink continues to try to dislodge the vehicle from the creek.

The engine winds down to an idle, Fink is staring down at the gas pedal. From outside the drivers side window, Solomon can be seen standing on running board, quietly watching with concern. Fink startles when he catches a glimpse of Solomon to his right.

"What happened to you?" Solomon asks. Fink realizes that the boy may have witnessed his rant and becomes amused.

"I'm stuck, that's what happened to me. What happened to you?" Fink mocks. Solomon, wide eyed and eager to help, offers some information.

"Axles are buried," he says with an innocent conviction.

"Is that a fact? Well, to tell you the truth, it didn't look that deep when I looked it over," says Fink.

"Yeah. It's deep enough to swim in, and it's a good fishing hole when there's no cars in it," says Solomon.

"Well, I wouldn't be here if I'd have followed the directions that said: 'don't get stuck,'" says Fink.

"My grampa's at the camp, and he's cooking supper right now. Come on Fink, let's go see him," says Solomon.

"Okay, but what about my car? I have to get it out, I just can't leave it in the middle of a stream," explains Fink.

"Grandpa will get my uncles to get your car out, come on, let's go see grandpa," Solomon says excitedly. Fink retrieves a bag of groceries from the back seat of his disabled vehicle, and they start in the direction of the camp. As they come upon the camp, Fink can see several cottage type houses set in a grove of locust trees. The closer they get, the quaint little scene becomes more clear. There are several wooden shacks in bad need of paint. In the center of the structures are chairs situated around a rock fire ring.

Solomon breaks into a run, and then skips backwards over a small wooden bridge that crosses a creek.

"Grampa! Look who came to see us, it's Fink! He got stuck in the creek, and he brought us food," says Solomon.

Nikani takes the information and processes it without acknowledging his presence, then continues to prepare dinner. He turns slightly to acknowledge Fink with a raised brow. Fink stands with the grocery bags in his arms while Nikani pulls a hot pan from the oven, then places two rabbits inside.

"Hello Nikani, I hope you don't mind me dropping by out of the blue, I was hoping to talk with you," says Fink.

Nikani does not respond, he continues with the food preparation.

"Solomon, take this pan of potatoes over to your auntie May. Tell her I said that they better eat it while its hot." Fink watches as Solomon carries the hot pan over to another shack. He continues to stand in silence, waiting patiently to be acknowledged.

"Sit down James Fink, have some coffee, and tell me what it is I can do for you," he says.

Fink offers the groceries, and Nikani accepts them with a smile and an appreciative glance.

"I took liberty of buying some supplies for your kitchen," says Fink. Nikani removes the groceries from the bag.

"Apple pie is Solomon's favorite, this is a good thing. Maybe you should have something to eat. I have fresh baked biscuits, fried potatoes, baked rabbit, and water cress salad," offers Nikani.

"Sounds good to me," says Fink as he splashes some canned milk into his coffee cup.

Nikani sets a hot pot of coffee down onto the picnic table.

"We ran out of sugar, but we have honey," says Nikani. "Coffee and milk is fine with me," says Fink.

"The last time I saw you, I could see you were searching for something, something in the wind. Am I right?" Nikani asks.

"You're partially right, but I wasn't searching, more like chasing," says Fink with a chuckle.

"How did you find humor in what I just said? It was not meant to be funny," says Nikani.

"Nothing you said was funny, it was what you said that made me think of the train station and my hat. All I know now, is that I'm not in such a hurry, like I was at the train station," says Fink.

"What is it you want to know, maybe I can help," offers Nikani, looking over a tin cup.

"I'm looking for some early history of the valley that isn't tainted with this water war. I was hoping you might be able to help me out with it," says Fink.

"Now, that is funny. We'll have to go back a quite a few years to pull out stories like that," replies Nikani.

"I know that everything started to change drastically for your people when the settlers came into the valley," says Fink.

"That's true, everything started to change, slowly at first. Then things started happening so fast, most of the Indians could't believe it," says Nikani.

"Did they come up in large numbers or in wagon trains," Fink asks.

"No, they first start with small herds of cattle and every year the heard would double in size. The cattle were ruining our foraging fields. The settlers began coming in from over the mountain by way of Walker Pass. You have to remember that some of those people just stumbled upon the valley, like the Jayhawker party. They settled in the southern parts of the Owens Valley during the gold rush. Back then there was no conflict over the water, there was plenty for everyone. It was mainly the land that was being taken, to graze cattle," says Nikani.

"1849 was when the gold rush occurred, can we go back that far?" Fink asks.

"Now, you see there, what could I tell you that you don't already know, all that stuff should be in books," says Nikani.

"That's true, to a point. It may or may not surprise you to know, our knowledge of American Indians in todays history books only takes up one paragraph," says Fink to the unknowing elder. "A paragraph is one little space about the size of a match box, and that is on one page in the entire book," he adds

"Water is power, where ever there's water, that water must be shared, or there will be conflict.

It's a history in itself. Around here, that's what it turned into. Us Indians don't know why there was so much of it. All we knew was that it was provided by the creator.

"Briefly, or as simply as you could put it; what was it like living in those days? Fink asks.

"It was like nothing you could imagine. In a nutshell, it was like having parents that never let you go hungry, kept you warm in the winter and happy in the summer. There was not any want for anything, as now."

"Before the coming of the whites, we thought everyone lived like us," says Nikani.

"Were you here in Lone Pine when they came to take the water?" Fink asks.

"No, but I was around when they came to look at the lake. I was in Cartago in 1905. My father worked on a ranch there," says Nikani.

"Cartago. Is that an Indian word?" Fink asks.

Nikani nods. "Indians lived there from the beginning. It means 'Fields of Grass', it is a Shoshoni word," replies Nikani.

"Anyway, I looked up from what I was doing and I saw two men in a buggy, and one tired looking horse. They were drinking from a whiskey bottle, laughing and talking loud. We watched them go north on the road towards Cottonwood Creek. It was around lunch time when we saw their buggy down by the shore of the lake," says Nikani.

"The Owens Lake, that must have been a sight to see when it was still filled with river water." Fink muses.

"It sure was. That year it was real full because of the winter run-off, lots of rain that year as I recall," says Nikani.

"Who were the two men?" Fink asks.

"I later found out, one was named Eaton and the other was Mulholland. They didn't stay long at the shore before they found a place to camp on Cartago Creek. I know this because they stopped by the ranch and asked to buy some grain, coffee, sugar, canned beans, and dry meat. The rancher sold them some lamb, and enough coffee and honey for a couple of days," says NiKani.

"Did they say what they were doing up here?" Fink asks.

"I overheard them say that they were up here looking for some land to buy," says Nikani.

Fink takes out a note pad and begins writing. A car horn is heard and his attention is turned to the creek crossing. They watch as his car pulls up packed with Indians from the camp. They all pile out of the vehicle and leave without saying a word.

"Thank you, I'm much obliged," says Fink as he and Nikani watch them walk away laughing and joking with one another. Solomon comes walking up with an empty frying pan. Nikani takes a dish towel from the apple pie.

"We have pie for desert, grandson, thanks to James Fink," says Nikani as he begins to serve up the supper plates.

Fink takes his first bite of baked jack rabbit and nods with approval.

"I didn't know rabbit could be so tender," he says.

"Slow cooking is the only way to bake a rabbit. Here, have a biscuit, put some honey on it, makes the rabbit taste even better," says Nikani.

"I watch my Grampa cook all the time. When I grow up, I'll be able to cook just like him," says Solomon in between bites.

"You just eat your dinner, and don't talk with your mouth full," scolds Nikani.

"I know work must be hard to find around here, but what do Indians do when there is work?" Fink asks.

"I have a nephew up north, he was able to find work with the City, cleaning yards for the big wigs," says Nikani.

"Does the City pay much?" he asks.

"Not money, they don't pay Indians money. My nephew gets supplies instead. He calls them rations, and they let him fix up and stay in one of their abandoned farm houses outside of town. As long as he keeps working for them, he will get food and medical treatment if he gets sick," explains Nikani.

"About seventy years ago, they used to have a name for that sort of work. It was called servitude, or slavery," says Fink.

"They don't own us, nobody owns us," Nikani responds adamantly.

"I'm not so sure about that. In Natural Law books, it sates that if land is taken over by another, that owner is responsible all the trees, creeks, rivers, and even indigenous people. That means that Indians become the new landowner's responsibility," explains Fink.

"Is that so? If that is true, then I think we should go to Sheriff Collins and report Los Angeles for not taking care of their children. Maybe the government will step in and take us away," says Nikani with hidden meaning,

"I thought they already tried that," says Fink.

"They did, but they forgot to close the gate, and we got back in," says Nikani, with a deadpan expression.

"You're a funny guy," Fink says with appreciation.

"Wasn't trying to be," he replies.

"Nonetheless, in one form or another, slavery is still going on right here in the Owens Valley," says Fink.

"Working for the big wigs has it's rewards. For one thing we know what is going to happen before it happens," says Nikani.

"You wouldn't be talking about the aqueduct, would you?" Fink asks.

"Well, those things we like to keep to ourselves," says Nikani.

"You can't be serious. You know about the bombings before they happen?" Fink asks.

"It's not that we know for sure. We just put things together and figure it out, then it happens," says Nikani.

"Like what? What do you put together," he asks.

"Indians who work on the ranches know when they are going to sell to Los Angeles," says Nikani.

"What's to put together? An overheard conversation, and you have a conclusion?" Fink asks.

"No, it's different. Indians watch and observe. Indian ranch hands see that when a rancher is being pressured by the agents, we watch them come around everyday. The workers know that when a ranch next door gets sold to the City, jobs are taken. Those Indian hands then get hired by the ranch that does not want to sell, they work at a lesser amount. To the City, it means nothing. When the drills come out, and there are wells on either side of the property, the pumping starts. They take the water until the water table drops. Alfalfa fields fail, soon there's no alfalfa to feed the cattle, and soon there are no cattle, no money to pay the workers. Sooner or later the City buys their land, lock, stock, and barrel.

One by one, that's the way it happened," says Nikani.

"How many of your people are out of work because of the insurgence?" he asks.

"Yup, look around, all these Indians you see in the camp, used to work on one ranch or another. And it's still going on. Ranch after ranch, they are all disappearing back into sage brush. Before the City, we Indians benefited from the farming, we would work for a certain amount of the crop, we never had it so good. During the harvest season, there was grain for our chickens, alfalfa hay to feed our horses, rabbits, sheep. Heck, some even started their own cattle herds," explains Nikani.

"So, the socio-economical impact reached far and wide," offers Fink.

"What?" Nikani asks.

"I don't know what that means, but if you are asking if it hurt us Indians, the answer is yes. For the Indian people here in the valley, winter months were not so hard. Then the City came, and the work dwindled to near nothing at all. We worked on grape farms that covered land that went on for miles. There were orchards of the sweetest peaches, nectarines, and apples. Groves of Walnut and pecan trees. I remember eating something they called pomegranate, never really understood that sort of food.

"In the winter we had raisins, dried potatoes, onions, carrots, beets, beans, everything you could think of, we picked and canned.

We had a store of food in our cellars. Now that the City has taken that all away, we don't know what will happen to us," says Nikani with deep concern.

"What if in the future, Los Angeles opened up the Owens Valley for agriculture?" Fink asks.

"That would be good for Indians all over the valley, it would mean work, a chance to buy land, raise crops, and alfalfa. We Indians, we know how to farm, we know how to graze and cull cattle, but we don't ever get the chance. That is a day dream. I don't see the City giving up the water to raise food," says Nikani.

"It isn't hard to put it together. Once the ranchers and farmers are gone, they will get rid of us Owens Valley Indians, all of us, just you watch," adds Nikani.

"They can't do that. Los Angeles is just a City, not a federal government," says Fink. There is reluctance felt in the course of conversation and as more sensitive matters are disclosed.

Later, as Solomon finishes his apple pie desert, Nikani smiles along with Fink, as both have been watching the little boy devour his favorite food. Nikani pours coffee, and from across the camp, there is laughter and singing. Someone strums chords on a guitar to a country song. To Fink, he feels fortunate to be among Nikani's friends and relatives at the camp. He has always been drawn to cultural anthropology, it is a perfect living laboratory.

While the camp's occupants make the best of what they have, it remains a mystery of how they keep a positive attitude. A wine bottle is passed around the camp fire.

"Alcohol has taken many of our people, a taking that has settled deep in our hearts, yet it brings relief from a pain we all suffer. Sorrow can make life hard," says Nikani.

"Yes, but I can see your people are strong. They seem determined not let the outside world get the best of them. Your people have had to live and continue to live through extreme adversity. To do so, a strong belief system has to be in place," says Fink as he tries to relate.

"To me, it allows a dignified past, something that may be lacking in a great many of us, I believe none of us can escape the past. Life, if turned bitter, can be that much harder," replies Nikani. "Life, is all us Indians have anymore. The bitter part is just a temporary change of scenery," he adds.

"Temporary, maybe," adds Fink.

"No, because nothing lasts," says Nikani.

"Point taken," agrees Fink. " What about before the coming of the whites, what was it like...give me some idea of the way it was before all the water trouble started?"

Nikani reaches for a plate of leftovers. "Grandson take the rest of this rabbit over to your uncles," he says.

"Can I stay over there for a while?" Solomon asks. Nikani nods and waits until the boy is out of hearing range.

"You didn't have to go through all the trouble of becoming our friend, you should have just asked.

"Understand, the story you are after cannot be told in the same way as the white people tell it. The way Indians tell the story is different. I'm not so sure that a people who have become so used to ways that are other than humble can accept a simple truth. Our story has no place in your world," says Nikani.

"Which is exactly why I need to hear the story from you, and it does have to be told in a different way. The story has to be told in a way that will show not only how it happened, but why it happened. I understand that; if compared to yours, my way of life is less than humble. In the beginning my people survived in a way the Native Americans did in the old days. If I could walk in your shoes, I'm sure it would expose me to things beyond my understanding ," says Fink.

Nikani looks upon him suspiciously, then smiles. "I speak of an understanding that has been whispered in the wind for all time. To my people it is the earth, the nearest touch to God that we have, it is the Indian way, a life that must be lived in order to understand," says Nikani.

"See, it's that sort of thing, it's the impossible I can't understand. The who, the what, and the where, but I can't go back into the past and live the way you did, give me something I can go on," pleads Fink.

Nikani stands. Fink looks upward at the stern old Indian who is disappointed at his clueless approach. Nikani smiles then goes to place a piece firewood into the fire pit, a match is lit.

"What you are doing now is seeking truth, a good start. The truth, when written, has strange way of becoming something else," adds Nikani. Fink becomes frustrated, he feels his story is slipping away from him.

"Where do I begin? All that I need is basic information. I don't want to go back into the past and live another life, not for a story that may not go to print," says Fink.

"You fooled me, James Fink, you must have snake oil running through your veins, go back to the City. There is no story here, just a poor way of life," adds Nikani.

"Go back to L.A? Now there's a thought. You don't think that hasn't crossed my mind? You, Nikani most of all must know that ever since I arrived in this valley nothing has gone right. It's as if I've been jinxed," says Fink.

"Jinxed? That is a word used in this valley a lot. No one can argue that long ago things went very wrong here. It brought misery, the land has been denied a peaceful way ever since. Men have failed the land in this valley. They lost sight of her beauty, and now they have made it a dangerous place to exist.

"This jinx you speak of is real. All of us feel it, no one can fix it," says Nikani as he takes a tobacco can and begins to fill his pipe. A twig is taken from the fire pit, and the pipe is lit. Drawing in deep puffs of smoke, Nikani releases the smoke, gently pushing it into the night air. He then begins to so hum an Indian song. Fink remains silent, thinking about the trip back to Los Angeles. As the campfire embers rise high into the night air, Fink has come to a point of exhaustion. It has been a long day for him, and he is suddenly feeling drained of energy. He settles back in the chair, his eyes slowly close and he falls fast to sleep. Nikani puts a finger to his lips as Solomon comes walking up towards the campfire. A minute later, Solomon covers him with two blankets. He goes over to his grandfather and says goodnight. Shortly afterward, Nikani decides to call it a day.

In the morning, Fink awakes to the aroma of coffee, and the sound of sizzling bacon. With a slight groan he manages to sit-upright, his body aching from sleeping in a chair all night. The camp occupants had kept the fire going all night, so that he wouldn't get too cold. Now they are casually talking among themselves. The table is being set for breakfast, there are two men quietly beginning their day, one is rolling a cigarette and the other has a cup to his lips. Nikani is at the stove cooking breakfast.

"Have some coffee Fink," Nikani offers as he places a huge, round frying pan on the table.

"Our boys and girls have to have a good breakfast before they go off to work," says Nikani. As Nikani and Solomon take a seat, everyone takes a turn at serving themselves to the huge pan of potatoes, eggs and bacon.

"No biscuits this morning, maybe tomorrow when there is more flour in the tin," says Nikani, he then motions to Fink to sit and join them.

"Don't let these quiet, well mannered neighbors fool you. Deep down inside they're wild Indians. You should have seen them the other night. Today they probably would thank you for the food you brought into the camp, but they're too bashful," says Nikani.

Most at the table become embarrassed while the others simply ignore Nikani's teasing remarks.

"But don't worry, you'll get to know them all by the time your story is done. They're a good bunch. Eat up Fink, there's a lot to do today," urges Nikani.

Those seated at the table become slightly amused at the fact that Fink will be under Nikani's strict and regimented ways for the rest of the day.

After breakfast, under the watchful eyes of half the camp's occupants, Fink has been designated the mechanic for the day by Nikani. With his head under the hood, Fink is replacing the engine part scavenged at the dump.

The sound of a car engine is heard, and the entire camp looks towards the aqueduct. A Los Angeles Police Department car, with two officers inside, slowly drives past, watching the camp. A barbed wire fence is the only thing that separates the camp from the armed guards on patrol.

"Seeing an LA cop cruiser in this valley, is like seeing a duck out of water," says Fink as he looks up from under the hood of Nikani's car.

"What kind of car is that Fink?" Nikani asks, referring to the patrol car.

"It's a Dodge Brothers. While were on the subject of cars, I don't see why we just can't take my car. At least it runs," says Fink. "True, but it's not your car, if it was then we'd take it," says Nikani.

"Now that makes a lot of sense, let me see; I have a car, but it's not my car, so that means we can't use the car?"

"That's right, where I will take you today, we'll need a car that can be fixed, if it breaks down. If we took your car, and it broke down, we wouldn't know how to fix it. If my car breaks down, at least I know how to fix it," says Nikani. Other camp members, listening to the exchange, nod their heads in agreement.

Nikani is not their chief, but his well earned respect carries weight with those in the camp, he trust them, and they in turn, trust him to be a leader among them. Nikani pushes the key into the ignition while the entire camp looks on. With a turn of the key and a few foot pumps on the gas peddle, the engine fires on the first try.

Fink is pleasantly surprised, he gives a thumbs up to Nikani. Then he is then motioned to take the drivers seat. As Nikani climbs into the passenger seat, several of the camp's occupants jump into the rear seat. Nikani turns and looks upon the group disapprovingly, and they climb back out. Walking away, they can be heard mumbling words of protest in both Indian and English. Solomon waves good-bye as they pull out of the camp for the ride into Lone Pine.

At the "Square Deal Garage," James Fink pulls a fuel hose from the gas tank on Nikani's Model 'T' Ford.

"Are you sure you can afford it? A full tank at . 22¢ a gallon adds up," warns Nikani as Fink hops into the drivers seat.

"That's okay, even though I'm used to paying . 15¢ a gallon in LA This full tank will last you for a while," says Fink.

"I don't think this car has ever had its tank filled since I've had it," says Nikani.

"Well, see there? Now you can go back to the camp and brag about your full tank of gas," grins Fink.

"Drive north to the Alabama Gates, go past there, and there will be a road on the left, Moffat Road," instructs Nikani.

"Thank you great scout, we are on our way," says Fink.

A short time later they are rolling up the highway with the top up, doing a maximum speed of 45 miles per hour. The Moffat Ranch Road is fifteen minutes away from their location. As they drive along, Fink brings up Nikani's story about the past.

"Your recall. How far back can you go? Is there some major event that can be used as a bookmark?" asks Fink.

"I can tell you this; when the soldiers rode into this valley, I saw them. When they tried to kill all the Indians, I was there. I can tell you of the time I escaped when they tried to take me from the land of my birth. They tell me it was around the 1850s, maybe the late 1850s." says Nikani.

"That may be right, according to the accounts that I've researched, the period you speak of would be correct," says Fink. A pencil and pad are pulled out of his coat pocket.

Nikani's story begins high on top of the rugged Inyo Mountain range, at a newly opened mine, claimed by a one time Spanish Expeditionary soldier, Pablo Flores. After being discharged from military service by the Spanish Crown, he journeyed back to the rich, mineral laden Inyo Mountains to mine silver. The claim, which he had reopened, was still rich with ore. He had knowledge of the mine, because he had worked it before his discharge. Originally, the Spanish named the mine, "Cerro Gordo," meaning "Fat Hill." Flores returned, claimed it in his name, and began working it on his own. After mining the site for a year, the ore revealed to be rich not only in silver, but also zinc and lead. A crew of five men were working under him, at two sites, to get the ore out of the mines. And so it started, the first silver mine to be established in the mountains of Inyo.

CHAPTER FIVE
Cerro Gordo Mining Camp 1861

A cold, winter wind howls through the mining timbers protruding from the landscape of the Cerro Gordo summit plain. The dry squeak of a wooden hoist is heard as an ore bucket is hauled to ground level. At the bottom of a shaft, the light from above shines down on the bearded, wrinkled, face of a Cerro Gordo miner. Those miners who shovel the ore into an ore bucket is known as a "mucker." On this day, the miners are taking three hour shifts at the bottom of the pit. The work is hard, and perilous, and if not on constant alert, injury caused by falling equipment or rock, can kill a miner. The old man watches the ore bucket as it reaches the open air, he breaths a sigh of relief. There is a miner's myth that has circulated among men since man started digging for precious metals. Most men when working a mine stay alive by way of the myth: when down below, you should never look up. If you fail to resist the temptation, you will die from a falling rock breaking your face wide open. The miner up top can see the old miner's face, as he reaches for the ore bucket.

"That old buzzard is tempting fate again, it's the third time this shift I caught him looking up," says another miner.

"Well, look at him, he's probably died already, he just don't know it,' says a third minor, as he pulls another 250 pound bucket of ore away from the A-frame and onto a planked landing.

A crew boss pulls his hat from his head, and wipes the sweat from the brim. With keen eyesight, he continues to watch a mounted Shoshoni warrior at the edge of a steep canyon wall. The miner admires the Indian's horse, standing alert, and motionless.

From across the ravine, Nikani stands watch over the miners and their mining camp. Now at nineteen years of age, he is called Tatsiumbi Nikani: The Sky Dancer. He is a warrior scout a position that is appointed by the chiefs, and requires a great deal of stamina. Infinitely competent in the ways of the Shoshoni people, Nikani has learned well from, Joaquin, his father and Lala, his mother. Their customs are very important to them, and they have taught that these traditions are the key to life itself.

On this day, much like the rest, Nikani is in full battle dress, and is postured on top of his mustang pony. He is a safe distance from the camp. The main objective is to show his presence, while standing watch over the Shoshoni burial grounds. The tribe is aware that the mining camp is slowly encroaching upon their sacred ground, and are doing everything, short of war, to prevent further encroachment.

The vigil over the burial ground began when a Spanish expedition discovered silver and lead ore deposits at the mountain. When the Spanish presence became known by the Shoshoni, the council deemed them not a threat. They would take what they wanted from the dirt holes, then leave the mountain. It wasn't until the Spanish began prospecting outside of the mine site that the Shoshoni began taking their lives one-by-one. The day finally came when the miners felt that their lives were worth more than the silver they were digging out of the ground for the Spanish Crown. The Spanish soldiers disappeared from the Inyo Mountains in the 1840's, and the vigil was relaxed. It wasn't until Flores returned in 1858 with a contingent of men, and the vigil over the burial grounds became necessary again.

In the distance, the clanging of the supper iron calls in the workers, and the cook waves them in toward the chuck wagon. For the miners, it means the end of a hard day's work, and their attention is now focused on supper. As the men make their way down to the chuck wagon, the welcome aroma of a hot meal drifts in the air. A dining hall is under construction, but not yet completed, so seating is where the miners can find it. A few yards away from the mess area is a wash trough, where some of the miners choose to splash the dirt from their faces and hands before supper. So exhausted are some, that they choose to simply satisfy their hunger. Some of the men waiting in line become preoccupied with the silent presence of the lone Shoshoni Warrior.

"Don't none of you pay that Indian any mind, just go about your business and eat your grub," the cook exclaims as he stirs the pot with a serving spoon.

"Last thing we want is to get them all riled-up by showing them fear. The evening meal tonight is beef, beans, potatoes, and biscuits, made especially for you by my two little hands," taunts the cook.

Looking down at his plate, one of the miners reminds the cook.

"Looks like yesterday's supper to me," says a miner. The cook takes a cigar from his mouth to address the complaint.

"Yesterday, it was mule deer, beans, potatoes, and biscuits," the cook grins. "Fooled you didn't I?" he says with a hardy laugh.

The miner scoffs and finds a place to sit and eat his supper. A timber beam suffices, and he is joined by others. The miner then offers in a loud voice, "See that Indian across the way. He's making sure we aren't digging too close to their sacred grounds. A place for only good Indians, if you know what I mean."

From a distance, a sudden burst of raucous laughter is heard by Nikani. With keen eyesight, he can see the circle of men looking in his direction.

"Word has it, them ranchers in the Owens River Valley have a plan that'll take care the whole lot of them," says a second miner.

"What do you expect the Indians to do? There's more cattle being herded in every month, taking up their land," says the crew boss. "It's no different from claim jumping I say. If someone were to move in on my dig, I don't think I would take to kindly to it my own self," the crew boss adds.

"You feel like that, what are you doing here mucking out this hell hole? Why don't you go join up with the Union. They could always use another man to fight with Lincoln's nigger lovers," says the first miner as he puts his plate down. The crew boss rises in an intimidating manner.

"Hell, I don't have to go all the way back east to fight. I can have me a little fight right here," says the crew boss as they close in on each other. "Because there isn't nothing' I like better than busting' up some inbred with bad manners," he adds.

The cook is observing the encounter and quickly intervenes before a brawl breaks out. "You boys fixing to take some time off? Cause if you are, you just might as well start walking right now, or after the fight, 'cause it don't make no difference to me," he says.

Both men hesitate while standing face to face. The disagreement is diffused when a camp guard yells out: "Soldiers, Army soldiers! I can see them right here from my lookout," he shouts. At the lookout point, situated on a craggy ledge above the camp, the guard has focused in through a telescope mounted on a tripod.

Through the dust and sunlight, the camp guard sees the second Army of the California Volunteers. They are riding in column on the far side of the Owens Lake.

"Hot dam boys! It's the United States Army, and they're riding' into the valley! Them ranchers must be smarter than they look," he shouts. Hats are flung in the air and the miners hail exuberantly at the event.

A sudden silence falls upon them when they see that the warrior scout has vanished. The camp cook becomes irritated at the quarreling men, and reaches for a sawed off shot gun. The weapon is slung onto his shoulder, in full view of the workers. The two disorderly miners acknowledge his intent and put away their differences as the cook continues to serve up the evening meal.

On the other side of the canyon, Nikani can be seen riding away at full gallop. From an eagle's eye view, a dust trail is kicked up by the hoofs of Nikani's horse. The high mountain plateau stretches into a vast desert plain. In the distance, the Shoshoni winter camp can be seen at Hunter Mountain. Nikani still has eight miles to cover, but his fast pony will get him there in 30 minutes.

As the morning sun rises over the Inyo Mountains, Fink continues to listen to Nikani's journey into the past.

"That was pretty much the way of it back then. When it came to precious metals, nothing was sacred," says Nikani, offering Fink more coffee.

"How many people lived in the Owens Valley back then?" Fink asks.

"Other than Indians? Not more than a couple of thousand would be my guess, from Bishop on down," says Nikani.

"In those days, did you ever make the ride to Bishop on horseback?" Fink asks.

"No, I never did make that 60 mile journey, but I know some who did. They had to get up pretty early in the morning to make that trip. It took them the better part of two days. After riding at the base of the Sierra's, where there were no fence lines, a camp was usually struck at Taboos Creek, from there to Red Hill," explains Nikani. "In my whole life, I never made that trip to Bishop. I know that the Paiutes called it something else, and I heard plenty about the place," replies Nikani.

"How far north did you ever make it by horseback?" Fink asks.

"We used to ride over from Hunter Mountain into the Owens Valley by way of the Long Canyon, now I think they call it New York Butte. We had to time it just right, because in the early spring, we could not cross the river. The river would overflow its banks. We would ride north until we found a place to cross over, usually just below the lava fields on the other side of Fort Independence," says Nikani.

"So, getting back to the mining camp at Cerro Gordo, you were riding to the winter camp to warn your people," suggests Fink.

"As I remember, it was in the fall, my horse began to lather up about two or three miles from the village. I wouldn't have been able to gallop him that far in the heat of summer, so it had to be fall. Time had been lost because I had to hold him back to a trot all the way to the summer camp. I remember as I entered the outskirts of the village, the people could tell I was there with a warning. My horse was winded, I had to walk him into the village. There were dozens of women and children making their way with baskets filled with foraged food and fire wood, they were all asking me if there was anything wrong.

"Back then, that particular village had been built in an alluvial area amid Pinon trees and sage brush, there were hundreds of mound dwellings were on the summit of the mountain," says Nikani.

"Mound dwellings?" Fink asks.

"That's right, others called them pit's, but we built our homes out of the earth.

"Basically a hole in the ground? Fink asks.
"Sort of, we covered the dwellings with wood bark for the roof and clay on the sides.

"Anyway, as I was saying, when entering the main part of the village, two young boys rushed to tend to my horse. I told them not to let her drink too much water. Then I made my way towards the council chamber," says Nikani.

In Fink's mind's eye, he could see Nikani walking up to the entrance of the council chamber, a cave opening at the base on the summit of the mountain. Fink see's Nikani entering the cave, and he is dwarfed by the huge geological feature, where Nikani disappears into the darkness of the cave.

"I walked into the lava tube corridor, the torches were getting low on light, so I knew they had a long council. I was thirsty from the long ride, so I stopped to drink from an intermountain stream. I will always remember that stream, so cool and sweet.

"Voices of the council were heard echoing off the walls. The cave corridor opened into a larger cavern, and it was filled with warriors and Chiefs. Their voices echoed deep concern of issues facing our people. I could hear one of them say:

"'The Spaniards, when they went to the hills to dig for gold, it was done. They did not take the land, there was no reason to fight. It's true we killed, but our women were dishonored, it was a fight and we were forced to kill.'

"'Let our enemies come to us, then we will fight and we will kill again,' said another chief.

"I heard another member of the Council stand to speak over the mutter of voices within the Chamber: 'Once they settle they stay. Only one mountain range away, they have settled, how long will it be before they are in this valley taking everything for themselves," says one of the council members

"'The Paiutes are a strong people, they are good fighters, they will drive them out,' said another.

"Then, Chief Monache, the elder of all the Chiefs, saw me making my way into the center of the council. Monache stood and brought the council to order.

"'Young man, come into the circle, tell the council what you have observed,' he advised.

"They all stepped aside to let me by. I walked to the center with as much bravery as I could gather up. Those closer to the center stood in respect.

"The Sina'si (soldiers) are upon the land, runners tell of their crossing from south of the Kawaiisu Nation. Their horses are tall and they are strong, and mounted by as many soldiers. They wear the colors of the sky, and their leaders have long knives, all have good rifles, I assured.

"The Council Chamber erupted with talk of war. Monache held up his hands to calm the warriors.

"Let the young man tell you of the Sina'si, we do not know why they have come, let him talk,' scolded Monache.

"I told them that they were traveling north towards Paiute country, their count is not as many as us, not half, but they have many wagons, which to me means that they were well stocked for a long stay. I told them that there was no sign of a day camp on the West shore of the lake. These soldiers would be gone by morning.

"Their way has been chosen, it is not the Shoshoni they seek, the Sina'si do not know now of this village, but before the next snow, this village will be known to them," said a chief.

"Then Monache stood to speak. He explained to the council that word from the Shoshoni tribes in the North, have sent word that a great war is on the rise. The whites are fighting each other, and they die in great numbers. They told of soldiers dressed in colors of the thunder cloud, and they tell of rifles traded for very little. There is plenty of whiskey to make fools of them Indians. The blue sky soldiers are here not to fight. Their numbers would be greater."

Nikani breaks the account to comment on the event. "The mood in the chamber turned solemn. I didn't see it then, but now I understand that the warriors were trying to understand the consequences of an invasion of their territory," he says.

"Had any of your tribe ever seen a soldier?" Fink asks.

"Other than Monache, I don't think any had seen a soldier up close," says Nikani.

"Since I was a small boy, there had always been talk of the soldiers, and before them, it was the

Spaniards. The ancestors have made this known so we can hear, yet we had no reason to believe that it is nothing more than talk. We were a strong people, our warriors were more than the few soldiers. We thought for sure the soldiers would fail when the hard winter wind stung their backsides," explained Nikani.

"I guess your people would have had every reason to believe the natural forces would defeat the enemy, after witnessing the account of the Jayhawkers," acknowledges Fink.

"That's true, we understood nature could inflict terrible harm to those not prepared. If you get lost in our country, you can't forget that it is a land that holds the ashes of our ancestors," says Nikani. "I remember our chief saying that our happiness lay in what is good for us all, that those few Sina'si could only mean one thing; from where they come, there are many more. After he said that, the council went quiet," Nikani adds.

"In time, we would find out there were many more soldiers than the Inyo Shoshoni. It was then he said that we would keep a close eye on them. Monache reached for a medicine bundle and held it up.

"We must prepare for ceremony. All you young men, stand for your people. A warrior scout will be chosen to observe our enemy,' announced Monache. Many of the warriors looked to me. I was standing tall in anticipation as to be the chosen one, says Nikani.

"We had no idea what was going to happen to us back then. I was nineteen," says Nikani.

"They were days I will never forget," he adds shaking his head. Fink is writing so fast he breaks a pencil lead. Nikani takes his pocket knife out and hands it to him.

CHAPTER SIX
The Occupation Of Alabama Gates

From a distance, Nikani's vehicle can be seen slowly gaining ground on a steep, wagon road in the foothills above Moffat Ranch. The engine is straining under full torque, powering the wheels at a steady slow crawl. As the vehicle reaches the top, Fink pulls onto level ground where a vista opens up to a magnificent view of the valley.

It is early Sunday morning, November 16, 1924. A convoy of 16 cars and pick up trucks have rolled out of Bishop, and towards Big Pine where they expect to meet with others that will join the convoy and continue south. The final rendezvous will be Independence, there they will join up with yet more vehicles, and push on to the main objective; to stage a protest against Los Angeles water policy. Their final destination is the Alabama Gates Spillway, just north of Lone Pine, where they will seize the gates and divert water supply to Los Angeles.

Unknown to Fink and Nikani, they are about to witness part of history from above the aqueduct. Nikani is explaining the early history of the valley below, pointing out places of cultural interest.

"As far as you can see north, Indian people had their camps on almost every creek flowing to the river. Summer camps were abundant within the mountains, a paradise for many. On the Inyo side, I recall seeing the Sierra's when I was a child. We stood on top of the mountains looking down on the great body of water of the Owens Lake. Indians called it Esha water, because no one could drink it. Once, I asked father who put the water there. He laughed and said the great water was put there by clouds, known as sisters to the mountains. He said, in the spring its sisters bring rain, and in the winter snow. Indians knew no one could ever use that much water. We just thought it would be there forever," says Nikani.

"Grandpa, there are an awful lot of cars on the road coming from Independence," says Solomon, pointing northward. Handing the binoculars to his grandfather, Fink becomes curious.

"What's going on Nikani?" Fink asks.

"I don't know, here, have a look," says Nikani. Fink adjusts the binoculars and sees a solid line of vehicles approaching the Moffat Ranch Road.

"Looks like fifteen or twenty vehicles coming this way, with more behind them, trying to catch up with the main group," says Fink.

"What's going on grandpa?" Solomon asks.

"Don't rightly know grandson, but I can tell you this, it isn't a parade," says Nikani.

"There's what looks like men in overalls riding in the back of the hay haulers, maybe farmers," says Fink, as he peers through the binoculars.

"They're either going to the spillway, or Lone Pine; has to be one or the other, there isn't much going south after Lone Pine," says Nikani.

"The movies are in town, do you think it might have anything to do with it?" Solomon asks.

"I know Tom Mix, he wouldn't think of paying that many extras for a western, unless he was doing a film on the Alamo," replies Fink.

"Maybe they're going fishing. Grampa, let's go fishing," suggests Solomon, feeling somewhat restless.

"We can go later this evening grandson, when they're biting," suggest Nikani.

"It looks to me like they're slowing down; parking on both sides of the road, and they are getting out of their vehicles," says Fink, still observing through the glasses.

"What the heck?" Nikani says in question.

"It was just six months ago that they blew the place up. What are they going to do now, open the spillway?" Nikani asks.

"It looks like that's exactly what they're doing. Here take a look for yourself," says Fink as he hands the binoculars to Nikani.

"Well, I'll be doggone. You're right, they're storming the gates right now. That one City worker better get out of their way, 'cause it looks like they mean business," says Nikani in an excited tone."

"Can I see, please?" Solomon asks as his grandfather hands him the binoculars. Solomon starts to observe the chaos down below at the spillway, but then his attention is grabbed by the Inyo Mountains across the valley floor. Fink gently pulls the binoculars from Solomon.

"Maybe we should focus on what's happening down below, Little Man," says Fink.

"For goodness sakes, there goes the water, right down the spillway," says Fink as he gives the glasses to Nikani.

"Tell me everything that you see," says Fink as he begins writing as fast as he can.

"What do you make of this Fink? Nikani asks.

"I've covered stories like this before, but it involved labor strikes. I can tell you this, they have seized the Alabama Gates, and taken control of L.A.s water supply," replies Fink.

"Why don't they just come out and say what they want from the City? Why go through all of this? Nikani asks.

"When all measures have been taken to bring a resolve, and communication breaks down between two groups, the only alternative is to demand an audience, and that is exactly what is happening now," explains Fink.

"What are they trying to say by taking over the 'gates'? Why don't they just keep blowing up the aqueduct? You would think that alone would've gotten the City's attention," says Nikani.

"Public opinion is one of the factors, meaning, the bombings are working against them at this point," explains Fink.

"I'm guessing that the first part of the message, is to let the people of Los Angeles know that they have drained an ancient lake, and a Natural Law has been broken. The second part of the message should address the Los Angeles Water Department to let them know that the massive amount of ground water pumping has to stop," says Fink.

"The ranchers and farmers are very determined to shine the light of day on all the dirty deeds done by the Los Angeles Water Department," adds Nikani

"And they're right, the citizens of Los Angeles have to know that the Owens River, by law, has to return to its natural course," adds Fink.

As the day wears on, the occupation of the spillway gates grows into a full event. The takeover of the gates has proven to be a successful operation. Fink has finished his outline on the event and suggests to Nikani that they'd better take another route back to the Indian camp.

"The Movie Flat is the shortest way back. Turn left at the bottom of the hill," instructs Nikani.

Traveling on a dirt road through the Alabama Hills, Fink is considering visiting the movie set of *Riders of the Purple Sage* and Tom Mix, but an urgency drives him on to get back to Lone Pine.

"Anyway, as I was saying, the sooner I get this to my boss the faster it goes to press. This is the story I was looking for. It would have never happened without you Nikani, and you too Solomon," says Fink as they drive on.

"Hey Fink! There's that movie set you were telling us about. Are you going to stop and say hello to your friend?" Solomon asks.

"I know I told him we would get together today, and I was considering it, but it's not possible. I have to call this story in to Los Angeles, Tom will have to wait another day," says Fink.

"Who is this guy riding up on a horse?" asks Nikani.

"Oh no, not now Tom," moans Fink. Tom Mix rides up to them on "Tony the Horse."

"Perfect timing Jimmy. We worked a half day, then we called it quits," says Mix.

"It's not what it seems Tom, you see there's..." begins Fink, as he is interrupted by Mix.

"I've got a scoop for you Jimmy. Right now as we speak," says Mix.

"I know. The new Tom Mix movie; sensational, ground breaking, etcetera, etcetera," predicts Fink.

"Oh, everyone already knows that. How about this; The ranchers and farmers have taken over the Alabama Gates spillway. It's why I wrapped early. Half, if not all, the extras are locals. Come on, let's go down, catch all the action. Hell, I even sent the Mariachi boys down to entertain the crowd. What do you say?" Mix asks.

"Tom, we just came from the gates, we weren't down at the site, we were above it watching the whole thing as it happened, and..." says Fink.

"And, you're on your way right now to report the story," says Mix, finishing Fink's sentence.

"No time to waste Tom," says Fink.

"Say, I'm not going to be in that story of yours, am I?" Mix asks.

"Are you kidding me? That's another 10,000 copies sold. You're up here siding with the ranchers. It'll be good for you and good for me, everybody's happy," says Fink.

"Well, on second thought, I think I'll stay here, maybe take Tony down to the creek and get him a bath," says Mix. With that he spins his horse around and heads for the movie set at full gallop. "Adios muchachos!" Mix shouts to Fink.

Later, upon reaching the Indian camp, Nikani and Solomon walk Fink to his car. Fink cranks the engine. The rental starts right up, and a silent cheer goes out to Solomon and Nikani.

"I wish we had more time to spend on that fantastic story of the old days. If it gets published, I'll send you a copy," says Fink as he pulls away. Solomon and his grandfather watch as the vehicle slowly crosses the creek without getting stuck.

"How come Fink didn't want to go fishing, grandpa?" Solomon asks.

"It's the way of others, grandson, it's their idea of how to go about their lives, not being as lucky as you and I. Fink knows all men have to fish, but on this day, he just couldn't to go fishing," Nikani says.

"Do you think he will ever want to go fishing with us, grampa?

"I think, in time, James Fink will want to fish for us all," Nikani says, pulling his smoking pipe from his vest. The other camp occupants gather around Nikani's car to talk about what happened on the drive. As they begin to explain the witnessing of the spillway seizure. A short distance from the camp, Nikani and Solomon can be seen explaining while making gestures with full excitement.

While driving into Lone Pine, Fink pulls up to a stop at a main intersection. He notices the town seems almost deserted. He continues slowly towards the hotel. A sign hanging in a shop window: "Gone to the Aqueduct," and another sign in a barber shop: "At the Alabama Gates." The temptation to follow a buckboard with horses at full gallop is overwhelming, but he avoids the urge. He begins to reassure himself out loud: "Make the call. Make the call first," he mutters to himself.

Inside the hotel, the clerk is out of the lobby. Fink puts his briefcase on the counter and pulls out a note pad, he pulls out a pocket watch from his vest and checks the time. The attendant bell is rung, still no clerk, his pocket watch is checked again as his patience grows thin.

"Hello, is anyone here. Front desk please," hollers Fink out into the court yard. Fink pulls the phone out from behind the front desk.

"Operator, this is an urgent, collect, person-to-person, call to Walt McIntee in Los Angeles, Madison 8-5421." The phone begins to ring. "Walt, yes, I have transportation, thank you for everything. I have a scoop on the Owens Valley water war. The Story Line is: 'City Water Seized.' Early this morning a mob of 100 farmers and ranchers seized the Los Angeles City Water Supply. At approximately 7:00 a.m., a group of Owens Valley protestors stormed Los Angeles City property, vandalized locks, took hostage a city employee, and opened the spillway gates. . ."

The hotel clerk returns to find Fink on the line with his boss.

"Lets hope that is a collect call," he advises. Fink nods as the conversation comes to an end.

"I was going to give you one more day to return to the hotel. If you didn't return, a deputy was to be sent looking for you," the clerk points out.

"Thank you for the concern, but as it turned out, my stay at the Indian camp wasn't so bad after all. As a matter of fact, they were down right hospitable," indicates Fink.

"Well, your room is clean and your bed sheets are turned down and waiting for you," says the clerk as he places a large envelope on the counter.

"It's only six o'clock, everybody must go to bed with the birds," says Fink as he sees the clerk tapping his fingers on the envelope.

"This came for you yesterday. I don't know who dropped it off, just has your name on it," says the clerk. Fink takes the envelope and examines it with curiosity.

"Any unusual occurrence today? The town seems a little empty this evening," says Fink with raised eye brows.

"Nope, nothing happening around here," he says, looking down. Fink picks up his brief case and starts for the door.

"Nothing? Not even a cat fight?" Fink inquires.

"Nope, not even a cat fight," he says. Fink walks to his room, still studying the envelope. His thoughts return to the clerk, blatantly lying to him, and pretending not to know of the takeover at the gates. He smiles, visualizing the look on his face when he reads the article that will be put to press tonight.

CHAPTER SEVEN
The Army Records And The Massacre

Inside his room, Fink opens the envelope and reads the cover page of the multi page document: UNITED STATES ARMY RECORD 1861. LIEUTENANT BARRY FRENCH.

Fink reaches for several pieces of venison jerky and begins chewing on the dry meat while reading the records:

June 25, 1861, the Second Army of the California Volunteers departed meadows lush with salt grass at Cartago and dispatched the company to a settlement in the lower Owens Valley. In the evening hours of the night before, a settler by the name of Johnson entered the camp with reports of hostile Indians at his settlement on Lone Pine Creek. Johnson's statements were in part:

'These thieving Indians have been stealing everything that ain't tied down, Lieutenant. If you hadn't come along when you did, they'd have murdered every God fearing one of us,' said Johnston.

"I observed Mr. Johnson with doubt, his account did not add up. I then continued with my entries into the military record book," wrote Lt. French.

"You say Indians attacked your home continuously for at least three days straight, and you say they had rifles?" Lt. French asked. Before the settler could answer, a sergeant approaches, and looking down at his records tablet, scratching his head under his hat, he drew me aside and stated:

"The most peculiar thing I ever saw lieutenant, there are no arrows, no bullet holes, not one sign of an Indian attack, heck even the one's killed weren't armed.' Sgt. Jones then remarked that it looked to him like the settlers hornswoggled the U.S. Second Army," says the sergeant.

"It seems to me that the Colonel is concerned about the incident, as he wants every incident having to do with hostiles to be reported in a concise manner," added the sergeant.

"Take a better look around and find out where those articles of clothing were obtained, I myself observed one of the men pass with a beaded belt slung over his shoulder and a pair of small moccasins dangling from his fingers," said the lieutenant.

"Orders had been given not to desecrate the bodies in anyway," added the lieutenant.

"It was then that Col. Stevens gave me the order to have my report before him by the following day. The Col. advised that I would do well if all the circumstances leading up to the incident were included. I informed the settlers that we'd be pulling out of the immediate area to allow the Indians to retrieve their dead. If the settlers wished, they could camp near the detachment tonight," wrote French.

"It was then that one of the settlers shouted, 'Let them rot in the sun, it'll teach the rest of them,' and yet another said, 'This land belongs to us, not them heathen Indians, kill 'em all I say, every last thieving' one of them,'or words to that effect,

"I explained to Mr. Johnson that our orders were clear, we were here to evaluate any injustice perpetrated against the Indians of this valley, and that includes any incident having peculiarities that rank among the incident that took place here yesterday,

"The detachment made their camp approximately 100 yards from the battle site. At sundown the men became quiet, observing the majestic mountain range of the Sierra Nevada. Colonel Stevens stood outside his tent, taking in the sight of a sunset. The camp had settled and I joined the Colonel.

"'The country is growing at such a pace, it will be sooner than we can imagine. This valley will bloom with settlements, and the natives will be gone,' the Colonel said to me.

"In a previous fight, which took place in the month of March, the whites involved were settlers, not 'Secessionist,' as reported. It is not known for sure, but from what I gather, the Secessionist have been flocking over the mountains from all directions, stirring up both Indians and whites," Col. Stevens writes.

In his hotel room, Fink thumbs through the documents to find the rest of the report, but is unsuccessful. Instead, he discovers a hand written letter from Colonel Stevens to his wife.

April 2, 1862. Day twenty. My dear wife, today we arrived in the beautiful Owens River Valley. With all that is happening with the war and all, it does my heart good to know there is a place that is seemingly unaffected. With things moving fast as they are, it is an inevitability that the Indians in this part, and all over for that fact, are doomed by encroachment of advancing civilization.

Word was sent from Los Angeles that Congress is passing a Homestead Act to aid eastern settlers in their settlements. They have valued the land to be at one dollar and twenty-five cents an acre. Our orders to establish a reservation for the Indians seems to be diminished with the Washoe and Coso mines now discovered. No doubt the railroad will follow. People have come into this Valley with livestock to convenience the mines with the sale of beef. The poor Indians, having their foraging fields turned into pasture are at a loss. It is possible whites are to blame, also probable that in strict justice they should be compelled to move away, leaving the Valley once again to its rightful owners," writes Stevens.

After reading the document in its entirety, Fink checks the envelope again for any note he may have missed that would reveal the sender. With no indication of the owner of the document, he settles down onto the soft bed and quickly falls fast asleep.

CHAPTER EIGHT
A Story for Solomon

Back at the Indian camp, Solomon is sitting at the picnic table, watching his grandfather, Nikani prepare dinner. He seems restless and asks his grandfather to continue the story of when he was in his younger years. The mention of his grandmother sparked a torrent of questions within the little boy, and Nikani now feels obligated to continue with his story about the past for Solomon's sake.

Now, in Nikani's mind it is 1861, the year when all the fighting started between the Owens Valley Indians and the U.S. Calvary 2nd Army. It was also the year Nikani decided to marry. In a strange way, he feels that if the wars hadn't begun, he would have not been joined with his wife. The conversation that took place earlier with Fink, softened his heart, a place where he keeps the memories of Tenapa. Conveyed in story, Nikani transports Solomon in time to 1861 a time Solomon can only imagination.

It is early evening at the Shoshoni winter camp. The council meeting had lasted most of the day, and the warriors are exiting the cave. Nikani walks toward his dwelling, one of many circular clay-dirt mounds in the village. A close friend approaches Nikani. It is Hu'na, a childhood friend, and he greets him in boisterous voice.

"So my friend, tell me what it was that you saw, what did they look like? Did they have good horses that can be taken in the night? When we steal them, we will be able to trade them for wives," states Hu'na, loud enough for a group of young Indian women can hear. They smile as they go about their work, making sure the elder women do not see their interest. Nikani jokes with Hu'na in warrior sarcasm.

"The Sina'si are well fed, they have hair on their face, not smooth like your face, Hu'na. They have been on the trail a long time, if they catch you stealing their horses, they will make you a wife," says Nikani. Hu'na twists Nikani in a head lock. Their horseplay is being observed by several young women who look on disapprovingly.

One of the women is Tenapa, a beautiful seventeen year old girl. She is grand daughter to a Shoshoni legend. Her grandfather led a hunting party from the Inyo Mountains, to what is now Northern Nevada, and into Southern Idaho to hunt the buffalo.

As the legend was told, it was in the early spring of 1786. Ishi-Wahni, or Silver Fox, had a vision that famine was to ravage Shoshoni villages throughout their homelands. A hunting party of seven set off on a journey that would have him return with 500 pounds of dried buffalo meat, hides, and bone tools. The winter of 1786 was a hard one, but because of Ishi, his village and others survived.

Tenapa is now a young woman, and she has been waiting for Nikani to ask her father for her hand in marriage. It has been in his heart since he was fifteen years old. Now, with the honorable position of warrior scout bestowed upon him, Nikani feels he is worthy to have a mate. Tenapa does not miss a chance to smile at Nikani with her sparkling almond eyes. Her straight, long, dark hair is one of the reasons Nikani always smiles back.

Tenapa makes eye contact with Nikani, and the horseplay ends, he pushes Hu'na away.

"When I return with horses, they will all go to your uncle for the hand of his beautiful Tenapa," says Nikani with a softness in his voice. Hu'na looks at his friend in disbelief, oblivious to his cousin Tenapa's beauty. Nikani tries to fend off the horseplay, but it continues despite his unwilling participation. At the family dwelling of Nikani, his mother has prepared the evening meal.

Inside the earthen structure known as a "dug out," it is comfortable, and can sleep up to eight people. The inner walls are stepped down three feet, then a three foot shelf, then a fire pit. The flickering fire from the hearth heats a hanging clay pot, slow cooking a stew of deer meat, camas root, wild onions, pine nuts, and mesquite beans.

A buckskin door flap is pulled back, and Nikani's enters. His mother, Lala, is sitting by the fire, sewing a pair of moccasins. Lala is in her thirties, she is strong willed, but kind. Nikani, being her only child, is well cared for and loved.

"Was that Hu'na's voice I heard just outside our dugout?" Lala asks. "It was. I wanted to ask if he could join us to eat," says Nikani.

"Has he forgotten his home, or have his parents run away from him?" asks Lala calmly. Nikani sticks his head out of the door flap and shrugs his shoulders. Hu'na accepts the rejection without a second thought and continues on his way. Lala hands her son a piece of damp buckskin, Nikani rubs his hands clean, then pours some tea into a gourd cup and sits at the fire. Lifting the cover from the clay pot, he scoops some stew from one pot and watercress from another. Lala offers a woven plate of fry bread, afterwards, silent prayer.

"When your father returns from the hunt, he will be proud to learn of your achievement. The others in the camp have been talking, they are saying that you have grown to be a dedicated young heart to your people. I am proud of my son, and your father will be honored," she says affectionately.

Later, on a bed plush with skins, Nikani sleeps soundly while his mother lay awake. She is worried about Nikani's father, who is a day late returning from the hunt in the Sierra Mountains. Lala quietly rises from her bed to put wood on the small fire. Nikani stirs and opens his eyes to see his mother staring longingly into the fire, her husband's buckskin jacket next to her cheek.

Lala steps out of the hut, she stands looking up at the night sky, and begins whispering a prayer to the Little Dipper, shinning in the night sky.

Long ago, before Nikani was born, Lala and her husband, Joaquin, made a promise to one another during their marriage vows. It was said that if ever they would be away from each other, their words would be conveyed through the stars of the Little Dipper. Through long hunts, her thoughts to her husband never failed to reach him at the moment he turned his eyes to the stars.

The fire has dwindled, all is quiet in the mountain village. Nikani and his mother are asleep. The lodge poles that supports the roof of the dwelling, begin to tremble. Earthen dust falls, sifting downward. A subtle ground rumble starts to grow then subsides. Suddenly the ground quakes violently. Nikani bolts to a sitting up position, he sees the roof supports shifting downward. Lala wakes, fear and panic fill her eyes, she is helped towards the door by Nikani.

The entire village has been disrupted as the earthquake continues to rumble deep in the ground beneath them. Frightened women, holding their children are fleeing to open ground. There is screaming and crying, the men are hollering out orders to go calm the horses. Out of the chaos, Hu'na finds Nikani.

"The Earth talks to you my good friend! It's telling everyone that you have been chosen," shouts Hu'na. The loud rumble is dampened by a huge explosion. The night sky lights up as white, hot embers rocket skyward, and smoking debris rains down on the village.

"Run! Run to the bluffs!" Hu'na shouts to Nikani. Lala witnesses the foolishness and becomes irritated when she see's Hu'na leading her son away. Tenapa observes Lala's concern and goes to her. They watch as the young men make their way to the bluffs.

Running at a fast pace, the pair hurdle over tumbling boulders on the narrow trail. The ground beneath their feet continues to quake intermittently as they rush to the bluffs. Hu'na looses his footing and tumbles to the ground. He rolls and bounces back up on his feet, yelling out war hoops.

"Hu'na, you are a crazy like the coyote! The ground should swallow you and spit you out!" Nikani hollers.

"It would be good! I would be happy!" Hu'na replies.

Once Nikani and Hu'na have reached the overlook, they stand looking down upon their Sacred Ground, it is a geothermal field. The two young warriors are dwarfed by gigantic columns of steam, blowing hundreds of feet into the night air. The entire Sacred Grounds are lit by spontaneous blue and orange flames, caused by gases omitting from just below the earth's surface. It is deafening, but exhilarating at the same time. Hu'na pulls Nikani close, so that he can hear his words.

"This is your power Nikani, the Earth shows you; this is your protection! The sina'si will not be able to harm you!" Hu'na shouts.

"If I am the one who is to be chosen, then you are the one to watch over me, in the warrior's way," replies Nikani.

"Always my brother...always," says Hu'na, a warriors handshake is given as they stand against raging columns of illuminated steam that disappear into the night sky.

The next morning, the entire village prepares for the ceremony ordered by Chief Monache. A lodge is being erected in the center of the now quiet ceremony grounds. Clay pots filled with food are placed directly into the boiling, colored mud, slow cooking until ready to be eaten. Others from the village haul reeds and willows to a lodge that will contain the ceremony.

A young Indian boy, running through the village, seeks out LaLa with a word from Monache.

She enters the family dwelling with a small bowl of tea for her still sleeping son. Quietly she places the bowl along side Nikani, who then awakes after feeling her presence. Nikani sits up in his bed roll, LaLa smooths his long hair.

"You still have ash in your hair from last night. If you had fallen into a hot mud pool, you would have deserved it for acting so foolish," scolds Lala.

"The runners have arrived, they bring word the hunting party has been spotted near the base of the blue mountains. Tomorrow, as the sun sets, they will be here, and you will still be in ceremony. I want you to offer this tobacco for your father's safe return," suggests Lala.

"I made tea for you, it is strong with honey. It is not too hot, so you can drink it fast. This will give you strength for the ceremony, you will need it," advises his mother. Nikani first sips the tea, but it's sweetness prompts him to drink eagerly. Lala prepares another mixture of the tea.

"Mother, I would like very much to tell father of my accomplishment. Let him know that I have honored him in doing as I was taught," says Nikani.

"I think the runners have taken care to let him know, but I will tell him again, and again," says Lala.

Nikani emerges from his dwelling. Tenapa hurries over to him with a ladle of water. Nikani grins when he sees the beautiful girl approaching.

"It was drawn from a hidden spring when the sunrise sky became bright with color," she says enticingly. Their eyes meet as Nikani places the ladle to his lips.

"Drink of it, and you will see it is pure and sweet, like my yearning heart," says Tenapa. The other young women nearby begin to snicker at Tenapa's audacious advance.

"My father speaks highly of you, he says you will make a good husband to someone, someday," she says looking up to him with soft eyes. Nikani begins to blush, he slowly continues on his way, leading her away from her onlooking friends.

"And you, do you think I will make a good husband someday?" asks Nikani. Tenapa's eyes light up. Thrilled, she turns and runs back to the group of young Indian women standing by the water jars. LaLa has also been watching the pairing ritual. She smiles, knowing that her son and Tenapa would make a fine couple.

Nikani continues towards the ceremonial grounds, he looks up as if to give a silent prayer.

"Someday, my sweet Tenapa," he says aloud.

Hu'na has caught up with Nikani and accompanies him on the way to the ceremony. "I was told how to survive the ceremony. My uncle says that on the third day of sweat, your vision will come to you," he says in confidence.

"Hu'na, my only vision right now belongs to your cousin, Tenapa, and now you are making it go away," says Nikani.

Hu'na is confounded at Nikani's rejection to his all important information, but not to be discouraged, he continues to walk with his friend as they make their way.

CHAPTER NINE
Old Joaquin The Hunter
1861

From high on top of a craggy, granite wall, the valley floor can be seen, shadowed by the majestic High Sierra Mountain range. The seven member hunting party appear out of the mouth of a canyon, dwarfed by towering granite canyon walls. The horses are packed well with game meat and skins. Nikani's father, Joaquin, is leading the hunting party out of the Sierra side of the valley. A seasoned hunter and experienced warrior, Joaquin is in his 40s and very fit, his shoulders glisten in the afternoon sun. Three eagle feathers adorn his braided hair, still dripping wet from the water he splashed with to keep cool. The horse he is riding suddenly becomes alert, flaring its nostrils and throwing its head.

The second in lead watches as Joaquin catches a human track that has crossed the trail. Looking down from side to side, he pulls his horse to a standstill. With a held up hand, he brings the hunting party to a halt. They observe as Joaquin motions that the track leads over the ledge and down into the canyon. A telescope is taken from his saddle bag, and in the distance, he spies a small band of 10 to 15 Indians on foot, making their way towards the pass.

"It looks to me like they are Paiute. They are running from something, the women have no packs, the men's quivers are empty, they have no water bags," says Joaquin.

"We should not interfere with the them. If they are running from a battle, their warfare should not concern us," says another hunter.

"It is not their own they run from, look close," Joaquin says as he hands over his telescope. "From here you can see that there is one woman, she has a child in her arms, but it does not look alive. There are other women with children, the children are wounded, some have died on their mother's backs. We should ride to our own, let the Paiute make their way."

Joaquin summons another rider, Pangwi, a hunter who knows the Paiute people and their language. He points to the tattered group. A question is posed to him as he focuses on the fleeing people below.

"Pangwi, you have known the Paiute, are their children safe among their own, even in warfare?" Joaquin asks. "Paiutes do not harm children, if those young ones have been hurt, it was not from any rival. White's kill the children of Indians. We should go down and hold council with their warriors," says Pangwi. Joaquin nods his approval. Pangwi mounts his horse and starts down toward the distressed group.

Disgruntled, one of the Shoshoni in the hunting party fires-up his horse, whirling at full speed in a short distance. Pulling his horse to a halt, he dismounts and directs his anger towards Joaquin.

"E-shaa! They are Indian people too, we are not enemies with the Paiute. Their enemies are our enemies," says the young warrior.

"Your anger is felt by us all, but let us wait for word that will give reason to fight," says Joaquin.

Later, as the sun moves closer to the Sierra's, an eagle circles above. While holding their lead ropes, the dismounted hunting party rests in the shade of their horses, some are napping. Joaquin observes the activity below, now grouped in a small circle. A wail is heard in the distance as one of the women describes to Pangwi how her child's life was taken. The men in their party begin shouting out in their anger.

Joaquin turns to observe the reactions of his warriors. There are some in the hunting party that are saddened by the ordeal, while the others mutter words in unforgiving tones. He stands to see that Pangwi has mounted his horse. Dust is kicked up by his horse as he returns at full gallop.

Back at the lookout point, where the others have been ordered by Joaquin to stand down, Pangwi relates the Paiute's plight to the hunting party. They listen as he tells them what was told to him. With a stick, Pangwi scratches a map in sand.

"The fight happened here, north of the e-sha water, below Chief George's camp at Manzanae.

The Paiutes went to trade with the whites, when they began shooting at them for no reason. Then soldiers came and they too began to shoot, trying to kill everyone. The soldiers chased some of the Paiutes to the lake. With no place else to go, the men, women, and some children went into the lake," says Pangwi.

"They tried to swim across the lake?" a warrior in the hunting party asks.

"Some did. The soldiers began shooting at them, killing them in the water. They laughed and made it a game," Pangwi says looking down.

"Sina'si? From where did they come, and why are they making war? The Paiute have done nothing but protect what is theirs. It is the whites, they should be blamed for what they do!" another warrior shouts out.

"Be still. We all know that where the whites settle, Sina'si draw their long knives, Indian people lose their land and their lives! They do not want us to live here anymore. Word will be at Chief George's camp by sundown, and Paiute warriors will drive them out!" another warrior exclaims.

"We must ride without rest, our people must be made safe," says Joaquin. He senses reluctance among his hunting party.

"The Paiutes will seek revenge, I want to ride north and join them in battle," says another.

"Do what you think is right, but our village was safe when we left, when we ride back to protect them, where will you be?" Joaquin asks.

The warrior mounts up, he turns to see if anyone else will join him. He observes the remainder of his hunting party with conviction, reminding them where their loyalties lie.

"What happened next, grampa?" Solomon asks with a saddened tone.

"The hunting party rode without rest, it was our fear that what had happened to those Paiutes might've happened to our village. We did not know, but that one fight was the beginning of the end, for us Indians," reveals Nikani.

Solomon is captivated with his grandfather's story, he has not taken his eyes from his grandfather for almost an hour.

"After that day, I could see that there was a terrible fear in my father's heart for Indian people all over the land," says Nikani to Solomon.

"Grampa, do you think that if this land was dry with no water, the soldiers would've wanted it?" Solomon asks.

"I think not, the army came to aid the settlement. Maybe, I learned that from someone who read a book of army records, it told all about the Indian wars in this valley. Those records showed that volunteers in the U.S. army came here to make a reservation for Indian people," Nikani explains.

"Where's our reservation?" Solomon asks. "It's out there someplace. When they make up their mind, we might get one," laughs Nikani.

"It never got to be known, but from that day on, it was nothing but fighting," adds Nikani.

"Auntie says there was fighting everywhere, there was even a war way back where the sun rises," says Solomon.

"Auntie is right, the whites were fighting themselves and the Indians at the same time. We won some battles, but lost many. You may as well be told now, because it won't be learned anywhere else," says Nikani looking directly into his grandson's eyes.

"In those days, it was not illegal to kill Indians for their land," says Nikani.

"Why did they have to do that? Solomon asks with a perplexed expression.

"There's so much land, nobody can live on all of it," Solomon adds.

"One day, you will want to look into it yourself grandson," says Nikani with a pat on Solomon's shoulder.

A voice is heard, and they turn to see it is Waneema, cousin to Nikani.

"Everyone says thank you for the baked rabbit and the trout, cousin," says Waneema as she places a pot and frying pan onto the cook stove.

"You can thank Solomon for the trout," says Nikani.

"You are such a good fish catcher, little man," she says thankfully.

"I hope you caught them at Hogback," she says.

"That's where we fish. Auntie Waneema, how come you tell me not to fish Lone Pine Creek?" Solomon asks.

128.

"Well, I don't mean the whole creek, just the lower end, right above the aqueduct," explains Waneema.

"Remember, I told you about the Indian wars?" Nikani asks. Solomon nods his head eagerly. "Well, that's where it all started, and this is where the story ends for you, grandson. Because it is time for you to go to bed, we've had a busy day. Your bed is already made and there's fire in the wood stove, sleep well," he adds.

"Grandpa, I don't want to go to bed yet. I want to hear some more stories," pleads Solomon. Nikani gives in and agrees to let him stay up for just a while longer, but only if he remains quiet.

Later, when most of the camp has gone to sleep, Nikani and Waneema continue to recall stories. As the stories are retold, forgotten memories are replenished by Waneema's added point of view.

"I don't know if your grampa has told you this story, but we found out years after the wars," Waneema tells Solomon.

"It was told to us by several old Paiutes, who used to trade with the whites, here on Lone Pine Creek. Those who told the story were very young when it happened," says Waneema.

"They said a few other Indian children were playing up on the creek one day. Right there where you used to catch fish. They were sneaking up on a stone house built by the settlers. One of the old Paiutes told us that he had his headband on, with a feather in his hair, and a play-bow with arrows," continues Waneema.

"He said that he parted the willows to see many mounted soldiers come into his view. They snuck around, climbing to a better spot in the rocks, and could see everything down below," she says.

"The way it was told; it became busy with soldiers, and it looked like they were counting the bodies of dead Indian people that he did not recognize.

"He saw Army officers writing things down on paper, he did not know at the time, but they were writing words of the battle that took place the day before. The owner of the stone house, was there telling him what to write. He pointed in our direction, and we ducked down so the soldiers could not see us," conveys Waneema in the words of the survivors.

"They were just kids back then, not knowing what could happen to them if they were seen. That old Paiute told the story like it all just happened yesterday," she adds, as Nikani nods in agreement, recalling the story.

"Every Indian in the Owens Valley ought to remember that story, because it was the beginning of the Indian wars, and the end of a way of life for our people," says Nikani.

"Owens Valley Indians were shown many things that they had never seen or done before. Us Indians had never tasted whiskey before, it made fools of the men and made the women cry out of sadness," says Waneema.

"There is lots of history that you will learn grandson, but not tonight, it is past your bedtime. There is a pot of heated water on the stove, go wash up and get ready for bed," says Nikani.

"Promise to tell me more tomorrow?" Solomon asks.

"I promise, little by little," replies Nikani.

CHAPTER TEN
L.A. Needs Water

A return trip to Los Angeles has been planned by Fink, but before leaving, a visit must be paid to Nikani at the Indian camp. Once at the camp, Fink is in the process of fulfilling a promise made to Solomon that entails his childhood while living in Los Angeles, and fishing. Fink recalls his experiences as a youth, fishing off the coast with his father twenty years ago. The mention of ocean fishing to Solomon is a special treat, he can't imagine fishing in waters where there are fish large enough to eat him. Solomon listens enthusiastically to Fink's fish story. Even though Solomon has never been to an ocean, much less fish in one, he has a feeling that Fink knows nothing about trout fishing.

While driving the backroads at the base of the Sierra's, Nikani has again allowed Fink to take the wheel. He has bombarded Nikani with a series of well timed compliments. Nikani listens as Fink brags about the Model T, and how effortlessly it climbed the hills above Moffat Ranch. Then Nikani's cooking is the subject of praise, followed by his ability to recall the past. It was not meant to be intentional, but more of a result of Fink's outpouring of gratitude for the hospitality he has been shown. He is honored to have been invited into their lives, their food that was hard to come by, and their friendship. It is Nikani's traditional values that allowed Fink to be among his people without obligation.

"You know, what gets me about you, Nikani? All the dignity in the world won't put food in your pantry, why won't you take money from me to buy food?" asks Fink.

"You are my guest, Fink. If I were to show at your house as a guest, you would not take money or food from me in exchange for hospitality," says Nikani.

"Totally different, for one thing, my pantry is stocked," says Fink.

"As mine, we have a stream full of fish, pastures teeming with rabbits and deer forever," replies Nikani.

"You just keep riding along this dirt road, it will take us to Hog Back Creek," adds Nikani, as he directs Fink to a small meadow with a stream running through it. The vehicle comes to a stop, and an excited Solomon jumps out of the back seat and opens the trunk. He pulls out two fishing poles.

"Hey Fink, can you fish?" asks Solomon. Fink turns to Nikani.

"Thank you Solomon, but your grand father and I have a little more to discuss," says Fink.

"It's time to fish, if you don't catch any fish, you don't eat," says Nikani with raised eye brows. Fink appeals to Nikani with pleading eyes, but is met with a gesture of denial. Fink opens the driver's side door.

"I know it's the way you do things, but Nikani, it's not a problem for me, I have an expense account. In fact, Solomon can put his fishing pole away, because I will take both of you to dinner tonight," says Fink. Solomon looks to his grandfather, being eager to catch some fish.

"Come-on Fink, let's go fish! I know where the good holes are at," he says. Solomon hurries down to the creek as a reluctant Fink takes a pole and follows. Nikani props his feet up and tips his hat over his eyes in preparation for a nap.

It is now early evening, and after the fishing expedition, Fink finds himself back at the Indian camp. Nikani is at the cook stove, frying the day's catch. At the long wooden table, Fink and Solomon are playing a board game. A whoop is heard by Nikani as the checker game comes to an end.

"You beat me again. How did you do that?" asks Fink.

"I do it, because I'm good at it," replies Solomon.

"Clear the table boys, supper is ready," says Nikani. The table is quickly cleared and two plates are place before them. Looking down onto the plate, Fink's appetite grows as a waft of potatoes, blanched water cress, and fried trout rises from his plate.

"And fresh baked biscuits. Nikani, you should open a restaurant," comments Fink.

"A restaurant? I can't even walk into one, much less own one," remarks Nikani. "Eat up, before it gets cold," he adds.

Fink watches as Solomon reveals to him how to pull the bones from a cooked trout.

"Grampa first taught me how to eat a fish, isn't that right, grampa?" Solomon offers.

"It doesn't look like much, how many of these are you supposed to eat?" Fink asks.

I can eat two, grampa can eat about four of them," says Solomon.

Fink leans forward and experiences his first taste of camp cooked trout. He approves with raised eyebrows. Nikani and Solomon look on as Fink enjoys his meal.

"I was telling grandson today of the river that still runs unchanged. The Paiutes practiced their own method of farming by tapping into the valley river," begins Nikani. Fink does not reach for his note book but opts to enjoy the plate of trout.

"They would let the water spill into fields of thick rich grass seed, wild oats, buck wheat, and camas," says Nikani as he walks to the stove. Taking a coffee pot, he pours for both Fink and himself.

"The rich fields were never turned, but every year we would help them burn the grass. The deer would come down from the mountains and feed on the new grown grass. Every spring the river would return in full strength and provide for the people," says Nikani. Solomon goes to feed the fish bones to his dog, he then goes to sit by his grandfather.

"It was 1861, Nikani, after the Army rode into the valley. The Shoshoni ceremony had confirmed you to be a scout, is that right?" Fink asks. Nikani looks down at Solomon now snuggled next to him, he has fallen fast asleep. Nikani then continues the story.

"That night, when my father returned from the hunt, he said later that the village appeared to be deserted as they rode in. The hunting party is uncertain as they look for signs of life in the village. Then a fire watcher appears and greets the men.

"Our hunters have retuned, and with plenty of meat," shouts the fire watcher. Joaquin turns with an inquisitive look, "Ceremony?" he asks.

"Chief Monache will call on the spirits for guidance for one of our own, it is Nikani, your only son," says the fire watcher. Joaquin dismounts, pulls his blanket from his horse, and his jacket and his Sharp's Rifle from the saddle. Joaquin's horse is lead away by the fire watcher. In the distance war whoops can be heard.

Joaquin slings a buckskin over his shoulder. Women and children hurry by as Joaquin makes his way to his dwelling. A soft smile comes over his face, he has caught sight of his wife approaching. Lala breaks into a run at the sight of her husband, they meet in an embrace, she holds him tightly, her head resting against his chest.

Joaquin gently lifts her chin, he touches his cheek to her, taking in her scent.

"Circles placed between two hearts will always test a strength in true men. It is never settling, always burning within, that strength is yours, from me to you, always," Joaquin says softly. Looking into her husbands eyes, Lala smiles seductively.

"Your strength will be tested again, and again in my arms tonight, I will replenish your heart with the warmth that has held me since the moment you left," says Lala.

One of the elder women calls to Lala as they walk by, reminding her of her duties to honor her son. "Our son has been called upon to stand watch over the people," says Lala to her husband. "He will do a ceremony to receive his path and direction, we will talk later, for now I have to help with preparation, keep me in your thoughts." Without another word Lala pulls herself away reluctantly to join the other women on their way back to the village, she turns to steal a glance.

Lala's walk takes on a youthful bounce, which Joaquin seems to enjoy, his gaze is interrupted by Kotach'wi (Ko-tosh-way), father to Hu'na. Kotach'wi is a tribal leader and a bullet from a settler has left him with a limp. A walking staff is needed to get around.

"The return of our warriors will carry the ceremony, come watch as our sons enter into the warriors way. Chief Monache has chosen Nikani as the Observer for the people...Nikani has chosen Hu'na to join him," says Kotach'wi.

"It's what his mother said, but why now?" Joaquin asks.

"Monache was given word of the soldiers, and one of the hunting party just spoke about a battle. They have killed ours?" he asks.

"We came across some Paiute. They said it was settlers in the Valley of the Inyo that took the lives of some of their men, along with the lives of their children and women," says Joaquin.

Kotach'wi curses a single word, he turns to Joaquin and can see the anger in his weary eyes. Joaquin politely excuses himself with a nod then continues toward the ceremony.

As Joaquin approaches the ceremony grounds, he is joined by Lala. A circle gathers around Joaquin to hear the story of the fleeing Paiutes.

"We did not see the battle, all we know is what the women told Pangwi. As far as I can tell, there was no battle, just slaughter for no reason," explains Joaquin.

"Did you see the sina'si?" a warrior asks.

"I did not, and I can tell you this; if there was sina'si anywhere in our vision they would have been seen," says Joaquin with Lala by his side.

"Your son, Nikani, has seen the long knives riding into the valley from this side of the mountains," says another.

"If that is what he saw, then we have his word for it. We came across their tracks, there must be as many as half our village. They have come to stay for a while, their wagon tracks are deep, their supplies are many," says Joaquin.

"They're worried they will find us," says Lala.

"If they do, then we will bring them to council. If that does not happen, then we will fight," says Joaquin.

"My son is in ceremony, the vision will come to him. Right now, we must place our strengths inside the ceremony lodge to help him. It is for the people that he sweats," says Joaquin.

Inside the ceremonial lodge, an intensely high chant radiates outward from the lodge. Nikani, Hu'na, Monache, and a medicine man are sitting on a ground covered with Tule Reed, steam fills the lodge. The villagers form a circle outside the lodge and join in, strengthening the chant. A hue of an orange glow from the red hot rocks begins to pulsate, penetrating the lodge and projecting outwards into the night sky. Nikani has drifted into a dream, leading to the spirit world.

His dream world takes on a surrealistic surrounding of a dismal barren landscape. He sees a glaring reflection of polished steel strobing into his eyes, then a saber cuts slowly through smoke filled air. From horseback he sees one of the women running with a child in her arms. A gloved hand, wielding the flashing strobe of a sword, strikes her down. She falls lifeless with her child tucked into her arms. Nikani can see himself falling backward through the air, arms outstretched. Bodies of his men friends and relatives fall downward through a dark space, their hair streaming upward. Hawks glide through the burning village then spiral upward to circle the carnage. Shadows of mounted soldiers continue to charge. Nikani wanders through a massacre, he comes upon a baby unaffected by the carnage. Nearby, an Indian woman struck with grief, is kneeling with her head bowed as if in prayer. Nikani becomes entranced, the woman's skin is encrusted with white, wind blown dust. He can now see the dark tracks of tears that have streaked her chalky white skin. The tracks of her tears take on the course of the Owens River, winding through the valley. A small puddle forms in the sand at her feet, taking on the shape of the Owens Lake. Slowly approaching, Nikani sees the woman is gently wiping away the chalky white sand from the faces of buried children. During the spirit dream, the intense visions cause Nikani to slump over into the lap of Hu'na. The dream breaks suddenly, and Nikani bolts upward and becomes fully conscious of his surroundings. The spirit world has released him with a death cry.

Outside the ceremony lodge, the death cry bleeds through the dream and into the ambience of the ceremony. The overpowering cry stops the chant for just a moment, then silence.

The door man for the ceremonial lodge turns to Joaquin. "That was the last round," he says as he pulls the door flap up and over onto the roof of the lodge. Through a cloud of steam emerges Chief

Monache, Hu'na, and Nikani. Joaquin and Kotach'wi lead their sons to the bathing area.

"Father, you're back from the hunt...I gave thanks for your safe return,"says Nikani.

"Thank you my son, your prayers worked for us all. I am proud of you my son. The spirits gave you a vision that was felt by all in village.

"The vision was strong it has left me weak and lightheaded," say Nikani.

"You men can sit in the bathing pond until your skin is soft and wrinkled, you deserve it. We will talk later my son," suggests Joaquin.

Water baskets have been drawn from the thermal pools. Nikani and Hu'na are disrobed and baskets of cool water are poured over their heads. A welcoming pool of warm water awaits their weary bones.

At sunrise the next day, with the blessing of Monache, Nikani and Hu'na have been sent on a quest to find the soldiers. Their mission is to observe and learn the reason they are in the valley. A defense has been planned by the war council, they have ordered the arrowhead makers to the obsidian grounds, and women to gather arrow shafts at the wild bamboo groves. Most importantly, the two observers are to find out what kind of muskets they are using against the Indians. The dream was translated by Monache, who saw danger for his people. His decision was to prepare for the day they will have to fight.

Nikani has mounted-up, his father walks up to hand him a buckskin jacket. Both young warriors are preparing to leave the village.

Joaquin has helped his son pack all that he will need for the journey. Hu'na rides up, leading another pack horse, he is escorted by his mother and father, walking along side his horse.

Lala steps up alongside the horse and takes Nikani's hand, she holds it to her cheek. Joaquin and Kotach'wi stand back and wait for their turn to bid them farewell. Hu'na rides up, and signals to Nikani just as Joaquin finishes checking the tie downs on the pack animals.

"You will do good my son, listen to the voice within and follow your heart so you can return to us. Our people have supplied your horses well with their best skins. They are for musket rifles, find the white traders, look for those with fear in their eyes they will seek your friendship," advises Joaquin. From atop his horse, Nikani looks down into his fathers eyes instilling the moment. Lala lets go of his hand and steps back, and gives a timid wave. Nikani takes the lead as he and Hu'na ride out of the village, one last glance back, and they see their parents standing proud as they wave goodbye.

On the outskirts of village Tenapa waits patiently for them to pass on the trail. She sits on top of a rocky ledge overlooking the village and an unobstructed view of the sunrise. Hu'na smiles as he catches sight of Tenapa. Nikani turns in his saddle towards Hu'na, a slight ration of sarcasm is about to be served up.

"My friend, look; there is a sleek she cat poised on the rocks above, ready to pounce," says Hu'na. Nikani smiles with sharpened eyes. He turns back in his saddle, and he looks up to see Tenapa posed seductively against a rock ledge. He rides up to the rock where Tenapa is waiting. She has chosen a rock that is perfectly level with Nikani as he sits horseback. Tenapa is pulled onto the horse and they embrace.

"Here is my promise to you, come back to me, I will wait. Go to the spring in the hills, the one with the arched rock over the stream. It has always been special. I will be there alone, waiting for you," says Tenapa.

CHAPTER ELEVEN
The Raid

November temperatures in the Owens Valley are mild compared with the rest of the country. The growing season lasts until October, warm enough to harvest a third cutting of alfalfa. Tonight, the temperature has dropped to just under 40 degrees. Fink has placed his exclusive in the hands of his Editor in Chief, Walt McIntee, and has made plans to leave for Los Angeles.

At the Indian camp, Fink is sitting with Nikani inside his shack. It is late at night, the camp is still vibrant with conversation and laughter. Solomon has gone to bed in his tree house and is sleeping soundly.

"How late into the fall season does Solomon sleep in the tree house? Fink asks.

"This time of year, Solomon is usually sleeping indoors. Somehow the tree house went from a perch to a cave, and he likes his cave," explains Nikani as he tosses a piece of wood into the stove.

"I know how he feels, when I built my fort no one could get me away from it. One day I moved back into my room and actually began to keep it clean," says Fink.

Fink is thankful that his new found friend is again communicating with him. He was beginning to get concerned that he was overloading Nikani by delving back into the past. He also worries that the emotional roller coaster ride may have affected his self-confidence in his desire to recall his past in the future. His reporter instincts tells him to wait before going any further with past accounts of his people. If there is anything he has learned from his experience at the Indian camp, it is patience.

"An observer holds the historical account for his tribe, he possesses a story that will be told for generations. When realized, it becomes a song that is taught throughout the tribes' existence. It is a very important realization," says Nikani.

"This may be wishful thinking, Nikani, but do you think my position in life qualifies me as an observer?" Fink asks.

"There may be some truth to that, but you have to remember this; being an observer is a very dangerous position. It is important for you to know this because the chosen person cannot become involved in what he is observing. If for any reason he becomes involved, it better be a good one. If a person violates that position, a life is taken, it is not always the observer at first, a loved one is more likely. An observer can act only to defend himself," Nikani says gravely.

"So, it's best for me just to be a lowly news reporter than an observer?" Fink asks, hoping Nikani will agree.

"My honor of having been an observer, above all, is the honor and respect that I have gained from my grandson. A simple little comfort, but one that I am very grateful for," says Nikani.

"You've done a great job raising him, he's happy, balanced and smart," praises Fink.

A car engine is heard, and the entire camp becomes silent. Throughout the locust grove, a spotlight strobes into the camp. Nikani and Fink turn their attention towards a vehicle bearing an emblem of the Los Angeles Police Department patrolling the aqueduct.

"I don't know why they keep their eye on this camp. It's not us that they have to worry about," says Nikani.

"I think they know that," says Fink.

"Then why do they make us feel like we are part of their water war?" Nikani asks.

"Because." Fink says.

"Because why?" Nikani asks.

"Well, because you are Indians. Ever since, well you know…" says Fink with hesitation.

"Know what? Nikani asks.

"Ever since Custer," Fink says, goading Nikani into a response.

"Ah yes, that guy. I heard it wasn't much of a fair fight," acknowledges Nikani.

"You know what I heard? I heard that one of his own men actually shot him, hoping that the rest of the Indians would leave them alone," says Fink, with a look of challenge.

"Probably so, it's what they did to us all the time; take out our leader first. But with us, there was always someone in the war party who thought they could do a better job," says Nikani, returning an equally challenging glance.

"But really, you know what I herd?" Nikani asks, with a raised eyebrow, and squinty eyes. Fink shrugs his shoulders – no reply.

"Sheep," says Nikani.

After a short silence, Fink scoffs as he stirs the campfire with a stick.

"I don't even know what kind of sentence that is supposed to be," replies Fink.

"Well, I used to herd sheep, but not anymore," laughs Nikani.

A smile comes over his face, then he breaks out with hardy laughter.

"Laughter is good. In the Indian way, that is a good sign, and it means you are being guided," says Nikani.

"An observer is chosen to seek the truth, right?" Fink asks.

"In matters that need to be settled. He is likened to an Eagle in flight, high above this earth, watching and seeing all that is beneath its wings," says Nikani.

"What if, in my heart, I feel that I am an observer?" Fink asks.

"It is a choice. Which way to turn, it is your choice, danger, risks, and the heartbreak of lost loved ones who will always feel betrayed by you," says Nikani confidently.

"The ugly truth, but truth it is. It's in my heart as it is yours. It is what I feel," says Fink.

"When I look back on it, I have to face those memories of being shot at by ranchers, farmers, vigilantes, the Army, and a couple of times by other Indians," says Nikani with a smile.

"I have revisited places in my heart long passed. Tomorrow is another day Fink, for now I am a tired old man," says Nikani, followed by a stifled yawn. A hand is extended towards Fink, and he accepts a handshake, but instead finds himself pulling Nikani up and out of his chair. He waves Fink off, and points to some folded blankets and a bed roll under the picnic table.

"If you get cold tonight," says Nikani as he makes his way back to his shack. Nikani's silhouetted figure moves slowly into the darkness. Fink gathers his thoughts and he begins to wander into Nikani's past. He hangs his head as he recalls Nikani's dream. Later as the camp has settled in for the night. A full moon shines and glistens off the rushing stream water that flows through the camp. It is the only sound heard in the still of the sleeping camp.

Inside Nikani's shack, the sound of a creaking floor awakens him from a deep sleep. He lies perfectly still on his back. By the light of the moon shining though his bedroom window, he sees a Deputy standing at the foot of his bed.

"Fred Burkhart? I thought you were a spirit. What are you doing at the foot of my bed?" Burkhart holds up a halting hand, and begins to speak to Nikani in a hushed voice.

"Sorry about this Nikani, but I didn't want to wake the whole camp," says Burkhart.

"Well, what are you doing here?"

"I'm here with Under Sheriff Jack Wright. We aren't here to bust any heads, so don't go doing anything stupid like alerting the rest of the camp.

"We're here at request of the Walker River Indian Agency. They've sent the B.I.A. Indian Police to take little Solomon back to the Indian school. If we have to, we'll back them if things get rough. So, while the boy's still sleeping, I think it best we clear those things up now," says Burkhart.

"My grandson does not want to go back to the Indian school, this is his home, Fred. I ask you, let my grandson stay here with me," pleads Nikani.

Outside Nikani's shack, Fink is in a bed roll under the picnic table. He is awakened by the murmur of hushed voices. Opening his eyes, he can see several uniformed officers from the Bureau of Indian Affairs, they have surrounded the shack.

Inside the shack Nikani slowly sits up, he begins pulling on his boots.

"Look, I don't like this any more than you Nikani, fact is those Indian cops out there are going to nail your old hide to the wall if you don't cooperate," advises Burkhart.

"It doesn't make any sense to me, why they make laws that keeps me from protecting my own grandson," says Nikani.

"You broke the law when you took Solomon in, Nikani, it's called 'harboring', it's the law. Myself, I don't give one hoot about aiding and abetting when it comes to little Solomon. Heck, I probably would have done the same. But after he ran away from the Indian school it became a BIA matter. They are here and he's gonna have to go back with them. Now you go on out there, wake Solomon and let him know what's going-on," says Burkhart.

Nikani stands and smooths his bed, then pulls up his suspenders.

"My grandson sleeps in his treehouse this time of year. There is no reason to let him see the Indian police. He will think he's done something wrong, let me bring him down, it will be better that way," says Nikani.

As Nikani and Deputy Burkhart exit the shack, Fink climbs out of his bedroll and stands by the table. Without warning, three BIA police officers quickly approach him, they motion to Fink to sit down.

"Nikani, what's going on?" Fink asks. Nikani just shakes his head despondently and continues on to the treehouse. The Federal officers begin to move into position, but a hand is held up by the Under Sheriff, Jack Wright, to wave them off.

Looking up at the tree house ladder, Burkhart turns to Nikani.

"Nikani, that ladder was built by a little boy, to hold the weight of a little boy," says Burkhart with a whisper.

"What choice do we have? I am a skinny old man. The ladder will hold me a lot better than it would your big butt," says Nikani, looking Burkhart up and down.

"Well, you didn't have to put it that way," says the Deputy.

Nikani takes a foot hold on the uneven rungs of the tree house ladder and takes a deep breath.

Throughout the tactical advance into the Indian camp, Solomon has remained asleep. As his grandfather opens the hatch door accessing the treehouse, the sound of rusty squeaking door hatches invade the little boys's dreams. Solomon turns on his side, opens his eyes, and sees his grandfather. He places his hand on Solomon's cheek.

"Grandson...wake-up...wake-up, it is time for all young warriors to be brave," he says in a soft assuring voice. Nikani prevents Solomon from rising, by a gentle hand placed on his shoulder.

"Do you remember when we talked of all good things?" Nikani asks. A sleepy Solomon replies:

"Ummhmm. There are angels. Do you know Grampa...? That there are angels," says Solomon in a far off voice.

"Your mother, when she was your age, used to say that all the time," says Nikani in a soft voice.

A full moon light shows wonder in the boy's eyes. Solomon props himself up on one elbow.

"I remember mommy," insists Solomon.

"If your mother were here now, what do you think she would say? Nikani asks.

"Mommy, she would say..." begins Solomon.

"What would she say, grandson?" Nikani pleads.

"Do what's right. That's what she told me," replies Solomon.

"They're here, grandson. They have come to take you back," explains Nikani. Solomon pulls his bedroll back, just enough to peer through the tree house peep hole. In the moon light, he sees uniformed men looking up towards his tree house. Solomon leans into his grandfather. Nikani holds him tightly, trying his best to reassure him that they will not hurt him.

"They're here..." says Solomon.

"Grandson, there will be another day when we'll all be together, but on this day, you will have to be a strong young man...your aunties and uncles are asleep, when they awake they'll be angry at what these men do," says Nikani. Solomon looks down towards the armed men below, he wipes his tears and buries his head into his grandfathers chest.

"Now I see what my dream was about Grampa. Mother kept telling me not to be afraid. Don't be afraid, and now, I'm not afraid," he explains.

Solomon leans over and pulls a cigar box out from under a book shelf. He holds it up into a beam of moonlight and lifts the top. The cigar box is offered to his grandfather, who takes it and pulls it closer. Through his failing eyesight, Nikani can make out all the treasures that little boys hold of value. He takes out a fishing lure and holds it up.

"I found this in the creek yesterday, and I was saving it for you grampa," says Solomon, dangling the fishing lure before his grandfather. The innocence of his gesture overwhelms Nikani.

"That is a good lure grandson. Every time I catch a fish, I will think of you," says Nikani.

Below Solomon's tree house, Fink's voice is heard questioning the under sheriff's authority to assist the Federal officers in the taking of the boy.

"It seems to me that your department would do better by spending more time on capturing actual criminals, like those who are bombing public facilities. Instead, all I see is a bunch of armed men, hunting down and taking children from their homes. It's no wonder this valley is ravaged by the chaos that it is today," says Fink loudly.

"Listen, this is happening everywhere, nobody can do anything about it. Hell man, it's the government's policy, not ours. If you're gonna jump down someone's throat, go to Washington and do it there. Better still, why don't you just head on back to Los Angeles and write about it, Mr. Hotshot reporter," insists Wright.

Inside Nikani's bedroom, a police matron rummages through tattered dresser drawers, collecting Solomon's belongings, placing them in a pillow case.

Up inside the tree house, Nikani and Solomon remain silent, listening to the slowly escalating argument. There is stirring in the camp as voices are heard. Burkhart motions to the BIA officers to not react. Just then, Fink looks up to see Nikani slowly climbing down the tree house ladder, followed by Solomon. Nikani is apprehended by the officers as he steps off of the ladder, and then Solomon. Nikani stands bound before his grandson in handcuffs, watching Solomon being escorted away.

Solomon, looks to his grandfather, then breaks away and runs to him. Nikani's hands are still bound, but manages to bend downward to meet his grandson's open arms.

The officers are becoming more uneasy, anticipating a situation that may become combative. The effort to not wake the camp for fear of a possible gun battle is rapidly deteriorating. The B.I.A. Police restrain Fink as Solomon is pulled away from his grandfather. A woman comes out of her dwelling to see the numerous police vehicles. The woman begins to wail at the sight of the officers pulling Solomon from his grandfather. Indian men pour out of shacks and rush to Nikani's aid, but are held back by the Indian Police.

Warning shots erupt, as one of the camp occupants exits his shack with a loaded rifle. Solomon is rushed to an awaiting vehicle. The weapon is dropped and the camp member is apprehended.

Pushed back and away from the commotion, Fink can only observe as Nikani stands helpless, watching as the B.I.A. police car speeds away. On the other side of the creek, the Indian men are leading the weeping women away, some of them voicing their anger.

"They have no right! When will they stop punishing us Indian people!" An Indian woman shouts, falling to her knees Fink hangs his head as Nikani walks away to stand alone on the road leading away from the camp. Solomon's cries for his grandfather are quickly drowned out by the sound of roaring car engines. Nikani stands in the dust kicked up by the retreating patrol cars.

Later in the day, at the picnic table outside of Nikani's shack, Fink sits alone, facing the direction of where he knows Nikani has withdrawn to. From across the grounds, he can see the camp's occupants, they are gathered in a circle, sitting on tree stumps and logs by the campfire ring. They are frustrated at the government and their assimilation policies. A bottle is brought out, and their sorrows are slowly drowned in memory after memory, of children that have been abducted.

Fink moves closer to where Nikani has isolated himself. He is sitting on a boulder staring out over the valley and softly chanting. The mid afternoon sun has becomes unbearable for Fink, he is concerned for Nikani, but respects his wishes and keeps his distance. An Indian woman quietly walks past his position, she is holding a water bag, a bowl of fruit, and Nikani's hat. The woman expresses concern for Nikani as she gently places his hat in his lap.

"Everyone is worried about you," she says as she sits in front of him. "But at the same time they want you to know they will continue to follow your lead. There won't be any retaliation for them taking little Solomon," she says. He reaches out to take the water bag, still dripping of the cool water from the stream. Nikani takes a long drink from the water bag, then he holds his hat upside down as she pours water into the top cap.

"Thank you, that water felt good," says Nikani.

"Solomon wanted everyone to behave themselves, it is what he said before they took him," says Nikani.

"Solomon is a good boy, Nikani. You raised him right," says Fink.

With the near empty water bag, the woman walks back to the camp for a refill. As she passes Fink's position, she offers the remainder of the water to him, and the last bit is squeezed out into Fink's open mouth.

"We feel it would be better if you to looked after him," she begins. "Word around town is; they are going to dynamite the aqueduct again, soon. The patrols are going to increase, we don't want to find him shot," says the Indian woman.

"Wait. Let me get this straight. You somehow heard this?" Fink asks.

"Not me, I didn't hear it first hand," she says.

"How does that come about? I mean, this knowledge is talked about around the campfire, in the Indian camp, like yesterdays news," says an astonished Fink.

"Indians are hired to do work that others feel is below them. Every morning the women and men walk down through the fields toward town to clean houses and tend gardens for these people. Many return to camp with the latest goings on," she says. Fink nods in agreement.

"Sheriff Collins should join your camp, he could learn a few things," says Fink.

"We're not so sure he doesn't know a few things himself," the Indian woman says.

"The City will be watching the camp. When Nikani comes around, try to lead him away from this spot. If the City aqueduct patrol finds him this close to the aqueduct, they will shoot to kill." Fink raises the water bag again, and receives the last few drops.

"In about ten minutes, I'll see if he wants to talk, maybe get him back to the picnic table," Fink says, looking towards Nikani, who is now wearing his hat to protect him from the heat.

"If you're not down at the camp in twenty minutes, I'll bring more water, get him away from here," she insists.

"James Fink, is that you back there?" Nikani asks without turning around.

"Sure is. I've been waiting, why don't you come down here, we can talk," suggests Fink.

"Why don't you come up here where it's cooler," says Nikani, turning to Fink, who is now standing beside him.

"Why is it cooler up here?" Fink asks.

"Once in while, a breeze off the aqueduct water makes it over the side, and it is cooler," says Nikani in a matter-of-fact tone.

"Did you know they're still looking for the ones who dynamited the aqueduct last week?" Fink asks.

"Didn't hear a thing about it. Did you?" Nikani asks.

"Nope, but the rest of the camp is concerned that the City patrolmen might open fire if they see you up here. You think?' Fink asks.

"I don't think so. There's been times when they've passed by, they didn't see me then, why would they now?" Nikani replies.

"Well, because now they are going to have to shoot somebody because of the bombing," reasons Fink.

"We'll see," he says. "The City has new construction going on down by a place called Nine Mile Canyon, they're building a syphon to draw water over the mountains. It is where the bombers will strike next," says Nikani.

"How can you be so sure?" Fink asks. "It's a guess, just like Indian hand game. Just a guess," says Nikani, holding up his clenched hands.

"Guess which hand has the pebble," he adds.

"Okay, I'll guess. That one," says Fink pointing to Nikani's right hand. His hand opens to reveal an empty palm, the other opens to reveal the pebble.

"All of the bombings have been here, up and down the valley. The City has been guessing where next, not once have they been able to catch them," says Nikani.

"Just like a hand game, it is a fifty-fifty chance they will strike again in the valley, or somewhere else" offers Fink.

"That's right. My guess is that they will hit the syphon, and there is only one way to get to it without the guards seeing you," says Nikani.

"It's supposed to be well guarded, and I understand they've been given orders; 'shoot to kill,"says Fink.

"That is why the bombers will strike from above. The only way to get at the syphon is by the mountain side of that round valley. They'll sneak down through the mountain passes. They'll have to leave from Lone Pine, up into a horse shoe meadow, and over into Monache country, then drop down to the syphon," says Nikani.

"All the while the City guards will be focusing on the road down on the flat. If it happens that way, the pipe won't stand a chance," adds Fink.

"Do you think they've taken my grandson straight off to LA? He's not eaten breakfast," says Nikani.

CHAPTER TWELVE
Maybe I'm Stupid, And Don't Even Know It

A full moon is momentarily obscured by campfire smoke. Nikani and Fink sit quietly, transfixed by the flames. There has been very few words spoken since Fink talked with Nikani, convincing him to return to the camp. It is Nikani that breaks silence.

"The injustice that our people have endured , only pushes them to be stronger; but when will it end? Nikani asks.

"I say this now, because my heart is filled with the past. I can hear my daughter, calling from a place far away," adds Nikani.

"What was she like, Nikani; Solomon's mother?" Fink asks.

"Shonnie? She was very kind, with a big heart like her mother. You see, when they came and took grandson the first time, it disheartened her so much that she began to drink. I saw that her heart was broken, there was nothing I could say that would ease her pain."

"She didn't ever drink before that happened, then that was all she did. Those in the camp would watch over her, no one drank with her, they told me she always drank alone. I told them not to get her anything to drink, but somehow the bottle always found her. One night, she drank so much, her frail little body gave up and she died in her sleep.

"When word reached Solomon, at the Indian School, he ran away. He showed up here four days later," says Nikani, hanging his head.

"Here? How did he get here?" Fink asks in disbelief

"He knew of the train, at night he could hear it roaring past Riverside. I taught him how to tell north and south by the direction of the sun's travel,"

"Smart kid," says Fink.

"He told me the night that he ran away, he left the school and walked in the direction of the train. He walked the tracks for two days until he found a place where the train stopped to pick up some cargo and he jumped it, all the way to Mojave. When grandson saw the Slim Princess pull into Mojave, he was happy that he was going home," says Nikani.

"Solomon recognized the train?" Fink asks.

"Sure did, he followed his homing instincts, he told me that he also recognized the track too. The narrow gauge track is all we have around here," says Nikani.

"That I found out, just getting here," says Fink.

"Solomon slept in a coal hauler that night, he made it all the way to the Mt. Whitney Station," says Nikani with a warm smile.

"He showed up in camp, black with coal dust all over him, tired and hungry. That night, at the campfire, he sat in the circle and told the story to the whole camp. It made me so proud, he was telling the story as I tell mine, arms waving all over the place, making sounds, and getting a laugh or two," says Nikani with pride.

"There's schools in Lone Pine. Why does he have to go to school so far away?" Fink asks.

"They don't allow Indian children in the classroom with other kids," says Nikani.

"Either way, it's just not fair. The government legislation to protect Indians by assimilation is causing more harm than good," says Fink.

"You know, they say Indian people are drunks, that we don't believe in God and we have no good worth. Yet, it is they who have made this trouble, and it is they who have no mind of Indians having a true love for life," protests Nikani. Fink hesitates, then takes out a pad begins to write.

"Once I told you, our story is different from the way you know it. We knew one day these things would mix up our way of life, don't ask me how we knew, we just knew. We had a way of life that bad things were kept out, and were part of our world," says Nikani.

"There is no culture that I know of that would accept a future filled with suffering. It's the very reason the whites left their own countries. The things they do are so disrespectful, so terrible, that it continues to spill onto the Earth like a poison," says Nikani. There is a long silence.

"You must be exhausted Nikani. I should go," says Fink.

"It might be good for me to get some rest. Maybe you ought to come back tomorrow when things might be better," suggests Nikani.

"Yeah, you're right. I have some phone calls to make when I get back to the hotel. Good night Nikani," says Fink as Nikani walks towards his shack.

The days events have left Fink emotionally drained, his feelings about the apprehension of the little boy has him upset with policy on Indian education. He recalls a couple of years ago, when an assignment was handed to him regarding cultural diversity in California. The subject matter did not interest him, so he handed the assignment to another reporter. Fink now wonders how the article would have panned out, if he had made the decision to write about the government's policy on assimilation. He takes a deep breath, knowing a highly charged political story dealing with Indians and assimilation would have been edited into a slant, approving the imposition of Indian children into Indian schools.

Fink is left to his own demons on the drive back to the Lone Pine Hotel, he begins to focus on the days events and the story that Nikani related to him earlier in the day.

True to his profession, his mind is swirling around a news story. As he continues into the night, the dirt road becomes rough, worn with washboard bumps. The shaking of the car's headlights, strobe onto the road in an almost hypnotic rhythm. Fink imagines Nikani and his warrior escort, Hu'na, as they ride their horses on a mountain trail. Just as Nikani explained the beauty of their mountain habitat, a route that took them along a ridge trail down a steep canyon. Fink smiles to himself, noting the way Nikani's told his tales. The story he was telling always seemed to take a back seat to the elaborate depiction of the environment. It left Fink with a sense of appreciation for the American Indian culture and their way of life.

The street lights of Lone Pine come into view and the road smoothes out onto an oiled surface. Pulling up to a stop-sign, a sheriff's patrol car cruises slowly past. As they pass, Sheriff Collins and his deputy, Fred Burkhart both look towards Fink's vehicle, as if casting suspicion upon him. Fink gives a limp wave, and looks towards Rossi's Cantina. Except for a few pieces of deer jerky, Fink has not had anything to eat all day. The cantina is just around the corner, he decides to get a dinner to take back to his hotel room.

Inside the cafe, he sees a well read copy of the Times-Tribune at the end of the counter. A cup of coffee is ordered along with a steak dinner, as he spreads the front page onto the counter. 'CITY TO PAY WWI VETS TO PATROL O.V. DITCH,' is the headline.

"Now don't that beat all," says Fink thinking out loud. The waitress overhears his comment.

"That's all we need, a bunch of shell shocked vets traipsing around, toting rifles and hand grenades," she says.

"Rifles and hand grenades? Wait until the tanks start rolling into town," says Fink, under his breath. The waitress stops and looks him realizing the potential reality. "Just kidding," Fink says.

Later as he leaves the cantina, he sees sheriff's patrol car slowly crossing main street just one block up. Fink gets into his car, with his dinner and pulls out onto main street. Almost immediately he sees the sheriff's car pull over. As he passes he looks into his rear view, and sees red lights; he is being pulled over.

Fink stops his vehicle across from the Lone Pine Hotel and watches as Collins and Burkhart get out of the patrol car.

"I'm beginning to think that you're either stupid, or you're trying to piss me off. Which is it, Jimmy?" Collins asks as he leans into the drivers side window.

"Well, I'm not trying to piss you off," says Fink as Collins flips his cigarette into the street.

"It just may very well be that I am stupid, and I don't even know it," says Fink, looking up with big eyes.

"Out of the car," commands Collins.

"You think you can come around here with your high and mighty press credentials and stir up the locals," says Collins as Burkhart slams Fink against the patrol car.

"You're mistaken sheriff, it isn't me who was doing the stirring," says Fink as his legs get kicked part and a pat down is conducted by Burkhart.

"What the hell are doing at the Indian camp, they don't know jack about what is going on around here," insists Collins.

"I can tell you this; they know by their own history that it's a political conflict that's behind this so called water war. What they don't know; is that it was the political conflict that forced you, the Sheriff of Inyo County, to deputize L.A. City agents," says Fink lividly. A billy club is thrust into his rib cage.

"We're not City agents, and you're not an Inyo County citizen, so I guess it makes this all even," says Burkhart, up close.

"I'm not against you, I was just trying to approach the issue from a different angle, that's all," pleads Fink.

"Seems to me that since you've been here, the subversive activity has increased," says Burkhart.

"Pure coincidence," says Fink as he is released from the search.

"You have two days, even less if another incidence occurs. One word to the City agents and they'll have us haul you in on suspicion," says Collins.

"You don't want to be in the Inyo County Jail house while all this bombing is going on. Being from Los Angeles and all, the prisoners might not look upon you with too much favoritism," says

Burkhart. Fink straightens his suit jacket as Burkhart steps up to him in an intimidating manner.

"Two days," says Fink with agreement. Fink takes his dinner, along with the copy of the Times-Tribune from his car, and crosses main street. The two lawmen continue to watch his every move as he enters the hotel lobby.

Inside, the desk clerk welcomes Fink as he shuts the lobby door.

"Good evening, will you be needing a room tonight?" The clerk asks. Fink turns to see a young lady behind the desk.

"I'm in room ten. James Fink," he says.

"Well then, welcome back Mr. Fink, you have several messages," the clerk says, handing them over.

"Looks like you're the head clerk in charge tonight," says Fink as he thumbs through his messages.

"My name is Kimberly, you can call me Kim, and yes, I am your desk clerk tonight. Dooley, the other clerk, has taken a couple of days off. He told me that he was getting to be a little worried about you," she says, jutting her ample breast towards Fink from the other side of the front desk.

"The next time you see Dooley, tell him I ended up in good hands," says Fink nodding towards the patrol car across the street from the hotel.

"Yup, watched the whole thing from here. I figured it had to do with the Indian camp," says Kim. Fink looks up from his messages.

"Dooley told me," she says.

"Yeah, seems to me that you weren't the only one he told," Fink says as he reaches for the phone.

"Operator, collect call from James Fink, Madison 6-2343," he says. The clerk straightens the lobby area away from the desk. Fink is returning a call received earlier in the day from his bride to be Anne Porter.

"...I miss you too, things here are about to be wrapped up and I'll be home day after tomorrow. Yes, you too. Bye," says Fink as he hangs up the phone.

"No sense in trying to contact these others until tomorrow," says Fink.

"I thought big City newspapers worked around the clock," she says. "Not the bosses," replies Fink. Kim folds her arms and studies Fink momentarily.

"While you were at the camp, did you happen to see an old Indian by the name of Nikani?" Kim asks.

"Do you know Nikani?" Fink asks.

"Sure do. When I was a young girl, he worked for my father on our ranch at Haiwee Meadows," says Kim.

"Haiwee? How do you spell that?" Fink asks.

"With an 'i' and a double 'e'. It's a Shoshoni word, it means Dove. You know, like a Turtle

Dove, lovey-dovey, that sort of dove," says Kim, watching the reporter jot down notes in his book.

"Do you remember what year that was? I mean, Nikani working at your ranch," Fink asks.

"When I was born, it had only been a little over 40 years since the U.S. Army rode into the valley. Nikani would come looking for work when the sheep needed shearing, but it was around 1909 or 1910 when dad hired him on as a regular hand," she says.

"Nikani told me a story about seeing Mulholland and Eaton when they first appeared in the valley. Was it your father's ranch that they stopped for supplies?" Fink asks.

"That's right. I myself remember those two drunks. It was in the fall of 1904, Eaton and Mulholland had been on the road for a week and a half, maybe two. It was obvious to me that they hand't bathed all that time on the road," she says waving her hand in front of her nose.

"They asked my father if they could camp nearby, he was about to tell them to be on their way, but I stopped him from doing so. I felt that if the poor horse pulling the buggy went another mile, it would have dropped dead. There isn't much for a horse to graze on from Jawbone Canyon to Cartago. That poor buggy horse, and the two pack mules, well I doubt if any of the stock made it back to Los Angeles.

"After hearing some of the interesting stories that were still circulating among the old timers, I decided to write down some of the more important things. I came to a conclusion that the early settlers could not have been that ignorant. Outside of the modern methods of farming, they failed to recognize the methods used by the Indians to tend this valley, were the same methods their ancestors used. Preserve the land and harvest its bounty, pure and simple," insists Kim. Fink continues to write notes.

"Now I don't know if you would be interested in this bit of history, it doesn't have anything to do with the water war," says Kim.

"Go right ahead. One may never know what will end up on the print editor's desk," says Fink.

"I read in my uncle's journal that he had recruited one of the Shoshoni tribes to join the Confederacy," says Kim in a low voice.

"Really? Do tell," Fink says, resting his chin on the palm of his hand.

"I believe it was one of the Walker Pass tribes that signed, or put their mark on a confederate document, swearing allegiance to the South," says Kim.

"Makes sense, align with the confederates to fight the Blue Coats. Did Nikani tell you this? Fink asks.

"No, but I bet if you ask him, he'll tell you about it," says Kim.

"That is interesting. What happened? Did they ever go to war with the Confederate Army? Fink asks.

"In the journal, my uncle wrote that he was disappointed in the confederate command because they never sent the guns he had asked for. The Indians were ready to fight," says Kim.

"Your uncle, was he an officer in the Confederacy?

"My uncle was James Scobey, he was a gun runner sent out here to California from Missouri by confederate spy generals. His mission was to enlist secessionist along with any Indian tribes he could persuade to join the confederacy. The generals were to provide him with as much fire power as possible to overcome the California Volunteer 2nd Army," she explains.

"Was he a spy?" Fink asks.

"He probably was that too. From what I have gathered from family bibles and other stories from family, Fort Sumpter was the one main event that got him sent out west," says Kim.

"But my daddy told me this story about Nikani that his brother told him before he died. God rest his soul. Apparently there was a trading post just north of our ranch, it's where the story begins. It's the same way my daddy told me and now, I'm telling you.

"Picture this, you're inside a trading post, it's daytime and it's dimly lit, tobacco smoke lingers in the still air. One lantern is situated over a poker table where four men play their hands at poker. A much younger Nikani enters through the swinging doors. He stops to let his eyes adjust, and he can sense tension. He then walks straight back to the counter with a bundle of furs, skins and Indian tobacco. Uncle Jim and others watched Nikani walk past their table, someone at the card table told my uncle.

"Four bits says that Charlie sells that old musket again, how about it Scobey, you in? He asked. They knew Uncle Jim was a southern sympathizer, and his war was with the union, not Indians," says Kim.

"Has this story ever been documented before?" Fink asks with enthusiasm.

"It's like I said, the story line remains the same, any embellishment comes through my interpretation, says Kim. Fink nods in agreement.

"Jim Scobey was my uncle, back then he would be in his 30's, fresh from the battlefields. Uncle Jim was a full on confederate agent with strong ties to the growing number of southern sympathizers in California, known as Secessionist or "Seceshes" as they called them," explains Kim.

"I told you once hayseed, my name is James Scobey. Captain James Scobey to you, and I'll bet a gold piece he doesn't," says Scobey, flipping a gold piece onto the card table. Nikani becomes alert, his eyes sharpen and he listens to the tension building behind him. The Storekeeper begins to go through the skins and pelts that Nikani has placed on the counter.

A young Indian woman enters through the front doors, followed by someone who looks to be her grandfather. The old Indian man mutters a message to Nikani in Shoshoni language.

"If you trade for the gun, those men will kill you, and take your pelts" says the old man.

Looking around, Nikani sees that the men at the poker table are keeping a close eye on all of them. The Storekeeper begins to shake his head, he sets his demeanor to negotiate.

"Most I can give you for the pelts is three dollars," says the Storekeeper.

Insulted, Nikani pulls the pelts back, he refuses the trade. Cursing erupts from the poker table, as Scobey gathers the gold pieces won by the bet. Nikani walks away from the counter towards the door. The young Indian woman steals a glance as Nikani passes, she steps forward with small leather pouch clutched in hands.

Without a word, several gold nuggets from a leather pouch tumble onto the counter. The Storekeeper retrieves a 25 pound sack of flour, a sack of beans and a side of bacon. With no recourse, the meager food purchase is accepted by the young woman and her grandfather.

At the poker table, Scobey watches the Gambler, his anger over the loss of the his twenty dollar gold piece is reaching a boiling point. Tauntingly, Scobey flips a gold coin into the air repeatedly. The Gambler stands abruptly, pushing his chair backwards and starts for the exit.

Nikani is making his way towards a warrior friend who is holding the leather reigns of his horse. He slings the pelts onto the pack horse. Shouting is heard, Nikani looks to the other warrior, who is telling him with eyes and a slow nod to prepare for trouble. From a mounted position, they both watch as the Gambler stalks out of the trading post.

"Hey! You old bastard. You owe me some money. I seen you in there blabbing your mouth off. I would've won me some money if it weren't for you," shouts the Gambler. He pulls out his pistol and holds it to the old Indian's head.

"Now, give over what ever gold you have left. Do it, or you die, right here, right now," barks the Gambler. In his defense the young woman tries to intervene but is pushed away. The other warrior begins to dismount but is discouraged by Nikani. The gold pouch is handed over to the Gambler, three small nuggets fall into his palm, which he places into his vest pocket.

Sensing intervention from Nikani and the other warrior, the Gambler begins to slowly back away. Nikani steadies his horse and goes to assist the Old Indian Man.

"Young men, leave before bad things happen. Go now, we will be alright," the old man says. The Gambler upon hearing words spoken in Shoshoni, arrogantly challenges by approaching the old man.

"See? There you go blabbering that gibberish," says the Gambler, his revolver aimed at the old man's temple.

Without hesitation the Gambler shoots the old man through the head, dropping him lifelessly to the ground. Nikani and the warrior are jolted into abhorrence, at the senseless killing. Nikani and the warrior are enraged but, they do not react. The other men in the trading post empty outside to see the Gambler standing over the old man's body, now being protected by his sobbing granddaughter. He grabs her, and yanks her up by her hair. He turns to Nikani.

"See there, see what you made me do, blabbing your mouth," blurts the Gambler. The other warrior waits for a sign from Nikani, his forearm raises with a closed fist, meaning to get ready for battle. Except for the rustling of the cottonwood leaves, a tense silence is broken when pistol hammers can be heard being pulled back into firing position. The young Indian woman is now his hostage, and he jerks her close to him. "Uh-oh, looks like there's going to be an Indian uprising," says the Gambler.

Standing at the Trading Post door, Scobey watches as the Gambler turns the girl loose and walks towards Nikani. He then grabs the bridle of his horse.

"You think I did wrong, killing that old man? There's nothing wrong with killing Indians...cause every last one of you needs killing. He draws his pistol up slowly and deliberately, aiming at Nikani's head. The other warrior slowly raises his hands as if to surrender.

The blade of the warriors hunting knife catches the sunlight as it is flung from its sheath. Nikani stares coldly down into the eyes of the Gambler, who has suddenly jolted into a rigid stance. A gurgling gasp is heard, and his eyes now wide with terror - blood from his neck streams through the air. The Gambler's gun drops to the ground. Nikani reaches down and grasps the handle of the knife that is protruding from the Gambler's larynx.

A standoff ensues between the warriors and the occupants of the trading post. The Storekeeper rushes to the Gambler's aid, while the others level their weapons and take-up positions. Two men from the inside the store begin to pull clothing from the old man's body. One of the men have the old Indian man's head, held up by his hair, preparing to cut into his scalp. The granddaughter struggles with the men, warding off the desecration. Scobey watches as Nikani and the other mount a charge on horseback. A war hoop is heard as both warriors at ride low profile and close to their horses, firing their weapons. Nikani closes fast through a barrage of smoke and gunfire. A war ax is swung in time with accurate and deadly delivery, taking off the top of one man's head. The other warrior rams his horse into the last foe, sending him end over end.

The story is broken when another hotel boarder walks through the hotel doors to ask for towels. Kim waits for the boarder to exit the hotel lobby.

"The way it was told to me by my daddy; was that Uncle Jim took up sides with Nikani. When the smoke and dust had cleared, three men were dead, one shot by Uncle Jim. He told Nikani and his warrior friend to leave before the stage coach arrived. They took his advice and rode away hard and fast. The Indian girl received the horses of the men that killed her grandfather and the stolen gold nuggets. Uncle Jim helped the young Indian woman tie her grandfather across a saddled horse, and she took him back to their camp.

"What's ever left in their pockets ought to cover the burial because I ain't burying those thieving saddle tramps for nothing," said the Store Keeper.

"He said he was getting tired of them killing every Indian that came to trade," says Kim.

"Between all of dead men, five twenty dollar gold coins were handed to him by my uncle," adds Kim.

The clock on the wall inside the Lone Pine Hotel reads 11:00 p.m., the two amateur historians have settled at a table. Kimberly has brought out her writings and has asked Fink to critique some of her writing.

"It's always been my opinion the Indians in this part of California received the short end of the stick when it came to their homelands. The Owens Valley was inhabited by the Paiute in the northern parts and in the southern parts, the Shoshoni. The extreme desert was their shield from the southern California expeditions. Why come up into areas that were dry and not suited for agriculture?" Kimberly asks.

"When they could settle into the vast San Joaquin," offers Fink.

'Exactly. When the Spanish enslaved over 20,000 of the coastal Indians to build their missions and roads, the Indians there still had a land base that they had control over. It was when gold was discovered in 49' that the migration over the Sierra Mountain range by the coastal Indians began," adds Kim.

"The news of slaughter that was occurring in the coastal regions of California weren't reported by any of the major newspapers," she says with accusing eyes.

"On September 9, 1850 California entered the Union. With miners flooding the hillsides to slue the gold, they left the land almost completely devastated. Indians fled to the desert lands and places the white miners could not find them. They were deprived of their way of life, customary food gathering came to an end by not wanting to get caught out in the open. Starving Indians started raiding the ranches and white settlements. That is when whites began hunting California Indians like so much wild game. The legislature passed laws to 'protect' the Indians by making them slaves under the Indenture Act. The state by allowed it's citizens to round up vagrant Indians and auction them off for services for up to four months. Under the same law, Indian children became indentured to whites because of ownership of the parents. This started a whole new enterprise. Organized gangs of men began to roam California searching for Indian children in wide spread kidnappings and attacks," says Kim.

"There was a movement in Los Angeles that was organized by a group that called themselves, 'Women for Equality,' they tried to convince the paper that it would be good press to expose the lawlessness in California in the 1850's. They came armed with ten pages of statistics, among the brutally shameful numbers was this; by 1853 California began forcing Indian people to relocate to military reservations. The Indians here were rounded up and taken to Fort Tejon, north of Los Angeles and south of Bakersfield.

"They tried to exterminate the native people of California, it was shameful. The worst act of slaughter in United States history. There were 150,000 Indians living in California before 1849, and by 1870, fewer than 30,000 were left, surviving on little or nothing at all," says Fink adamantly.

"The slaughter didn't escape President Lincoln's term of office as the "Great Emancipator," says Kim.

"On December 26, 1862, he ordered the largest mass execution in American History. December 26th! Three-hundred Sioux men were ordered to their death. Kim says, raising her voice. Her adamant point of view causing Fink to look over his shoulder in an obvious gesture to warn her.

"I really don't care who hears me," says Kim indignantly.

"I feel it has to be said, even if it's just between the two of us," she adds.

"It's been accepted as an unwritten event, but the ugly truth, it remains the largest mass hanging in United States history," says Fink.

"Sounds to me like 'Honest Abe' apparently wasn't honest enough. What was he thinking?" Kim says.

"Don't know, but I can tell you this; it wasn't honest," says Fink as he gathers his notes. The written history of the Owens Valley by Kim, is handed back to her. "You're an exceptional person, Kim. Never lose your desire to write, this is an important project that you have started," Fink advises. "I know you are checking out of the hotel in the morning. I shouldn't be keeping you up venting my thoughts," says Kim.

"No, it's okay, I'm of the same mind when it comes to injustice. I have to say; after all that's been said tonight, I think you ought to know something," he says. He pauses momentarily, grasping her hand.

"They took his ten year old grandson into custody early this morning," says Fink.

"What? Who took him and why?" Kim asks. "The BIA Indian Police took him out of the camp and they escorted him back to the Indian school in Riverside," says Fink regretfully.

"My God. The old man must have been devastated," says Kim.

"I'm worried about him," says Fink.

"Believe me when I say this; I would go to the camp and check on him, but other than you and the missionaries, no one goes to the Indian camp," says Kim.

"I have complete confidence in the others living at the camp, they'll see to it that his is taken care of. It's just a sad situation," says Fink.

CHAPTER THIRTEEN
The Syphon Bombing At
No Name Canyon

On a dirt highway 57 miles south of Lone Pine, a 1923 Chrysler sedan pulls off the road and slows to a stop. The sedan is positioned on an access road leading to the mouth of No Name Canyon, the site of a water syphon owned by the Los Angeles Water Department.

Inside the vehicle there are four men, all are smartly dressed in expensive suits, their shoes are shined and they all wear newly purchased Stetson hats. Laying on the backseat of the sedan is a copy of the Times-Tribune. On the front page in large print is; LOS ANGELES POPULATION TOPS ONE MILLION.

The engine is turned off. Jack Marshall, the driver, focuses a pair of binoculars on the syphon pipe site.

"They must have a cook tent up there because the guards are chowing down on breakfast, right now," says Marshall.

"How many?" asks Noah Dixon, from the back seat.

"Looks like the station is deserted, being Sunday, everyone's gone, so that makes it three counting the cook. It's just like L.A., to put expendables on guard duty," says Marshall.

"Why do you say that?" Dixon asks.

"Those two guards look like Indians to me," says Marshall peering through the binoculars.

"Take a look," he says, handing over the glasses.

"I'll be, you're right. That there is Jeremiah Eagle Horse, and the other is Billy Williams. I hope they're making good money, cause they're sure going to earn it today," says Dixon. Suddenly, the binoculars are dropped into his lap as a mirrored flash forces him to cup his eyes with his hands. The others in the sedan catch a glimpse of the reflection coming from the summit pass, it continues for just a moment longer.

"Well, there's the signal, the boys on the summit pass are ready to go. It will take them an hour to get to the syphon site," says Marshall.

"We'll be there, waiting. Remember, things have go as planned, we have to keep the guards and the cook out of sight, and a safe distance from the blast," instructs Dixon.

Riding in the passenger seat is Samuel Bishop, he takes the binoculars from Marshall and focuses on the summit above the canyon.

"I can't see them, but the mules are kicking up too much dust. Who's the lead packer up there?" asks Bishop.

"Salty Peters, it's all his stock," says Dixon from the back seat.

"Check your weapons and keep them down," says Marshall as he flashes his headlights for a return signal.

"I want to know, why can't we just go back up to the valley, instead of heading for Mojave?" asks John Harley, sitting in the back seat.

"I was of the same mind, John. That is, until I figured that after the blast, Sheriff Collins will be high-tailing it down here as fast as that county cruiser can make it," says Marshall.

"Collins?" Harley asks.

"I'm aware '*No Name*' is in Kern County, and out of his jurisdiction," explains Marshall.

"Just because his jurisdiction ends at the county line, doesn't mean he won't be looking for any locals that just might be headed north on this very eventful day," replies Bishop. The engine is started and put into gear, the imposters make their way towards the syphon guard shack.

"God help anyone on the main road when that water starts crashing down in that wash," says Dixon.

"It won't be a wall of water, just flash flood size. We figured that 320 second-feet of water sounds like a lot of water, and it is, but by the time it travels the distance from the syphon to the main road, it won't be all that it's supposed to be," says Marshall, in a convincing tone.

"What if the guards start shooting?" Harvey asks.

"Let's hope and pray they don't level their weapons. We are here to damage LA City property, we're not here to kill anybody. Besides, I doubt that a guards pay at $2.50 a day, would spark enough loyalty to defend an outhouse," says Bishop.

"Remember, we are a contingent of Owens Valley ranchers defending our livelihood and families, we have the right to preserve our hard work and the pursuit of happiness," proclaims Bishop, as he steers the vehicle towards the syphon.

From the canyon summit, a rider by the name of "Big Mike, peers through a high powered telescope mounted on a tripod. He watches as the eight riders and their pack train make their way down the canyon trail. Big Mike repositions the scope and sights in on the approaching vehicle. He repositions the scope again, the main gate guard can be seen, it appears that he is not aware of the vehicle coming up the dirt road towards the guard shack. He keeps the telescope trained upon the main guard shack, he sees that the guard has put down his breakfast plate and arms himself with a shotgun.

The Chrysler sedan pulls up to the check point. Big Mike can see that the guard is relaxed and is talking with Jack Marshall, who is posing as aqueduct Chief of Operations, H.A. Van Norman. It is known that he is in Lone Pine conducting field evaluations, and staying at the Dow Hotel.

Down at the main the men remain seated in the vehicle guard shack "I'm sorry for the hold up Mr. Van Norman, but I have my orders, no identification, no entry," says Eagle Horse, looking at Marshall through wire rim bifocals.

"Well how about that, the City actually hired someone who can do his job, and do it well," says Marshall, turning to gain approval from the others in the vehicle.

"I always carry my wallet in my briefcase, which at this moment, is in the trunk," he adds as he sets the parking brake.

Through the high power telescope, Big Mike can see Marshall open the drivers door and start for the rear of the vehicle. As the trunk deck comes up, a handgun is pointed at the guard's head. The shot gun and his service revolver are seized in less than a second. Marshall follows the guard to the barred gate and watches as it is raised. The guard and his captor disappear into the guard shack.

Inside the main guard shack, Eagle Horse looks at Marshall, through his bifocals.

"I know you," says Eagle Horse. You're Jack Marshall, my cousin worked on your ranch. What the heck are you doing?" Eagle Horse asks.

"We're going to bomb the syphon," says Marshall.

"Holy smoke! Bomb the pipe?" Eagle Horse cries out.

"Don't worry, nothings going to happen to you. Nobody's going to hurt," says Marshall.

"Mr. Marshall, my shift ends in an hour. Could you come back then?" Eagle Horse pleads.

"No dice. Who's going to relieve you? Marshall asks.

"The cook. There's another at the work site to relieve Billy.

"What am I supposed to tell the dad-gummed City Agents?" Eagle Horse asks.

"You tell them we pulled up, put a great big gun in your face and tied you up," says Marshall.

"You couldn't see a thing because during a scuffle, your bifocals got knocked off," says Marshall as he takes the glasses from his face.

"Do you want me to rough you up a little, to make it look legitimate?" Marshall asks.

"No thanks, I just had breakfast. Jack, could you put my bifocals someplace where they won't get stepped on? Eagle Horse asks politely.

Up on the summit pass. "They're in," announces Big Mike. The other four men holler out with a cheer.

"Don't they have to get a hold of the others?" asks one of the night riders.

"They will, but they got through the main gate, the other guards have no reason to question their presence," says Big Mike, as looks through the telescope. He observes the vehicle pull up to the main equipment staging area of the syphon. Through the scope he can see the City posers take one guard at a time as their prisoners. Harley has Noah Dixon take the Chrysler and retrieve the guard that has been tied up and left in the guard shack. Harley, Dixon and Bishop take off their suit jackets and shed their vests, shirt sleeves are rolled up as they start preparing for the dynamite to arrive.

Soon after they take control of the staging area at the syphon, the pack train and eight riders arrive. Charlie Waters, the honcho of the Night Riders, and his right hand man Lefty Jones lead the six mules laden with 36 cases of dynamite to the syphon. The men are ordered to unload the mules, place a case of dynamite ten yards apart along the giant syphon pipe.

The station guards and the cook were placed a safe distance from the syphon to insure no injuries. A long slow burning fuse was lit, which gave the night riders and the impostors plenty of time to get a safe distance away from the blast. The LA Water Department syphon was bombed and the plan was executed without a hitch.

The Night Riders rode through the back country all night by the light of the last of the quarter moon. They camped at Big Whitney Meadows before dropping down into the Owens Valley by way of Shepherds Pass. The impostors, Marshall, Dixon, Bishop and Harvey made it to the Sierra Highway and were able to witness the explosion from afar. The two Indian guards and the cook were rescued by repair teams that showed up later in the day. There were no injuries caused by the No Name Canyon syphon bombing. It would be reported in the newspapers that the blast took out approximately 300 feet of metal syphon casing and shut down the flow of water to Los Angeles from the Owens Valley. The cost of repair of the damage was said to have cost $75,000.

Driving through the outer reaches of the Mojave Desert, Fink's rented vehicle can be seen from a birds eye view. The mid morning sun rises higher in the sky as he passes Little Lake, an old stage coach rest stop. A long dust trail can be seen in Fink's rear view mirror, kicked up from the tires of the car. He is traveling on the Sierra Highway, a broad two-way dirt road leading to Mojave, Lancaster, Palmdale and Los Angeles. Fink looks out over the desert landscape, a road sign amid the sage brush, comes into view 'LOS ANGELES 160 MILES.' Fink slows the vehicle down to 10 M.P.H. So a cup of coffee can be poured from a thermos. He recalls the echoing words spoken to him by Nikani a few days before.

"It is allowed, that men play God to those who will follow, but in the end we Indian people will continue to observe. What we see can only be equaled to our own great sorrow. In time you will see that only a country's government will destroy those it was designed to protect. One day, it will consume the culture it has created, like an animal eating it's young. Be ready to survive Fink," he recalls. A freight truck speeds by and passes with its horn blaring. Fink is snapped back into reality. Looking down at the speedometer he sees that he is barely traveling 20 miles per hour. Not far up the dirt highway, he sees the truck that passed him, through the dust he can see a line of tail lights.

A Kern County Sheriffs patrol car has blocked the highway, and another is guiding vehicles through a washed over road. Fink pulls up to the check point.

"What's the problem officer?" Fink asks. "The road's been washed out, you can make it through, but take it easy," advises the officer.

"Funny weather. Not a cloud in the sky. Yet, here we are, held up by a flash flood," jokes Fink.

"Not something caused by weather. More like dynamite. They bombed the LA Aqueduct syphon earlier this morning," says the officer. Fink shakes his head in disbelief, then pulls out his press card.

"That's interesting, because I just came from the Owens Valley, and it's happening there too," says Fink.

"Sir, pull your automobile over to that side of the road, shut off your engine and wait for an officer," orders the officer.

"Officer, I'm sorry, I should have presented my credentials," says Fink.

"As I said, pull over to the side and an officer will be right with you Mr. Fink," says the officer as he waves on another officer.

Fink sets the hand brake on his car as an officer approaches. Without a word his press card, drivers license, and auto registration are handed over.

"I know this may be a stupid question, but I have to ask. Where were you staying in the Owens Valley and what was your business there?" The officer asks.

"I was staying at the Lone Pine Hotel for the past week, covering a story on the bombing attacks that took place throughout the valley. My comment to the officer reflected exactly that," replies Fink.

"This is just an observation, where I live we get the Times-Tribune, but we still have to buy the Bakersfield Californian to get the real story of what has happened in the Owens Valley," suggests the officer.

"That's a surprise, I thought you guys read *True Crime* and stuff like that," says Fink.

"Don't get cute with me, Mr. Fink," says the Officer.

"There's a huge farming community just on the other side of the mountain range. Farmers in Bakersfield are very interested in the take over that LA has imposed on the Owens Valley. I hope you wrote how Los Angeles has stunted the agricultural future of the valley. Don't forget to write about that, Mr. Hotshot Reporter," says the officer.

"It'll all be in my story, and the article will be out in the next few days," says Fink.

"I'll be looking forward to it. Is it true they've got spy's on every corner?" asks the officer, as he rips off a ticket from his book. Fink takes the ticket reluctantly, looking at the officer with a blank stare.

"It's a warning. When you return the vehicle, let the dealer know the tag is out of date," says the officer.

The officer stands back as Fink starts his vehicle, he takes his hat off and scratches his head as he watches Fink turns his vehicle around and stops.

"How can I get to the syphon station?" Fink asks. The officer just shakes his head as watches Fink continues his U-turn and drives northward.

The last six days spent in the Owens Valley has Fink doubting the strength of his story subject matter. The chief editor will expect a story that will go to the editorial desk with front page potential. The occupation of the Alabama Gates outside of Lone Pine looks promising, coupled with involvement of Tom Mix support of the spillway incident, may scoop the bombings that occurred while he was in the valley. On a wing of a prayer, he just may have a story by the time he gets back to Los Angeles.

While entering Lancaster, by way of the Sierra Highway, Fink checks the time on his pocket watch, and realizes that the syphon bombing has set him back a few hours. A decision is made to spend a night Lancaster hotel.

Inside a hotel room, Fink places a call to Anne, his bride to be. "Hi honey, there were some complications on the way back. No, I'm all right, it's just that there was an incident at the aqueduct, I just could't let go of. Yes, I will. Lancaster right now. The pass is still congested with construction. I'll see you tomorrow, I love you," says Fink.

Later, Fink has settled into his room, where he is certain the story will come to him, once he gets some sleep. In his thoughts, 'Sleep On It' has some weight to it, but then, Fink would have to sleep for a week in order to truly write a story that would do justice to his experiences in the Owens Valley.

CHAPTER FOURTEEN
The All Seeing Chronicle

After spending the night in Lancaster, and leaving in the early morning hours, Fink chose to travel by way of the Pear Blossom Road. His plans are to arrive in Los Angeles while Anne is at her office, meet with the Chief Editor, Walt McIntee, and see Anne later in a surprise visit. McIntee made it clear to Fink, that he is expected at his office by 1:30 p.m., no later. The route he has chosen is the longest, but considering road construction on the passes; will be the quickest.

On the winding route back to Los Angeles, he will stop in Pasadena to call his boss in case there is a change in plans. As he winds his way through the San Gabriel Mountain passes, he is soon entering the farm lands of Sierra Madre. He recalls an earlier article in which research revealed the history of the Spanish settlement of Rancho del Rincon de San Pascual. The settlement grew into what is now Pasadena. Rolling down Colorado Boulevard, Fink realizes that he is in the middle of Eaton family land holdings. Frederick Eaton is a descendant of the old pioneer family, and the actual strategist of the LA aqueduct. Born in Los Angeles in 1856 on a two acre plot, of which grew into downtown Los Angeles. Fred Eaton learned to read and write in public schools. A self taught enthusiast, he later took up a trade in the field of structural engineering. At nineteen he became superintendent of the early Los Angeles Water Company. In 1898, Fred Eaton was elected Mayor of Los Angeles, and as mayor, he made William Mulholland superintendent of the reorganized Los Angeles Water Department. Immediately after the turn of the century, he teamed up with Mulholland to realize an ambition to bring water from the Owens Valley to Los Angeles.

Now in downtown Pasadena, Fink scans both sides of the street, looking to find a phone booth. He pulls into the first parkings space available. Luckily, he finds himself directly in front of the "Oaks Cafe" on Colorado Blvd, and Fair Oaks Ave. It is Sunday, May 25, 1928, and the cafe is packed with church goers. A Sunday copy of the Times Daily is at the end of the dinner counter, it is also where an empty counter stool stands vacant. Looking around to find a phone booth, he sees one to the rear of the cafe, but it is occupied.

"I'll have an egg salad sandwich to go, and two cups of coffee, one for here and one for the road, please," says Fink to the waitress as she arrives at the counter. Sifting through the stack of newspapers piled just to his right, he finds the front page to the Times-Tribune.

'PULITZER PRIZE AWARDED TO ROBERT FROST.'

"What the...," says Fink, thinking out loud. A cup of coffee is placed on the counter, he takes the cup to the now unoccupied phone booth.

"Where is my front page article about the spill gate takeover north of Lone Pine?" Fink asks the Chief Editor.

"Jim, it's Sunday. The editorial staff outgunned me with religious rhetoric and slanted the front page to a more lighter side. It was their decision not mine. Until now it's been nothing but the bombings, in the Owens Valley," says McIntee.

"Well, that's just too damned bad, because last night when I tried to get in touch with you, you wouldn't answer your phone. Why? He asks. "It was Saturday, my God Jim, even I deserve a little time off," says Walt.

"If you had made your self available we may have had a good front page story of the syphon bombing," offers Fink.

"Syphon? What syphon?" he asks.

"Three-hundred feet of syphon pipe was dynamited in a canyon south of Little Lake. I managed to get a few photos of the damage before being run off the site," says Fink.

"The hell you say? Come straight to my office, I'll be waiting. I want to be filled in on every last detail, we can get a teaser in on the evening edition, and run a full page on it in the morning," says Walt before he hangs up the phone. Fink is left looking at the receiver. "Ungrateful; didn't even say good-by," says Fink.

In Los Angeles, the downtown traffic is extra light as Fink pulls up to the Times-Tribune Building. Inside the office of the chief editor, Fink talks with his boss who is reading through upcoming articles for the evening edition. A shot of whiskey is poured and offered to Fink, of which he declines. He can see his chief editor looking at him through the bottom of his glass as it is tipped up. McIntee's body language does not look promising as he continues to read the hastily handwritten drafted document. The quiet in the office is unnerving as he waits for McIntee's response.

James Fink has been working for the Time-Tribune for seven years. Walt McIntee has taken Fink under his wing, but still considers him a 'pet peeve' in his office as a lead reporter. McIntee accepts Fink's bold approach to journalism, a touch that reminds McIntee very much as himself when he first started out.

McIntee is a tough second generation Irishman who was received an education through the public school system. After the great earthquake that devastated San Francisco, journalism had been his life's goal. The now white haired, cigar smoking, whiskey drinking veteran of journalism world, received his calling when interviewed by a Chronicle reporter in amidst the rubble on Market Street. His hardline view of reporting with the Times-Tribune earned him a reputation of "The

Boss" when it came to the paper's position on Owens Valley and the aqueduct issues.

"You're kidding, right? I mean what the hell is this, where's my story! The gott-damned aqueduct's been blown-up three times since you've taken the assignment. Nobody's been arrested, caught or implicated, and you put this before me?" McIntee says accusingly.

"I'm of the same mind Walt. My whole slant on this story was to not become redundant," offers Fink.

"Redundant? The Owens Valley ranchers have declared war on the City of Los Angeles. War may have become superfluous to some, but to others it is essential information. Those are the people who will buy a newspaper that tells the story," says McIntee. Fink shows no emotion, rather he listens and observes.

"In case you didn't know, let me fill you in on what's been happening since you went up to the mountain, Mohammed," after a gulp of whiskey, McIntee continues.

"If I wanted a different slant on the aqueduct bombings, I would have had some print worked up on water sports and the Summer Olympics," scolds McIntee.

"I just thought an angle like this...," begins Fink.

"With this article, L.A.'s water issues would be left wide open to ridicule by every bleeding heart walking the planet!" McIntee shouts.

"Look, I did exactly as you directed, sorry if the story isn't all you expected. The aqueduct bombings need to have more substance. Let the people know why their anger is being expressed with dynamite. We have an obligation to our readers to print what other papers have been printing," says Fink in a calm and appeasing voice.

"What is needed, is some balls Jim...as it reads now the story lacks the attitude our readers have come to rally around.Frankly this is the sort of stuff I would expect to read in the Owens Valley Herald. Now I want you to go home, take off your dress, have a nice warm glass of milk and think about it. Tomorrow I want you back at work with a real story. Fink takes the article from Walt's desk, he turns to leave.

"It's my intention to give our readers a little insight as to what it's like to live in midst of the chaos. I think if you read the piece objectively you might see where it is going," says Fink.

"Lot's of warm milk, and plenty of rest Jimmy, come back on Tuesday. The extra day of rest may clear your head. The door close as Fink exits McIntee picks up the telephone.

Outside, Fink makes his way through the company parking lot, an attendant meets him to collect a fee. He continues to his vehicle then hesitates when he sees a man waiting by his car.

Bernard Michaels, a long time friend and fellow reporter for the San Francisco Chronicle. He is a big man full of confidence.

"Bernard Michaels the Third, what are you doing in Los Angeles? The Chronicle run out of stories to print?" Fink asks in jest.

What? San Francisco without print? That's kind of like LA without water, don't you think? The comment triggers a reaction in Fink who stops and turns toward his old rival from college days.

"There's been a lot that's happened between here and San Francisco, let's go have a cool one and catch up," says Bernard

"You don't have to twist my arm, I'll go along just to see what you've been up to. You buying? Fink says. Bernard put his hand around Fink's shoulders gives him a buddy hug as they walk toward a cocktail lounge.

"So Bernard, when did they let you out of Alcatraz?" Fink says jokingly.

"Right after you escaped from that Tijuana jail. The two old friends are quick to catch up on old bonding banter, as they continue down the street.

When they come upon "The King Edward Hotel lounge, Fink can sense that there may be more to Bernard's visit than a friendship reunion. Once inside, a secluded table is found and drinks are ordered. The lounge has a casual crowd and almost half full.

"This place hasn't changed a bit," says Bernard.

"What Los Angeles or King Eddies? Fink asks. "Both, but I've noticed the traffic, its gotten worse," says Bernard.

"I know you too well Bernie, what's up? What are you doing in L.A.?" Fink asks. Bernard takes a long draw from his drink.

"Actually, I'm here to do you a big favor, Jim. I'm going to save you a lot of research," says Bernard," says Bernard.

"You're going to forget that Tijuana trip, and never mention it again, that's what you're going to do," says Fink?" Fink asks.

"You really don't know? Fink's eyes widen and he blinks twice.

"You and the rest of this sleepy little City are sitting on a powder keg Jimmy," Bernard says.

"Odd that you should mention that," says Fink.

"I've read most of the print on the aqueduct issues. Do you really believe that what's happening to the Owens Valley will just someday go away? Fink becomes uncomfortable, as he contemplates his friend's warning.

"I've been in LA for two weeks on this assignment and can't believe what's going on here," says Bernard.

"Tell me about it, I have to live with it," says Fink.

"Tell me something, is everyone in on it, I swear this must be one of the biggest snow jobs in the history of the world!" Bernard says.

"This has been my recent take on it; there's no wonder Americans aren't concerned over a war in Europe. Hell, all's we have to do is send L.A.'s Water Board over there, they'll sabotage the whole thing. The whole war will be over in a week!" Fink says with a laugh.

"Don't think for one minute that these issues haven't been brought to light. Maybe if you'd stop to read some print other than your own you'd know it's been done to death," says Fink.

"Well then tell me why everyone else can see the water department fiasco, but the city cannot. They're heading for a very rude awakening," says Bernard.

"I can't tell you how many times I have come to that conclusion," says Fink in agreement. "No one knows how or when but it's damned sure going to happen. The Owens Valley is being turned into a desert, and now their economy is folding.

"Not according to Mulholland," says Fink.

"Tell me what you know about the Anthrax outbreak," adds Fink.

"Anthrax? Where? Fink asks in an inquiring tone.

"See? You didn't know Jack about it. All the other newspapers up and down the state put copy out on the streets about the breakout. Big news, Fink," None of the agency's will come out and say it, but isn't it such a coincidence. They have a name for those sort of dirty deeds, it's called industrial sabotage, Jim," says Bernard.

"Come on Bernie, isn't that kind of stretching things a little, L.A. in the Hoof and Mouth business?

"Who do you think you're kidding Jim? You know deep down it's is a big story for anyone who breaks it. Ask around man, check it out and take my word for it," says Bernard. Fink takes a drink, and studies his friend for a moment.

"What kind of evidence have you put together? Fink asks, now very interested.

"There was a hoof and mouth out break in the Los Angeles stockyards years ago, by then the Owens Valley and ranches further north already had their cattle herds established," explains Bernard.

"Okay, I see what you're getting at. There was no need to import cattle to the Owens Valley, the herds were all exported to the San Joaquin Valley," says Fink.

"Bingo. Beware of this story, because if you get too close, they'll try to rub you out. They're out to break that valley, any way they can. It's outright war on all levels, Jimmy," Bernard Michaels gets up from the table to leave but is stopped by Fink. He hands him the story rejected earlier by McIntee.

"You may not know this, but there is a growing movement in L.A., demanding reform of the Water Department. Take this article, courtesy of the Times-Tribune. Feel free to use it because it'll never get printed here," says Fink.

Later in the Wilshire District of Los Angeles, Fink's vehicle can be seen arriving at his home, pulling into a car port. As Fink gets out of his car, he is met by Joel, a neighbor who has been watching his house while away.

"Hello there stranger, how'd the assignment go? Joel asks.

"Difficult but very interesting, how did things go around here? Were there any problems? Fink asks.

"Nope, everything was honky-dory, you owe me $2.50 for the paper boy and the Gardner says you need to pay him for last month," says Joel. Fink pulls his groceries from the car, he turns and gives Joel an inquisitive look. "Did the Water Company come by to turn off my water meter? Fink asks with a smile.

"No, but a friend of yours by the name of Bernard Michaels dropped yesterday," replies Joel. The information catches Fink by surprise, he does not recall Bernard mentioning his visit.

"What did he want? Fink asks. "It was my impression that it was an intended visit, he talked my ear off," says Joel.

"Don't tell me; he gave you an in depth account of the Tijuana incident," says Fink. "I didn't know you were such a hooligan back in your younger years Jim," says Joel.

"Sometimes even hooligans can have too much fun. Thanks for taking care of the place Joel, says Fink as he walks up the steps towards his front door.

Inside his house, Fink fumbles for a light switch, holding two bags of groceries. He steps over a pile of mail below the mail drop, and makes his way to the kitchen. While putting away the groceries, the telephone begins to ring.

"Hello?...just now...well I haven't had a chance but, could you please hold for a second, I have someone at my door," explains Fink.

"Come in! Fink shouts while taking directions and writing them down. "Yes, what's the nearest cross street?"

From the tiny foyer, Finks voice can be heard as he talks on the telephone. The mail that was on the floor has been gathered, and it is placed on a foyer table. In the living room, Fink continues to listen to his party at the other end of the line. Fink is pleasantly caught by surprise as two hands come up from behind. The fragrance of a familiar perfume invades his senses as the hands begin to caress his chest. A few buttons on his shirt are then undone.

Anne Porter, fiancee to James Fink is an attractive 24 year old, with a degree in business. Unable to land a position in the male dominated corporate management she took a job as a teacher in a Los Angeles public school system. Anne could have easily had an acting career, her long supple legs, blue eyes and shoulder length blond hair, attributes that screamed screen test.

"Yes, I mean no, no...don't worry it'll be taken care first thing Monday...goodbye," says Fink hastily, as he caresses her wandering hand. The phone falls off the hook after a fumbling attempt to replace it. Ann continues the seduction, one of which Fink shamelessly surrenders.

CHAPTER FIFTEEN
The Bedtime Story

Later in the evening, inside Fink's home, a single table lamp has been dimmed by a draped silk scarf. A song by Sam Lanin & his Orchestra, can be heard, playing softly. From behind the living room couch, a hand reaches over and turns up the volume to the song; 'It Had To Be You,' The smoke from a cigarette rises and lingers in the air.

"Okay Finkie, what is it?" Anne asks. "Come on, tell me what's troubling you, I know it can't be me...not after all that," Anne teases.

"Nothing, everything is fine. You're here, I'm here, what could be better than that?" Anne asks.

"Nothing huh? Well, I can tell something has you tied up in nots," says Anne.

"Must be my work, honey. You know, same old, same old. The Owens Valley assignment is still up in the air and I need to bring resolve to some issues," he says wearily. Anne tries to comfort him with a hug.

"How would you like to come along with me tomorrow?" Fink asks.

"I would love to, where are we going?"

"To an Indian school in Riverside. I just want to check it out, see if there may be a story there," says Fink.

"A story? She asks.

"Inhumane practices inside of government boarding schools for Indians," Fink says. He now notices that Anne is not giving him her full attention, she seems to be preoccupied. Fink smiles as he recognizes an unmistakable gleam in her eyes.

"I thought we had dinner plans tonight," says Fink.

"Dinner maybe, desert yes," says Anne as she pulls him back down into the couch.

By the light of dinner candles, Anne look at Fink through her half full wine glass. An impromptu late night dinner is being shared between Anne and Fink.

"What was it that happened in Lone Pine? What made you want to cover an article on the Indian School? She asks.

"An awakening, a realization of having been asleep for a number of years. I don't know. Maybe I'm placing too much emphasis on my work ethic," says Fink.

"Okay, so try me. I know a little about having to second guess my decisions, dealing with children, and all," says Anne.

"Yeah...dealing with children, would leave you vulnerable to emotional overload," agrees Fink.

"When it comes to that part of the ethical work process, there is nothing wrong with allowing the human side of life bleed into your work effort," says Anne.

"I guess you're right. Well, here it is in a nut shell;

"I befriended a Shoshoni elder and his grandson while in the Owens Valley, and somehow I became caught up in their plight. It all just melted together, the history, the bombings, the people caught in the middle," says Fink.

"Sometimes I wonder how you can keep focused on the objective part of some of the stories you have covered," says Anne.

"Yeah, I thought I was bullet proof until I ventured into the Owens Valley. But, then again, it's always been like that for me. I find that when it comes to separating myself emotionally from a story, it's draining just dodging the realization of exploitation," says Fink.

"Tell me, why do you feel your recent acquaintances affected you in such a way?" Anne asks. Fink hangs his head.

"The events that took place, it's the whole story of the Owens Valley and what's happening there also took it's toll on me," he says.

"The old man and the boy, what were they like?" Anne asks.

"Nikani is the Shoshoni elder and his grandson's name is Solomon. The old man is the most honorable man I've ever known. Solomon once told me that when he was at the Indian school his first time around, he would tell his favorite story to other boys his age. Solomon would tell me:

"I used to tell it to the other boys in my dorm when I became lonesome for my mom, and grandpa. It always put me in a different place, one where I could see my grandpa at my age," said Solomon.

"An Indian bedtime story. I can't begin to say, how interesting that sounds to me," says Anne.

"I liked the story myself," Nikani once said.

"Would you care to share it with me?" Anne asks.

"He always told that story to Solomon, but he told me, and now I'm going to tell you. I think he would like it if I shared it with you," says Fink.

"I would be honored," she says. Okay, but first I have to do something," he says as his hat is retrieved from the coat rack. He snugs his hat down onto his head, he holds his head up in a dignified manner and begins Solomon's story.

"A long time ago, there was a group of people headed west for the gold rush in 1849. They made there way out here from a state called Kansas, and they were called the Jayhawkers. The Shoshoni, still had our winter camp in the Panamint Valley, a few mountain ranges over from Death Valley, where it was still warm that time of year. A runner from another village had come into the camp and told us that there was a small band of whites coming through. It was odd to see them in that part of the country," recites Fink.

"I can recall reading something about that group when in college. They were lost weren't they?" Anne asks.

"Lost, ragged, and starving. There must have been ten or twelve of them, men, women, and some children," says Fink. "What did Shoshoni people do?" Anne asks.

"They watched them for a while, but were very cautious for they had learned of the pox that had been spread throughout the Plains. What else could they do but watch," Fink replies.

"Anyway, some of the group went south and others found their way over the Townes Pass. One of the men separated from the group that was going south, heading up the canyon where we had our camp," explains Fink. The story continues to be narrated by Fink and told by Nikani.

"Well, I was the one who first spotted them. They looked tattered and tired, but there was this lone Pioneer walking towards our winter camp. Far behind him and into a valley, I could see several wagons, they are stranded. One of their oxen could be seen floundering trying to get up off of the dry dusty dirt," says Fink. "Then what happened?" Anne asks enthusiastically.

"Solomon's grandfather, Nikani was only ten years old, he'd never seen a white man before. So he watched as the scraggly pioneer crawled into one of the village melon patches. He started eating like there was no tomorrow. He was crazy from hunger and thirst. To the young Nikani, it looked like he was going to devour the whole patch," narrates Fink.

"The melons were a source of the tribes food cache, they would just let them dry into the winter, then cut them open. The dry melon meat taste like candy. To everyone, it was always a good treat. Nikani wasn't about to let him eat all their candy," laughs Fink.

"He was so busy watching the strange man, he realized that the other children he had been playing with earlier, were gone. He didn't know what happened to the other kids, all he knew was that he was alone with a man who had a hairy face," tells Fink.

"So Nikani pulled an arrow from his quiver, put it in his bow and pulled back as hard as he could. Kuttinna! He shouted, which means: I will shoot," Fink says with a chuckle.

"What did he do?" Anne asks. "The way it was told to me was that; the Jayhawker looked up, and there was sticky melon smeared on his beard and on his face," laughs Fink.

"The first words of English I ever heard were: 'Thank God,' he said with a sense of relief," says Fink.

"He chose to take his chances with the Indians, more than suffer death in the desert," offers Anne.

"At ten years old, he captured an adult white man, a pioneer, a Jayhawker? Amazing, truly amazing," adds Ann

"Yeah, not only that, when he told me that, I could just see the looks on their faces when he walked into the winter village. The Jayhawker's hands over his head in the surrender position, followed by a little boy with a tiny bow and arrow," laughs Fink.

"That is the best bedtime story I've heard in a long time," says Anne.

"When Nikani told me that story, we were at the Indian camp outside of Lone Pine. He didn't get to tell me the rest of it because we heard someone warning us with a whistle from the camp. We became alert and listened for a few moments. The sound of a car engine was heard, it was a City patrol car, slowly rolling by on the aqueduct road. We took cover behind some boulders below the aqueduct embankment, the vehicle rolled by without seeing us," explains Fink.

"Would they have arrested you just for being near the aqueduct? Anne asks.

"Far worse, they would have shot us dead," says Fink. Anne gasps at the harsh reality.

"Anyway, later at the camp that night, Nikani showed me the telescope given to him by the Jayhawker," says Fink.

"What a great story, I can't wait to meet the both of them," says Anne.

"Good, at first chance we are going to be on the road to Riverside," says Fink.

CHAPTER SIXTEEN
Riverside Indian School

A few days later, James Fink and his fiancee Anne Porter are traveling to Riverside. Anne pulls out a folder and begins to go through what appears to be news clippings and letters.

"This is the file I borrowed from the administration office. There was a study done last year on ethnic background and percentage of the student body. Right now American Indian children cannot attend public schools. It's been predicted that somewhere in the future, it will be accepted as a normality, but for now, Indian education remains in the hands of the government," says Anne, shuffling through the folder.

"Ah, here it is, "Sherman Institute," apparently was first constructed in 1890, in Perris, California. It was later moved to its present site because the water became undrinkable due to discoloration of high iron content. Public Health caused the school to be closed, citing an inadequate water supply.

In 1902 the school then reopened about twenty miles from Riverside. Originally, the school consisted of about ten buildings. One hundred acres were set aside to teach farming methods and support the school. The school was named after Dr. James Schoolcraft Sherman," says Anne, reading from the file. "Schoolcraft? I wonder which came first, the school or the craft," says Fink, laughing at his own joke.

"Laugh all you want, he later became Vice President of the United States under President William H. Taft. Now, can you focus just while longer while I finish reading this piece? There are 43 tribes throughout the U.S. that have their children in attendance. California Indians are well represented, but also there are Indian children from the Pacific northwest, The Southwest, and The Plains.

 The students are supervised in the field to raise their own food. There are plans that include an elementary Indian school and a high school curriculum is slated for 1926," concludes Anne.

"Solomon explained that the school was like a jailhouse, or what he thought a jail would be like. My guess was that he meant they placed a major emphasis on discipline and punishment. Is there anything in the folder that can verify this?" Fink asks. Anne continues to shuffle through the documents.

"There are reports from the parents of the children who attended. The government accounted for almost, if not more than a hundred boarding schools. Complaints of abuse were common at every school, but none had been documented," Anne reads on.

"Children are punished with corporeal punishment, brutal beatings, and isolation, of which resulted in malnourishment. Parents of students are continually being told by their children that they never get enough to eat. The heavy labor that is forced upon them only compounds the matter of hunger," reads Anne as she puts down the document. There is a minute that nothing is said between them.

"Just before leaving Lone Pine, I witnessed the most callous act of enforcement I'd ever seen," says Fink.

"I think I know where this is going. Oh Jim, I'm so sorry. I understand now what's been troubling you," says Anne.

"I realized that remaining objective in reporting my stories, I became callous to the taking of Solomon that morning. I began to reason that many parents of Indian children had no choice, but to send their children to government schools. Their children were denied an education in the public schools because it wasn't allowed. Indian children were not to be taught along side of white children. It was, and still is pure racism," says Fink. "What happened to Nikani's grandson?" Anne asks.

"They surrounded the Indian camp and threatened Nikani with arrest and imprisonment if he did not cooperate. Anyone in the camp would have been shot if they interfered with the removal," says Fink.

"How awful he must have felt," says Anne.

"I don't know what was said between Solomon and his grandfather, but I'm sure Nikani had him understand the consequences," explains Fink.

"Are you sure he is here at Sherman? They may have taken him to another school," suggests Anne.

"It won't be long until we find out, there's the Cajon Pass and we are about to take on a long down hill grade, so hold on," warns Fink.

Later as they descend into the valley floor and continue onward towards Riverside, Anne provides some trivia on the pass.

"Did you know that the Cajon was once a stock trail that miners and ranchers used to pack supplies in and out of these rugged canyons?" Ann asks.

"No, but I had an idea it must have been something like that or a deer trail," says Fink.

"Actually, it's an ancient trade route established by the Indians, then became the northern most end of the Old Spanish Trail, which then was the route to Santa Fe, New Mexico," she says.

"Now that, I didn't know. Did you know that this route is soon to be designated U.S. Route 66? Fink asks. There is no immediate response.

"I wonder, where did you read that? She asks.

"The Times," is said simultaneously. Their laughter is a welcomed break from the vigors of the road.

Entering onto Magnolia Avenue, the Indian school comes into view. The architecture of Old Mission revival is accented by date palms. "The school is beautiful, but terribly ironic," says Anne.

"I don't get your meaning. Ironic? Fink asks.

"The architecture was chosen to further the ongoing effort of assimilation. Yet, the Spanish enslaved California Indians to build missions, very much like this," explains Anne.

"Interesting, yet deceptively not part of the process of assimilation. It seems to me that American Indian children are, at every turn, reminded of the past," says Fink.

"At the turn of the century, the majority of Indian schools were administrated by prominent religious leaders that had no idea of how to apply teaching methods to Indian children. It was an accepted concept that if the children were exposed to the Christian belief system, the children would see the "way" of white beliefs. To the religious leaders, an understanding of another culture by the Indian children would be left to God. A desire to learn would follow and assimilations would transpire."

"It was an unforeseen reality for the preachers that American Indians had a single belief system; that which they could only see and touch. The one and only belief they could rely on was the Earth. An energy force so powerful that offered prayers were extended to those they could see and touch. A dichotomy emerged that was ignored by the early non-governmental administrators of Indian education programs. The teachings of Christianity could only be taught," adds Fink.

"I see what you're saying. To teach someone to feel an emotion as powerful as love, is pretentious," says Anne.

Anne pulls out the folder again and reads from a news clipping on 'Assimilation.'

"In 1908 a policy was implemented to rid the Indian children of their traditional beliefs and Indian way of life. Termed as the "Outing System," this was a method that would presumably force out any desire to return to the traditional life.

An infamous quote, created by Captain Richard Henry Pratt, founder and Superintendent of the Carlisle Indian Industrial School, had its controversy among activists in 1880. He was quoted to have said: "Kill the Indian, and save the man." This became a popular anthem among the ignorant. The "outing" method would impinge on every part of everyday life of the children. In some instances, for the most part, none of the children had ever seen a motion picture film. When they were exposed to this form of entertainment, it would be presented by showing their ancestors being defeated time after time, in battles that always ended in bloodshed and slaughter. On this day, Solomon's visitors had reached the Indian school, just as the weather turned gloomy.

Through a dormitory window, Solomon can be seen watching Fink as he approaches the Administration Building. A smile comes over his face, he turns and runs through what appears to be a deserted dormitory.

Inside the Administration Building, Anne remains seated in the waiting room, as Fink is greeted by Donald Peters, the Superintendent of the school. Inside his office and standing at his desk, Fink sizes the man up as he walks around his desk to his leather cushioned chair. His first impression of Peters is formed by his clothing--a military type jacket, with cavalry styled trousers, and boots to match.

"As I explained over the phone Mr. Fink, we do not choose to maintain a low profile where the public is concerned, it is our policy to protect the privacy of the children. It is necessary to safeguard Institute policy. These children have been placed into our care, and are wards of the United States Government. Any interference with their routine learning programs would be irresponsible on our part. After all, they are here for vocational study and to learn a new way of life. We wouldn't want anything to impede our focus. Would we?" Peters asks.

"Mr. Peters, I'm not asking for much, the article would mainly be written from an observers view point. A simple tour of the campus would suffice," says Fink.

"There is a question that I have to ask; why would any news editor give approval to such an assignment? Indian children and assimilation can't be newsworthy, here in Riverside or Los Angeles. Unless your story will emphasize a waste of taxpayer money," says Peters, gesturing with an unlit cigar in his hand.

"Quite the contrary, Mr. Peters. I intend to show the taxpayer that their money is being put use in the manner they intended," says Fink on a whim.

"I'm sorry, I wish I could accommodate you, but it is simply out of my hands. Why don't you come back in a month? By then I should have authorization," suggests Peters.

Fink thanks Peters for his time and starts for the door, but just before he exits, Fink turns and comments on government policy.

"In view of it's purpose, I think that one day, the world will know the real truth of the word assimilation. No matter how it is recounted, it will bear the disgrace of the entire nation," says Fink with a condemning stare.

Walking back towards the car, Ann is concerned that Fink has taken the denial too hard.

"Jim, is there something you're not telling me about this little excursion into Riverside? I mean, you're beginning to worry me. I've never seen you so weary over a situation," she says. The door is opened and Anne settles into the passenger seat. She watches Fink as he walks past the front end of the car.

"I'm sorry. I shouldn't have let my expectations override my common sense. What did I expect from an administrator that thinks he's a military general," says Fink. The rain begins to pour down. A quietness falls between them, and except for the raindrops, nothing is heard, until Anne poses a question.

"This isn't like you, I've never seen you become so involved in a story," says Anne.

"It's not just a story, sweetheart, for me it's an awakening. I've been asleep for the last seven years," says Fink.

"I agree with you, it's not right what they're doing. What makes it worse, is the unbearable way they are going about it. In another country, it would be deemed criminal for such acts to occur.

As the engine is started, a bolt of lightning strikes nearby, and thunder rolls through the area. The downpour suddenly becomes harsh. The car remains parked while the engine warms.

"This does not look like the pleasant excursion I anticipated. What next?" Fink says dejected.

Looking up into the rearview mirror, in the dim light of the storm, another lightning flash lights up the interior of the car. Fink startles and jumps in his seat when he sees two eyes smiling at him. Solomon suddenly appears, his head popping up from the back seat area.

"Hey Fink!" Solomon says excitedly. Anne lets out a stifled scream. A realization stuns Anne when she sees the little boy. Thinking aloud, she softly says his name, "Solomon..." Fink turns in his seat to see Solomon smiling, he begins to giggle, then laugh, his boyish laugh becomes contagious. Solomon jumps into the front seat with Anne and Fink.

"I did it! I snuck-up on you Fink," he says.

"Anne, I would like to meet Solomon, the grandson of the great warrior, Nikani," says Fink. A hand is extended by Solomon, but Anne pulls him to her for a hug.

"I've heard so much about you Solomon. How did you know we were here?" Anne asks.

"I watched you when you parked by the administration building. I woke up today thinking it was time Fink showed up, and he did," says Solomon.

"They don't know you're here with us, do they?" Fink asks.

"No, my dorm is supposed to be raking leaves in the orchard today, but it's too wet out there for me," says Solomon.

"Won't they know you are gone?" Anne asks.

"Not until bed count tonight, let's go for a drive Fink," says Solomon excitedly. Fink looks to Anne.

"Oh what the heck, we can go get a hot dog, can't we?" Fink says as he surrenders to Solomon's wishes. "Hot dogs it is," says Anne. The roar of an engine is heard as Fink finds reverse. The chattering of the small boy can be heard; pulling away in the driving rain.

Later, the car can be seen parked in an orange grove. The rain has subsided and the sun is trying to shine through the clouds. Inside the car, Solomon is sitting between Ann and Fink. He is completely unaware that they are watching him as he devours a hot dog and drinks down a soda pop. Looking into the paper bag for another hot dog, Anne is amazed that he has eaten two hot dogs, a bag of chips, and working on a soda pop.

"It looks like we've eaten all the dogs. Candy bar anyone?" Anne asks.

"How is the food at school?" Fink asks.

"They never give us enough to eat and we have to do all this dumb work from early in the morning until dark," says Solomon.

"Have they ever hurt you? I mean, do they punish you?" Anne asks.

"I got the paddle for running away that last time. It hurt to sit down for two days," says Solomon.

"How about others in the school? Fink asks.

"Most everyone has stories," says Solomon, sadly.

"If you had a choice, where would you rather be, here or home with your grandpa?" Anne asks.

"Everyone wishes they could go back home," says Solomon, sincerely.

Finks vehicle rolls up to a field at the back of the Indian School. It is getting close to the dinner hour at the school. Although there is no head count at dinner, Solomon will have to be back at bed check.

"Don't worry about me getting into any trouble, I hide from them all the time. Tell Grampa I miss him and I'll write when I get better at it," says Solomon as he climbs out of the vehicle. Fink hands Solomon his business card.

"This card has my phone number on it. I want you to call me if you need anything at all" says Fink. Solomon takes the card and feels the embossed lettering.

"You're a pretty fancy guy Fink. Could you let everyone know at the camp, that I'm going to learn, get smart, and make everyone proud of me. Tell them I'll never forget that I am Shoshoni," says Solomon beaming with pride.

"Bye auntie Anne, so long Fink," Solomon shouts as he runs into the open field towards the school.

CHAPTER SEVENTEEN
The Saint Francis Dam 1928

It has been four years since Fink visited the town of Lone Pine and the Indian Camp. He keeps in touch with Nikani on a regular basis, knowing that any word of his grandson will lighten his heart. When a letter is written to Nikani, it is always by way of the Lone Pine Hotel. The acronym of Nick Hahn, in care of Kimberly. With Kim's help, the letters always found their way to the camp. Fink makes it a point to visit Solomon when he could. Fink was hoping he would get another chance to visit Lone Pine on assignment. Without any pressing issues to make the trip, his chief editor saw no cause for an assignment into the valley. It has been several months since the last devastating aqueduct bomb went off, and calm has been restored.

It is the weekend, and Fink has Anne as an overnight guest. In the living room the telephone continues to ring as Fink awakes to a beautiful Saturday morning. Easing out of bed, he walks softly into the living room. "Ludlow? It's the weekend, don't you ever take a day off?" Fink asks in a low voice.

"There is no rest for the wicked, Jim. You ought to know that," is the answer over the phone. Fink accepts the response knowing that a call from this associate bears importance.

In minutes, he is fully clothed and prepared to leave. He takes a moment to gently kiss Anne on the cheek while she sleeps soundly. Fink leaves a short note on the dining table, hoping that she will understand he has been called away to cover a story. Fink reluctantly closes the front, quietly as possible.

Outside on the porch, a newspaper boy rides by on his bicycle, flinging a newspaper onto the walkway. Upon landing on the hard cement, the paper unfolds. Fink looks down to see the headline: O.V. BANKERS TEN YEAR SENTENCES. Fink picks up the paper and begins to read through the story. "Damn," he says with discouragement.

Fink steps up into the driver's seat and starts the engine. He contemplates the methods going on under table by the Water Department. As the engine warms, he reads the article and becomes agitated. As an investigative reporter, Fink has become very aware of the dealings with the unscrupulous Water Department. The control of the department, and the power that the board possesses, is on the level of tyranny. The Watterson brothers, Wilfred and George, bankers in the Owens Valley, were convicted on charges of bank fraud. He shakes his head in denial as he continues to read the news article. The article only reinforces his convictions of the long arm Los Angeles had into the Owens Valley. Extensive research was not needed to find that the fraud charges originated from the L.A. City Attorney's office.

The paper drops into the passenger seat and Fink continues on to the meeting with Ludlow. A map is unfolded, and his finger follows a path to a location in the San Francisquito Canyon. From Los Angeles, it is a four and a half hour journey.

On the way, passing through the northern reaches of Los Angeles County, Fink passes a road sign. The incline allows for a slow passing. The sign reads: Piru, Elevation 710 feet above sea level. The Santa Clarita River Valley is a mass of foothills and steep ravines left by the San Andreas earthquake fault. Looking down at his dashboard gauges, he can see that the his car is beginning to overheat.

The Los Angeles Bureau of Water Works and Supply is in charge of operating the dam, now in full operation. Driving within site, Fink feels he has now come full circle with the Owens Valley water war, because he is about to see where Owens River water is being stored.

The rendezvous with his associate, John Ludlow, is of an urgent nature, but Fink can only guess what he may be told. A story broke about a suspicious death at the dam, and Fink has been working with Ludlow on the case, sharing information. The directions lead Fink to a nearby point at the dam site. He is to pass through Piru, cross over a bridge, and drive up to a vista overlooking the dam.

As he continues on to the site, he passes another sign that reads: ENTERING LOS ANGELES COUNTY. Fink soon comes to a turnout in the road where there is a parked vehicle.

John Ludlow is a retired police detective, now a part time private investigator. The death that occurred at the dam a month earlier, was contracted to him by the family of the deceased. A negligence lawsuit had been filed agains the City of Los Angeles in connection with the death.

"I hope you brought some high-top boots, there are a lot of snakes around here," says Ludlow, as Fink walks up.

"Snakes?" They just look like snakes Ludlow, actually they're politicians.

"What's the skinny on Richard Sullivan?" Fink asks, as Ludlow hands him a pair of binoculars.

"Focus in about three-quarters of the way down from the top of the dam, the blood soaked cement, can't miss it," Ludlow says. Fink adjusts and focuses on the Saint Francis Dam.

"I dug up all kinds of stuff on Sullivan, which, of course, took more time, which took more money, which..." says Ludlow. An envelope is then placed into his hand.

"It's all I brought, I'll be good for the rest, trust me," says Fink.

"Three days, Fink, and I send my boys out after you," says Ludlow in a bad Italian accent. Fink does not respond.

"Okay, first thing, right off the bat. Bill Mulholland has lost it, the guy is completely obsessed with his St. Francis project, to a point that he is blinded by his achievements," says Ludlow.

"Go on, I'm listening," says Fink, not taking his eyes from the dam.

"Do you know what riparian water rights are?" asks Ludlow.

"Somewhat, riparian has to do with river banks?" says Fink.

"Right. It's really a Latin word, ripa, meaning bank, so its ancient. Riparian water right is a fundamental truth, holding that all landowners whose property is adjoining a source of water, have the right to make reasonable use of it. If there is not enough water to satisfy all users, they have to divvy it up, so that everyone down stream has an equal share according to the acreage. Riparian water rights cannot be sold or transferred, and if they are, it has to be done with the owners of the adjoining land. The water cannot be transferred or diverted out of its natural watershed," explains Ludlow.

"Thank you professor, when is the test?" Fink asks.

"Very funny. Now listen-up, because the water rights are going to tie in later on. Now, I found out through more than one source, that Benny Sullivan was connected to the Owens Valley by a blood relative," says Ludlow.

"The guy they found at the bottom of the dam was a sympathizer?" Fink asks.

"According to the report written up by St. Francis Dam officials, Sullivan was not a long time resident of Piru as previously thought. He was hired on to work on the dam project, because his physical address was in Piru. When I spoke to his neighbors, they told me he had moved in with a Miss Betty Scott, a hot little twenty-two year old that he met in LA. This took place one year before the construction on the St. Francis began. I don't know if it was planed or just coincidence, but if I had to bet on it..." says Ludlow.

"Was it an accident as the report stated?" Fink asks.

"I didn't get that far. When I found out that he had a girlfriend, a local girl from Piru, things started falling into place. I found her in living on North Broadway, alone and paranoid," says Ludlow.

"For crying out loud. Why didn't she just stay in Piru, where she is a legal resident?" says Fink.

"You're going to love this. Sullivan's girlfriend spilled the beans a few days ago. She tells me everything. She's highly pissed-off, because they were going to get married, just before he gets dead, and just before the big payoff," says Ludlow.

"Payoff?"

"Apparently, he had plans to blackmail everyone on down to Mulholland. The dam officials and the entire water board," explains Ludlow.

"I think if he had just taken on the Water Board, they would have accommodated his demands, but Mulholland? He wasn't going to be blackmailed by a low grade hydro-engineer. Apparently, he wasn't going to let the board be blackmailed either. Scott is pissed-off, because she won't receive any death benefits, because of the fact they are not married," he says.

"I got that. What about his connections to the Owens Valley?" Fink asks.

"Sullivan was a real 'Deusy'. She said he was always ranting about L.A., and how they swindled his aunt and uncle out of their ranch in Big Pine," explains Ludlow.

"Vengeance saith the Lord. Okay what was the shake down about?" Fink asks.

"His job description listed him as a hydro-technician, but he was really just a crew leader. The money was good, and he knew the dam inside and out. The girl told me that the dam is going to collapse, and she didn't want to be around when it happened," says Ludlow.

"What about her family, has she tried to warn them?" Fink asks.

"She tried to warn everyone she could before she left, but everyone seems to be working at the dam, making good money," says Ludlow.

"Okay, so Sullivan hits them up for hush money and they kill him. Who killed him?" Fink asks.

"I can't tell you that, because my investigation stopped when the L.A. City Attorney slapped a cease and desist order on me. I will be arrested if I set foot within the Saint Francis boundary lines," says Ludlow.

"What about your spiel on riparian water rights?" Fink asks.

"That is what Betty Scott kept mentioning. She said; 'every time Sullivan would go into one of his rages about how his relatives got their land swindled out of their water rights, that term, riparian water rights, would come up,'" says Ludlow.

"I'll be a son-of-a-gun, they're doing the same thing here as they did in the Owens Valley," says Fink with astonishment.

"That was the better part of the shake down," says Ludlow.

"Prey tell," says Fink.

"U.S. Law protects riparian water rights. In this case, with the St. Francis Dam, Los Angeles was prohibited from shutting off the natural course of water flowing down stream towards Ventura County.

"This is in the books?" Fink asks.

"Yup. Poor bastards had no idea a twenty story pile of concrete was being poured in their backyard," says Ludlow.

"The workers didn't let on that it was happening? It was a massive construction project. How could Ventura County not know?" Fink asks.

"The cement trucks rolled in to the construction site within the boundary lines of Los Angeles County. It was all planned out, the construction had to be concealed in order to keep the project out of the courts. Never mind the undermining of water rights, the whole project was illegal from the get-go. Are you getting all this?" Ludlow asks as Fink continues to speed write onto an open pad.

"The St. Francis Dam' is a good example of how far LA will go to build upon its infamous success in water acquisition, etcetera, etcetera," says Fink.

"Hell man, it's not about LA and its need of water. It's about waging a private little war against the ranchers and farmers in the Owens River Valley," says Ludlow.

"Owens Valley," offers Fink.

"Yeah, one of those, anyway this dam should have never been built here. Geologically it's unsafe, it's a disaster waiting to happen," says Ludlow.

Fink looks in the direction of the dam, which can be seen at a half-mile distance. Ludlow hands Fink a pair of binoculars.

"This place has got more earthquake faults than Carter has liver pills, and get this, Mulholland eliminated a dam project in the Owens Valley that was a hundred times more stable than this site," shouts Ludlow, facing the dam site.

"You mentioned that they started construction in 1925, a year later they started filling the damned thing...damned thing," repeats Ludlow. "I get it. You're wasting your time as a P.I.," says Fink, looking through the binoculars.

"Where's the State engineers when you need them? I'm going to have to get close enough for pictures, is it possible?" Fink asks.

"It's possible, but you're on your own. They have armed security on both sides of the canyon," says Ludlow.

"I'm on that, I can see them now. My God, would you look at that? The dam is already leaking, I can see it from here. What are they thinking?" asks Fink in disbelief.

"Yeah, I guess they're hoping to shut it down before it reaches full capacity," says Ludlow.

"This is insane, there are towns at the bottom of this canyon, Piru is just twenty-five miles down from the dam site," he says, handing the binoculars back to Ludlow.

"At this point Jimmy, you're the only one who can stop it, and if you can't stop it, at least put out a warning," says Ludlow as Fink goes to his car.

"I have to put my boots on, it's getting pretty deep when you start talking about me putting a plug in this mess," says Fink as Ludlow comes walking up.

"That dam was built by the people who live the in towns below where we are now standing. Many of them are still on the City payroll. It's bread on the table. Now, I'm not saying they're not concerned, they're just not inclined to say anything about it," says Ludlow.

"You're absolutely right Ludlow," says Fink in a realization. "Good, let's start with some interviews with the hundreds of households situated in the Santa Clarita Valley. Families with women, children, and, in some cases, infants," says Ludlow. Fink looks into his eyes, and for the first time he see's a soft side seeping through the hard shell of the veteran LAPD detective.

"I'm going to get those pictures John, and I'm going to get them into copy. The public has to know that the Pied Piper of the modern water world is selling them down the drain," says Fink as he takes a small Leica 35 mm camera from the trunk of his car.

"Go get 'em, tiger," shouts Ludlow to Fink walking in the direction of the dam.

"There are many people depending on you, Jimmy. They may not know it now, but they will when your story breaks," Ludlow shouts. With an upraised arm, Fink acknowledges his comment with a wave of the hand.

The sound of a rattlesnake den, stops Fink in his tracks. He looks back towards his car, only to see Ludlow nodding his head with a thumbs up gesture. "Do me a favor and wait for me. I won't be long," says Fink. Ludlow leans back against the car and waves good-bye in an ominous manner.

Four hours later, Fink is walking down the hallway of a second rate hotel in the North Broadway District in Los Angeles. Ludlow had given him the information where to find Betty Scott. An interview with her will tie things up for the news article.

After pushing a door bell button, a door to the apartment opens slowly, but is restricted by a security chain. A wide-eyed young woman with unkept hair peeks through the opening.

"Hello, Miss Scott? My name is James Fink, I'm a reporter for the Times-Tribune. Can I have a word with you?" Fink asks in a sympathetic tone.

Once inside, Betty Scott and Fink are seated at a table by the window, overlooking North Broadway down below. "When we first met, I was head over heels in love with Ricky, but there towards the end, my doubts had gotten the best of me. He made things sound so wonderful about us and the future," says Betty.

"Can you tell me anything about what Mr. Sullivan knew about the dam that made him think he could extort money from the water board?" Fink asks.

"Yes, I'll tell you everything that I told Mr. Ludlow. Perhaps with your help, they'll be forced to lower the water level of the dam before it's too late," pleads Betty.

"What did he tell you about the water level, Betty? Why did Mr. Sullivan think it was dangerous as it neared capacity?" Fink asks.

"For one thing, the dam isn't strong enough to hold the water behind it. Ricky explained it to me in simple terms, and while sometimes I can be dumb as a box of rocks, I understood what he was telling me," says Betty.

"How did he put it?" Betty thinks to herself. "He said that the dam was originally designed to be 175 feet high. Not long after they started construction, they decided to add another 10 feet to the height making it 185 feet high. Then a year ago they added another ten feet," explains Betty.

"Making the total height 195 feet," adds Fink. "Ricky likened it to a lady with big breasts. If she puts on a bra that is too small, well you know what will happen every time," she says.

"Excellent analogy," says Fink agreeing with a smile. "Just out of curiosity, do you know what an 'acre-foot' is?" Fink asks.

"Sure do. If you had one acre, and walled it up on all four sides, one foot high, then filled it full of water, that is an acre-foot. My daddy grows alfalfa," says Betty.

"Did he ever mention how many acre feet the dam held?" asks Fink.

"I believe he said it was a 38,000 acre foot storage capacity. That's when I realized, that if the dam was only supposed to be 175 feet high, and it's built to 195 feet, well, there's only one thing that can happen. It's why I left, I don't want to be there when it happens," says Betty.

Upon leaving North Broadway, there is an urgency to get back to his place to start on the news article. He feels that he has everything he needs, except an interview with Mulholland.

The following morning, Fink is in the Chief Editor's office, anxiously awaiting a critique on his latest feature article on the St. Francis Dam. Walt McIntee does not seem to be impressed with Fink's first draft. Taking several photos from an envelope, Walt looks through the material. More discouragement is expressed by his boss, then the article is dropped onto his desk along with the photos.

"Jim, you have some vacation time coming, I want you to use it. Go somewhere, relax, and collect your thoughts, so you can come back and do your job. The job that we're paying you to do," says McIntee as he pours himself a drink, then gulps it down.

"I can't use this stuff, Jim, for crying-out-loud. The City wants to read about progress. What you've given me is mundane story about a maintenance problem. The St. Francis Dam is as sound as can be.

"You can say that after looking at the photos I took yesterday?" Fink says with astonishment.

"The interior of a newly built dam leaks, and it will leak for a few more years, until the bentonite forms their seals. Mulholland knows what he's doing. Why don't you try writing about that?" says McIntee as he gulps down another shot of whiskey.

"I can't believe you won't meet me on this Walt. Think about what's at stake here. There are thousands of lives that may be lost. We have to expose this potential danger," Fink pleads.

"Jim, you are beginning to piss me off. You think I am privy to what the Water Board has been up to and what Mulholland has been doing? You have that luxury to guess at these things. I have to maintain a professional attitude to protect the paper," says McIntee, slamming a clinched fist down onto his desk.

"What if it happens? Fink asks.

"No, Jim, what if it doesn't happen. Will you ever be able convince yourself that your idea of professionalism will win out over your conscience of single-handedly destroying the Times-Tribune?" McIntee says in a somber voice.

"I know this, Jim. I know there are forces behind the water project that are much bigger than you ever imagined. The powers-that-be will not let a news reporter or its paper get in their way. You are asking me to do just that, stand in their way. If you can't see that, Jimmy, I think you may be in the wrong line of work," says McIntee, waiting for a response, but Fink says nothing as he walks to the door. As he opens the door, Fink finally exhales and shakes his head in disbelief.

A few hours later, in a lounge not far from the Times-Tribune Building, Fink sits alone at the end of the bar. He is on his fifth shot of whiskey. He makes his way to a phone booth inside the bar. Anne's answering service is dialed.

"I'm sorry, but she can't be reached. There is no forwarding number for new messages," a service person says on the other end. The receiver is placed back on the hook, and he returns to the bar.

"Okay, Ernie, I'm going to take your advice and go home," says Fink.

"Your car will be all right in the parking lot. You could call Anne to come get you, or I can call you a cab," says Ernie.

"Call me a cab, Anne is angry with me, and I can't blame her," says Fink.

"Lover's quarrel?" Ernie asks.

"Worse, the problem arose when I wasn't around for her to quarrel with," Fink says.

"Flowers, a box of chocolates, and a ton of foot messages ought to do it," advises Ernie. "Your cab is right outside. Be brave Jimmy," he adds, as Fink makes it to the door.

Headlights flash across Fink's house as the taxi pulls up into the driveway. An inebriated Fink makes his way out of the cab, he continues to his front door. The taxi cab pulls away as Fink goes through his key ring to find the front door key. Without warning, he is seized by two men. Before he can get a word out, they begin to beat him down onto the porch. The assailants repeatedly punch and kick Fink into semi-unconsciousness.

One of the assailants pulls Fink up by his tie. "Water, L.A. needs water. Now repeat it," says the assailant. Fink hesitates and a blow is delivered to the back of his head. His head is then jerked back up again. "Repeat it," says the other assailant. Through bloodied lips, a reluctant response is spat out by Fink.

"L.A needs...water," replies Fink, reluctantly. The assailants then continue to beat Fink totally unconscious. The two men halt their assault when a neighbor hollers out that he's called the police.

Inside Fink's apartment the living room is dimly lit, he is laying back on the couch, his head wrapped, lips and eyes bruised. After being called by the neighbor, Anne arrived to tend his wounds. "All day I had this feeling that something was going to happen," says Anne as she dabs dried blood from his face with a wet wash cloth.

"They really did a number on me. How do I look?" Fink asks.

"Who ever 'they' were, bloused your eye, cut your lip, and I'm not sure, but your nose may be broken," says Anne.

"Yeah? I'm happy just knowing their fists are going to be really sore in the morning," says Fink.

"It's not funny, Finkie. You ought to go to the police," says Anne.

"Honey, I can't even remember what they looked like, and my neighbor wants to stay out of it," says Fink. "Why would someone do this to you?" Anne asks.

"I've tried to tell you so many times, but I didn't want my work to interfere with your life in the least bit," says Fink.

241.

"I can appreciate that, but now you have to explain this bizarre occurrence," says Anne.

"I've been working on an expose' with an associate, John Ludlow. At the heart of the matter is the St. Francis Dam. John is working on a suspicious death, associated with the dam site," explains Fink.

"So, you think this had anything to do with it?" Anne asks wearily.

"Right now, I'm not sure if it has to do with the Owens Valley or the St. Francis. They may've brought them down from the Owens Valley. Up there, goon squads have been doing this sort of thing for a while, and they've been getting away with it for years. Just because it happened here in LA, won't make any difference," says Fink.

"Jimmy, maybe you had better think about this, your job is on the line. I've been watching how the Owens Valley issue has consumed you. Now, it's the St. Francis Dam.

"No one has the right to screw with people in this way," says Fink as he painfully makes an effort to sit up. Anne gives him some aspirin.

"It has to be stopped, Anne, before our whole system goes the way of Europe," says Fink. "Jim, please, just rest, and we can discuss these things later," she pleads.

Fink lays back, he holds up a hand mirror to his face, 'geesh,'" he says disdainfully.

"I look like I just stepped off the set of a horror movie."

CHAPTER EIGHTEEN
The Return

A few weeks have passed, and Fink is into his second week of his forced vacation time. His wounds have healed, and he has chosen to travel to the Owens Valley to visit the Indian camp and see Nikani. He has a few letters from Solomon to deliver as well. The visit is just one reason for the return. Fink also wants to do a follow-up story on the last bombing and the damage done.

Sheriff Collins and Undersheriff Jack Wright, are the first on his list to be interviewed. Having called the sheriff's office while still in Los Angeles, Collins agreed to an interview. His decision to grant the interview was largely based on the rude way he treated Fink on his last stay in Lone Pine.

"Welcome back Mr. Fink, how was your journey coming up?" Collins asks, noticing Fink's healed cuts.

"Fine as frog hair. Ran into heavy cloud cover around Lancaster, but no rain," offers Fink.

"What happened to your face? Looks like someone worked you over," says the Sheriff.

"My memory is a little bit foggy on the matter, but if I see anyone up here that may spark a recollection, you'll be the first to know," says Fink to the curious sheriff.

"I want to thank you for allowing the interview. I know the last time we were in each other's company, things didn't go so well," adds Fink.

"Yes, that's true. I was surprised to see that the unpleasantries didn't go into print. For that, I think we can start off on a different foot," says Collins.

"I won't take up too much of your time. I'm up here to do a follow up on how the valley has progressed since the last bombing occurred," explains Fink.

"You mentioned over the telephone, something about the last bombing. You can understand that it's an ongoing investigation, and I can't divulge that information. I can tell you this, It's no secret that it happened a little over eight months ago, on June 5, 1927. If you read the Owens Valley Progress-Citizen, you'll find that the trouble started when the City turned down a number of reparation claims submitted by the Bishop and Big Pine Water Associations. That happened on May 6th of last year. Then all hell broke loose in the valley. Just after you left the valley to go back to LA, the City hired six hundred special agents and told the Inyo County Sheriff's Department that they were awaiting orders. That didn't sit very well with me or my men. Hell, we already had enough of their thugs placed on the county force. It was all political as usual. My Department was caught in the middle. We had City agents scouring the valley for the bombers. The idiots were pulling over innocent valley citizens, detaining and searching their vehicles for no cause. We had our hands full with investigations and trying to keep Los Angeles City agents from violating the rights of our locals. It got so bad at one point, a citizen's group petitioned the governor of California to send in the state militia to keep order and protect their rights," explains Collins.

"There was a news article sent to me from Contra Costa County, about an arrest warrant for a C. Percy Watson that had ties to the valley. Can you elaborate?" Fink asks.

"That was some kind of fiasco there. The Los Angeles City Attorney, in conjunction with LAPD detectives, contacted the Inyo County District Attorney. They stated that we had a fugitive living within our jurisdiction, that we should arrest the fugitive on an arrest warrant out of Contra Costa County, someplace near Oakland. How they found that out, I don't know, but by law we had to arrest him," says Collins.

"The news article read that Watson had a fifty-eight acre ranch in Big Pine and was one of the militant ranchers here in the valley," suggests Fink.

"Well, if that is what was printed over there in Contra Costa, then it must be true, but then again, I can't say," says the sheriff with a raised eyebrow.

"The charge was for illegal transport of dynamite, and the L.A. City Attorney claimed he had purchased 400 pounds of high explosives over in Contra Costa County and conspired to blow up the aqueduct," says Collins.

"Was Watson was a loyal supporter of the O.V. Protective Association?" Fink asks as Jack Wright enters the room.

"People in the valley were fed up with Los Angeles stepping all over their rights, spying upon them, and turning their property values into dust, due to their excessive pumping of ground water from the neighboring ranches that the City agents had bought up," explains Undersheriff Jack Wright.

"How did the Watterson's get involved? How did it come about that they were prosecuted for bank fraud?" Fink asks.

"That was another thing. The City jumped all over them for supporting Percy Watson, in an attempt to raise bail for him in Contra Costa County. From what I gathered, Wilfred and George sent out a hand written note to several of Watson's associates to pitch in for Watson's $5,000 bail. The next day, when the note was returned, there were a 150 signatures attached to it, with donated cash. When Watson was released on bail, the City went after the Watterson's like a pack of wolves," explains Collins.

"Had enough? 'Cause we have more if you want to hear it," says Jack Wright as Fink continues to write into his note pad.

"Say, are you going to see Nikani on this trip?" Collins asks.

"That's where I'm headed after I leave here. Why?" Fink asks.

"Well, I never did get to tell him, but when the Indian police showed up to take little Solomon, I was just doing my job. I thought it was real cold blooded the way it went down. You tell him that for me," says Collins.

"I'll be sure to mention it. I want to thank you both for your time. I'll be seeing you," says Fink, tucking his notebook and pencil back into his jacket pocket. After checking into the Lone Pine Hotel, Fink tries to contact John Ludlow to arrange a background work-up on the Los Angeles City Attorney.

While driving to the Indian camp, Fink's thoughts on the St. Francis Dam have him wrought with anxiety, but he feels that if Ludlow wanted to give him an update, he would contact him at the hotel. He is hoping a message will be awaiting him when he gets back. A steep grade tells him he is about to come upon the Big Dip in the road and the North Fork of Lone Pine Creek, on the outskirts of town.

As he slowly crosses, his wheels begin to bog down into the sandy creek bed. Once again, Fink's vehicle becomes stuck in the creek. Instead of anger, he smiles to himself, remembering the first time it happened, only this time Solomon isn't there to help him out. Fink rock hops to the bank of the creek, he slings his jacket over his shoulder and begins to walk towards the Indian camp. As he nears, he can hear the others calling to Nikani, letting him know he has company.

"The Observer has returned, where is your paper and pencil?" Nikani asks in a joking manner, as he greets Fink.

"My paper pad is all 'full-up,' I just got back from Independence, had a long talk with Jack Wright and Sheriff Collins, but I'll get around to that later. I've brought you a few letters from Solomon," announces Fink as he places the letters into Nikani's hand. The letters are held up, so the others in camp can see.

"A letter from my grandson," Nikani says as the others in the camp gather around to hear the letter read by Fink.

"Dear grandpa and everyone, I am fine and I hope you are too, I miss you all very much, I have been doing real good in school and miss fishing with you and Harry the dog. My teacher says that I am smart and helped me with this letter to you. I love all of you and dream of home every night.
P.S. Grandpa, please make 'Fink' uncle to me in the Indian Way," reads Fink.

A deep silence follows. Soft weeping can be heard from one of the women. Nikani wipes tears from his eyes.

"James Fink, there is a place for you in my grandson's heart," says Nikani, then turns and holds up the letter to everyone.

"We welcome Fink as uncle to my grandson, Solomon Joaquin," announces Nikani. The camp approves unanimously by hoops and hollers. Fink is congratulated with hand shakes, an elderly woman kisses his hand and touches it to her cheek.

Later, the entire camp gathers around Nikani's picnic table to listen to Fink tell the story of seeing Solomon for the first time at the Indian school.

"...so we just drove around and ate hot dogs, then he started telling his own personal stories about each of you. He misses his aunties, their fried bread, and uncle's guitar playing," says Fink. Except for the crackling of the fire and the rushing creek, it is silent.

"Solomon didn't say this, but I could tell he is remaining strong. His mind is made up to succeed and come back to all of you. The Owens Valley is his home, and no matter where he may find himself, he will aways return to his home," relates Fink. An elderly woman pushes her way through to speak to Fink.

"Many of us can still recall when the Army tried to get rid of us Indians by taking us to live at the place they call Fort Tejon. Those that did not die from hunger and thirst came back to our home. Solomon lives with that strength as we did back then," she says respectfully. There is agreement among the camp.

"All of our sons, daughters, nieces, and nephews have been taken away to Indian schools. They say it's the law, but we Indian people do not understand why our children cannot learn along side the others. They have schools here in Lone Pine, and other places in the Owens Valley, but our children are not welcome," another camp resident says.

"I hope you don't misunderstand, we Indians know there are good things to come out of learning the white way. When we miss them very much, those good things don't matter," says Nikani. Fink nods his head in agreement, Nikani offers a handshake to Fink, solidifying the understanding.

A communal supper is prepared for Fink, and later, after the camp members have returned to their shelters, Fink relaxes inside Nikani's shack.

"You know, after you left that last time, those crazy city people put up huge search lights alongside the aqueduct, looking for bombers in the hills. Sure enough, after all that, bombs went off just south of the Alabama Gates spillway. They don't know what they're doing, just kept us awake all night long with those light generators," says Nikani as he stokes the stove fire. Fink is seated by Nikani's rocking chair going through his notes.

"Nikani, Indian people don't see this water war, what they see is conflict and uniformed men with guns. Indians see the land being taken away, but not from our people this time," says Nikani.

"May I quote you on that?" Fink asks.

"Makes no difference to me, I can't read, but you must keep in mind that in the circle of life, everything returns to its place," says Nikani as he rises from the wood stove.

"If you change the path of a river, you disturb the spirit, the power of natural flow. In time the river will return and the lake will become full, but beware, for the river will strike out, like a snake that's been grabbed by its tail." Nikani sits back in his rocking chair, and resumes a relaxed position.

With Nikani's words, the St. Francis Dam intrudes on Fink's thoughts. Knowing the water that is stored behind the dam, is water from the Owens River.

"Do you believe the river will return?" Fink asks. "The river is there, it was never taken, it will be here forever, long after the City is gone," says Nikani. The squeaking from Nikani's rocking chair is interrupted when he addresses Fink's apprehension.

"Something is troubling you, Fink. Do you know how I can tell?" Nikani asks. Fink does not reply, but simply waits for his answer.

"Your spirit and self-confidence is not what it should be," says Nikani. The circle, it works for the good as well as the bad, but who's to say what is wrong, when in the end, all will turn to good," says Nikani, looking at Fink as if seeing him in a different light. To Nikani, if Fink is showing a stress that is taking place in the Indian camp, a weary state of mind means but one thing, Fink has come full circle and has acquired the responsibility of an observer.

After farewells are given at the Indian camp, Fink is back at the hotel. A message has been received, and is handed to Fink. 'Return immediately' JL. It is from John Ludlow, and Fink feels it concerns the dam.

The next morning, on March 8, 1928, Fink is on the road, and traveling back to Los Angeles. He has arranged a meeting with John Ludlow later in the afternoon. Somewhere in Los Angeles County, John Ludlow is on a backroad leading to San Francisquito Canyon, the site of the St. Francis Dam. Despite a Cease and Desist Order handed down from the city attorney, Ludlow continues to monitor the dam site. Being ex-LAPD, Ludlow still has friends within the department. Ludlow has deep contempt for city attorneys. Early in the morning, Ludlow was dropped off by an associate, to avoid being detected by the dam security. He has settled in at a well camouflaged vantage point. Sitting on a ground cover tarp, he has set up a high power telescope. He keeps his eyes on the dam, while having a breakfast that consists of an egg sandwich and a cup of thermos coffee. He intermittently scans the dam for any movement, hoping to find Mulholland or his second-in-command, Van Norman.

Ludlow can see that the St. Francis is near capacity level. He estimates that it will be just a matter of days before the water will be near overflow. A sign: KEEP OUT crosses into view through the scope. With further adjustment, he can see a construction trailer.

Into the view of his scope walks Mulholland and his foreman, they are walking into the trailer.

"I wish I could turn into a fly and get into that trailer," says Ludlow, looking through the scope. A car horn is heard in the distance, Ludlow looks at his watch and sees that it is 9:30 a.m., the time set for his associate to return as his ride out of the canyon. Ludlow scrambles, gathering his gear, he has ten minutes to get to the pickup vehicle.

Carrie Anne Phillips, a forty-one year old former police matron, volunteered to be Ludlow's accomplice in the prohibited surveillance activities. Looking at her watch, she has been given specific instructions to leave the area after ten minutes, if he does not show at the pickup spot. Ludlow does not want her to be arrested for trespassing. She looks out of the windshield, but does not see Ludlow. The car is put into reverse and she slowly backs out of the clearing. Just as she starts to pull away, she sees John Ludlow in her rear view mirror, running after the vehicle, frantically waving his hand. The brakes are applied, causing the car to skid on the gravel road. Carrie leans over and opens the passenger door for Ludlow, who, when reaching the car, tosses his gear into the back seat, then slams the car door as the accelerator pedal goes to the floor. Ludlow takes a few seconds to catch his breath.

"When I said wait ten minutes, I didn't mean exactly ten minutes. What were you doing, sitting here with a stopwatch?" Ludlow asks.

"Only following orders boss," says Carrie.

"We have to get to the bridge before security gets there. Step on it, but stay on the road," says Ludlow in an urgent voice. From the opposite side of the canyon, Ludlow's vehicle can be seen speeding down the winding dirt road. The vehicle continues on across a wood bridge, taking them over the Ventura County line.

"Go a little further, once you pass that bend in the road, and pull over, I've got to whizz like a race horse," says Ludlow.

While taking care of his business, he can hear Carrie inside the car.

"You will never guess what happened to me while having breakfast in Piru," says Carrie. Ludlow climbs back into the passengers seat.

"Let me guess. Your corn flakes began talking to you?" says Ludlow in monotone.

"Okay wise ass, for that, I'm not telling you," says Carrie vengefully.

"Only kidding," says Ludlow. After a short silence, he continues; "Okay, I'm sorry," he says with all the sincerity he can muster.

"Guess who was sitting right behind my table at the Piru Cafe," Carrie says excitedly. Ludlow begins to answer.

"No, don't guess, just listen," she says.

"A Dam operator for Generator House Number Two was sitting in the next booth behind me, and

I could hear every word," she says, pleased with herself.

"You've got my attention."

"He was having breakfast with one of the hydro-engineers. They were talking in code, but knowing what I do, I knew what they were saying, sort of," says Carrie.

"The hydrologist was explaining that the repairs would cause a cut   back on the water storage level, and that was not sitting well with you-know-who," says Carrie.

"Who? Mulholland? Ludlow asks.

"That's who I thought, they kept referring to him as chief. Who else could be chief engineer?" Carrie asks. Ludlow agrees with a half-cocked head.

"Lowering the water level for dam 'upgrades' as they put it, would mean a setback on the hard target date," says Carrie.

"Target date for what?" Ludlow asks.

"For the dam to reach storage capacity," says Carrie as she sits back.

"They're not going to lower the water level to repair the leaks. That's what it sounds like to me," says Ludlow.

"They're not going to start the shutoff until the dam is near overflow," says Carrie.

"We have to get back to L.A.," says Ludlow in a concerned voice.

CHAPTER NINETEEN
Something Has To Be Done

In Walt McIntee's office, a conference is being held with three representatives of the Los Angeles Water Board. Walt looks at his watch, anticipating Fink to come walking through the door.

"Mr. Knowles, I'm at a loss, my office sent the board specific request to attend this meeting, I thought they understood the importance of it all," suggests Walt.

"Let me assure you Mr. McIntee, we are here to represent the Water Board in proxy. This situation should not reflect in any way, the board's deep concern towards the matters at hand," replies Knowles.

"You have no idea why you are here, do you Mr. Knowles?" Walt says with certainty.

Before Knowles has a chance to respond, Fink comes through the office door with an arm filled with folders.

"Awfully nice of you to show up Jim," Walt says. "My most humble apologies to all," says Fink with a hint of sarcasm, as he decides not to bow to the proxy board members.

"Gentlemen, this is our senior journalist, James Fink.

"Wait for the introduction before you go all out … Jim, this is Michael Knowles, Vice President in charge of Public Relations, and this is Henry Peabody, Chief of Contract Procurement, and his Assistant, Randall Parks," says Walt, looking at Fink with raised eyebrows.

"Where is the Los Angeles Water Board?" Fink asks.

"Apparently they were all called out of town," replies Walt.

"While you may think our presence is nothing more than a token gesture on the part of the Water Board, the pressing issues our bosses are faced with – are not," says Peabody.

"Pressing issues? Why don't you come out and say it in terms that we use, such as; methods of procurement, fraudulent acquisition of Riparian rights, coercion, these are words we use to describe the Los Angeles Water Board.

"I beg your pardon, but it is the opinion of the board that the Times-Tribune shared in the achievement of water acquisition for this great city," says Knowles.

"Mr. Knowles, if I may ask; What is it you really do with the water board?" asks Fink.

"As I explained to your boss, I hold several positions, one of which is public relations, all of which make me indispensable," says Knowles.

"It's unfortunate that we have to express our valid concerns to a proxy board that recites a rehearsed opinion regurgitated by the water board.

The main issue here, as I see it, is your bosses have been coming under tremendous scrutiny. And, you expect the Time-Tribune to cast the board in a better light," says Fink.

"Yes, on the lines of morally responsible to the public and its safety," says Parks chiming in.

"Oh?" Fink says feigning interest. "How then do you propose the Times-Tribune prop up the chief engineer and his unbridled passion water acquisition?" Fink goads.

"Well, he has a certain way that's become liable to the City. In the event a worst case scenario occurs, damage control will be immediate," says Parks.

"Hold on just a minute. You come into the Times-Tribune, masquerading as upper echelon water board executives, then suggest a "scenario" to a catastrophe, that will paint the board in a favorable light?" Fink asks adamantly.

"We are in the news reporting business, we cannot sit on our hands while the board basks in their own cover up," Fink adds. Just then Walt intervenes, he not wanting his star reporter to go to far with his point.

"Gentlemen, I think we have discussed about enough for today," says Walt apologetically. As he opens the office door, the last word is offered.

"Mulholland should be sent packing for endangering thousands of lives of men, women, and children.
The project should be shut down immediately. Stop worrying about what might happen and focus

on what's happening right now," hollers Fink as the quasi water board leave McIntee's office.

After the door is closed, Walt goes to his desk and reaches down into a drawer and pulls out a bottle.

"It's not going to be that easy Jim; running an expose on Mulholland. He's come to full power, everything he does is heralded as a glorious achievement. LA in his pocket," he says, pouring a drink. The intercom buzzes and McIntee accepts a call from one of the actual Water Board members, looking for an explanation as to why the meeting went sour. Fink observes his bosses demeanor, trying to catch any hint of disloyalty to the paper.

"Jim, I've been doing a little research, and you were right," he says, looking down at the report the proxy Board Members presented to him.

"I've decided to run your expose' on the St. Francis Dam this weekend. On one condition, I want equal time for the board members to defend their standpoint," demands Walt. Fink concurs, and with that in agreement, they stand and leave the office. Among Fink's many achievements, what transpired a few minutes ago ranks the best experience in his career.

Excited and overjoyed, Fink is eager to share the good news, he immediately heads to his newsroom desk and places a call to an associate John Ludlow, a private investigator.

"No, I am serious," says Fink into the telephone line to Ludlow. "The story is going to run this upcoming weekend," he adds.

"This weekend? Jim, you really have to see what's going on out there. Within a day or so, three days tops, the dam will reach capacity. This weekend may be too late," says Ludlow.

"That dam was never meant to go to capacity. I'm going out to the site tonight," says Fink.

"Jim, the dam will still be there tomorrow, why don't you wait until morning, we'll go together," reasons Ludlow.

"They can only deny me entrance or tell me to go away," says Fink. With that he hangs up the telephone and goes to his car. After gaming up his vehicle, he is on the road to the top of San Franciscito Canyon. An hour and a half later, he is at the guard shack at the entrance of the St. Francis Dam.

Inside his vehicle, Fink looks up to see a security guard in full uniform. A press pass is presented, and the guard studies his face. Fink becomes concerned that he may not gain access to the site. Another guard is called over, and Fink waits patiently while both guards discuss the press pass. To his surprise, he is directed to a visitor parking lot by the ranking guard.

"Your clearance is in order sir, please display and keep this pass with you at all times. Do not cross any Off Limits signs, and stay on the walkways," instructs the guard in a routine manner.

Fink makes his way past the guard shack to get a closer look at the dam.

"LA Times-Tribune" Fink says to another guard standing at an entrance gate leading to the dam. He offers a cigarette to the guard.

"Been with the City long?" Fink asks, reading the guard's name plate.

"Officer James?" He adds.

"Sorry sir, but I can't divulge any information, or answer any questions," says Jones.

"They tell you that? Tell you not to provide answers to words like; geologically unstable, or dam seepage, or structure failure, they tell you that?" Fink asks in a deliberate tone.

The guard hesitates, he turns and walks toward the center of the dam on a walkway, Fink follows. They keep walking then the guard stops at midpoint of the dam.

"Listen, someone needs to do something about this," says the guard as he looks around. He then discretely motions to Fink, directing him to the opposite side of the dam. A light beam from his flashlight shines down onto the dam wall.

"The downside of the dam has numerous leaks," says James as Fink looks downward.
By the light of a flashlight beam he sees a place at the base of the dam where the water is churning upward.

"The smaller leaks are obvious, but what's going on underneath, you won't believe. At night when it gets real quiet you can hear the dam shifting and quaking," says James.

"Has the damage been written into the report at the end of you shift?" Fink asks.

"Every shift I'ver worked for the past week, the same information was entered into the report," says James.

"And the other shifts?" Fink asks.

"As far as I know, it's all been entered in, on every shift," says James.

"Mr. Fink, I have family living below the dam, something has to be done," pleads James.

"My assignment to cover the dam is important, and I give my word, everything that is learned here tonight will be off record. Your name will not be mentioned," says Fink. The guard thinks about it momentarily.

"Does Mulholland ever come to inspect the dam?" Fink asks.

"I've only seen him out here once, but then, I work the night shift," says James, as he turns his back to Fink and continues.

"The guy gives me the creeps. The night that I did see him out here, he was acting crazy. He walked the dam back and forth, right here in the middle, all night long," says James.

"Was he saying anything,"?

"I could see through the binoculars that he was talking, but from my post at the gate, I couldn't hear his voice," says James.

"To me, it was as if he were trying to will the dam into a sound state," says James.

Fink goes to the holding side of the dam, and a beam of light sweeps over the cement surface.

"It's hard to tell anything's wrong, looking at it from this angle," says Fink.

"That's the bad part. What's worse, it's been forecasted that we are in for one of the heaviest rainy seasons in a decade. I tell you, Mr. Fink, it really has me worried," says James.

"Keep your eye on the Times-Tribune front page, within a week everyone will know this story," Jones watches as Fink turns and walks away, still writing in his note pad.

After the long ride from San Franciscito Canyon, Fink has reached his apartment in Los Angeles. It's been a long day, and upon opening his door, he is happy to see Anne. She has made him a surprise dinner, and is placing candles at the dinner setting when he walks in. A romantic interlude is awaiting, and now that Fink is home, the night can begin. As they end the embrace, the phone begins to ring.

"Please don't answer it," says Anne as she pulls Fink close to her. Long into a passionate kiss, the phone continues to ring.

"Should I rip it out by the roots?" Fink asks. Frustrated, he goes to answer it.

"Hello?" Fink answers. He finds that the call is from the Indian School. Fink turns to Anne.

"It's from the Indian school," he says, turning his attention back to the telephone call.

"Yes, Mr. Peters, that is true, I am his designated contact for the Joaquin family. I am Solomon's uncle," says Fink as he turns to Anne with a melancholy expression.

"I understand. Please, may speak to him? It's understandable that he is upset, thank you," says Fink. On the other end of the line, Solomon is handed the phone receiver by Peters.

"Uncle? Mr. Peters told me that grampa got sick, he won't wake up," says Solomon, crying.

"Solomon, I need for you to listen, I will do everything I can to get you home. Right now I want you to do something," suggests Fink.

"Go to your room and write your grandfather a letter, tell him how much you love him and miss him. I will make plans to be at the Indian school soon as possible," urges Fink.

On the other end, Solomon continues to sob into the phone. "Okay," he says as he hands the handset to Peters.

"Superintendent Peters, is there any way possible that we can talk, tonight?" Fink asks. "Thank you, we are on our way," says Fink as he slowly place the receiver back on its cradle. He turns to Anne.

"The superintendent explained that he received a call from the Inyo County Sheriffs Office, notifying him of Nikani. He has taken ill and fallen into a coma," says Fink, as Anne comforts him. "Solomon must be devastated. We must go to him now, Jim," says Anne.

"I know baby, and thank you for being here for me tonight. I know it all doesn't seem fair to you, but now more than ever, we have to be strong for Solomon," says Fink.

"Come on, gather your things, the superintendent will be waiting for us at the Indian School," says Anne. Fink goes to the table and blows out the dinner candles.

"I am placing a call to Sheriff Collins, then we'll be on our way," says Fink.

After another long ride, Fink and Anne have arrived at the Indian School. They find that roll call had been taken earlier, and Solomon has gone unaccountable. In a hallway, Anne waits patiently for Fink, who is having a discussion with the school official about granting Solomon a temporary hardship release.

Out of the corner of her eye Anne sees a small figure standing next to her, it is Solomon.

Inside the superintendent's office, Fink is seated with his hat in his lap. Superintendent Peters is seated behind his desk, pondering the situation. His hands are clasped resting on his chest with index fingers touching his bearded chin. Nothing is said between them. Fink is motionless as he faces the stern Superintendent.

"School policy is worded clearly, Mr. Fink. 'Only a relative of an enrolled pupil may take temporary custody of said pupil. Temporary custody is allowed only if the situation is on an emergency basis.' To say that an absence should be authorized, simply on a matter of illness, is certainly not within the scope of policy," says Peters.

"Surely your school policy must also address situations of hardship, brought on by a family emergency. It is my understanding that Sheriff Collins had contacted your office to notify you of the urgent situation concerning Solomon's grandfather," says Fink.

"He only mentioned an illness," says Peters.

"Do you know the definition of 'coma' in medical terms?" Fink asks.

"Not precisely, no," admits Peters.

"We could give Sheriff Collins a call, I'm sure he will provide you with the definition," says Fink.

"My knowledge of a medical term has nothing to do with your claim as a blood relative to young Solomon," says Peters.

The supernatant becomes distracted, Fink hears the office door open, he turns to see Solomon.

"Uncle!" Solomon hollers as he runs to Fink. A short conversation takes place, and it appears that Solomon does not agree with what has been said. With some protest, Solomon exits the office, to wait with Anne.

"I'm going to be straight with you Mr. Peters, so forgive me if I seem rude, but as it stands, I have enough information to launch an investigative report on the policies imposed on your students, or should I say inmates," says Fink.

"Now see here," Peters stresses adamantly, but Fink quickly continues.

"The public knows nothing of a government that forces Indian parents to give up their children in the name of assimilation," says Fink. The superintendent becomes agitated.

"Now, you can look at it this way; the article can begin right now, with you reciting detrimental school policy, or you can read about the school's compassion to aid and consider emergency leave, so that Solomon can go and see his grandfather, whose health is failing as we speak," says Fink with conviction.

Peters reaches inside his desk drawer, pulls out a form tablet, with the heading 'Excused Absence' on it, and begins writing.

From the Superintendent's office window, he can be seen looking down on the parking area. Fink, Anne, and Solomon are walking from the building to their car.

It has been a long day for Fink and Anne. He and Anne have agreed to share the drive on the way back to Lone Pine.

After stopping in Mojave for dinner, they are back on the road. Solomon is curled up into Anne's waist coat, as she drives up the Sierra Highway.

"I spoke to Jack Wright, the Undersheriff. He explained that he was waved down in Lone Pine by one of the members of the Indian camp. The woman told him that they didn't know what to do, except let Sheriff Collins know of Nikani's condition, with the hope that he could contact the school," says Fink.

"Is there a medical facility in Lone Pine?" Anne asks.

"Yes, there is. Collins dispatched a Sheriff's Deputy to escort a doctor to the Indian camp to examine Nikani. After the diagnosis they contacted the school," says Fink.

"What do you think will happen when we get there?" Anne asks.

"I don't know, I've never been to an American Indian healing ceremony of any sort. We're about three and a half hours away. Barring any mechanical failures we should be there around 11:30, or just before midnight," says Fink. For the remainder of the journey back to the Owens Valley, Anne has taken the wheel. Solomon is now curled up next to Fink, who fell asleep shortly after leaving Mojave.

A few hours later, Anne pulls into a gas station in Olancha for a personal stop. "Where are we Auntie Anne?" Solomon asks in a sleepy voice.

"Well, I see you're back from dream land," says Anne.

"Hey, this looks like Olancha," says Solomon excitedly.

"I have to go to the lady's room, and if you have to go, better go now, 'cause we're not stopping until we get to Lone Pine," says Anne as she hurries to the restroom. Fink begins to stir in his sleep, then springs awake.

"What happened? Where are we? Why have we stopped?" Fink asks frantically. He hears laughter.

It is Solomon, laughing uncontrollably, after tickling Fink's nose with a piece of string.

"Hey Fink, were almost home. We're in Olancha," says Solomon.

Fink rubs his face to wake himself. "It's good to hear you laugh Solomon," says Fink.

"I wrote a letter to grandpa. Want me to read it to you?" asks Solomon as he begins to dig through his bag.

"No. I think you ought to read it to your grandpa. We'll be seeing him in a few hours," says Fink.

"Next stop, Lone Pine," says Anne as she opens the driver's side door.

"Not before we have a chance to go to the boys room, come on Solomon, let's go do our business," says Fink.

CHAPTER TWENTY
Nothing Lasts But The Earth And Sky

As Fink, Anne and Solomon pull up to the big dip, just outside of the Indian camp, they can see that the campfires are blazing. Indian chants can be heard as they navigate across the creek. Upon entering the camp, Solomon walks together between Fink and Anne. His many relatives are taken aback by his presence. The women begin to weep with happiness. He continues to walk past relatives, now standing quietly at campfires. They follow and gather around Nikani's shack.

Inside, Nikani is being watched over by relatives as he lay in coma. Solomon falters as he is lead to Nikani's side.

"Grampa, it's me Solomon. Fink brought me to see you," says Solomon as he slowly approaches his bedside. Solomon reaches into his jacket pocket to pull out his letter.

"See grampa, I wrote this letter to you when I was in school. My handwriting and spelling are getting better, see?" he says as he tries to present the letter to his grandfather. Nikani does not respond, and it confuses Solomon, his grandfather always showed interest in his efforts. Solomon begins to read the letter aloud, trying to get Nikani to wake up and give him encouragement. Solomon, while reading the letter, is putting his best effort forward to be fluent. Fink and Anne watch painfully as Solomon's fragile voice breaks. Anne buries her head in Fink's shoulder and weeps softly. Fink comforts her, but is equally touched with emotion. The letter is place on Nikani's hand by Solomon, trying to get him to take it, hold it, and tell him how well his handwriting has progressed.

"Why won't he wake up Auntie Anne?" Solomon asks.

"Honey, he may not look like he is awake, but he knows you are here. Go over to his bed side, put your hand in his, and ask grandpa to squeeze your hand if he can hear you," says Anne.

Fink and Anne watch as Solomon walks softly back to his grandfather's bedside, and holds Nikani's hand.

"Grampa, can you hear me? Please hear me grampa. Squeeze my hand if you can hear me," pleads Solomon. When Nikani responds with an ever so gentle flexing of his hand, he becomes elated. He begins weeping expressions of respect and gratitude. One of Solomon's relatives goes to his side and comforts him. Anne and Fink join her as they gather around Nikani's bed.

It is now way past midnight. There are still a few camp members awake, keeping the fires going. Inside Nikani's shack, Anne has fallen asleep in a chair. Fink keeps vigil with Angie, a cousin to Nikani.

Solomon is cuddled next to his grandfather. He has pulled Nikani's arm around his shoulder and is sleeping soundly. Two other women enter and quietly communicate with the woman at the bedside. Both women quietly begin to check Nikani for vital signs. One of the women listens closely for any sign of breathing, while another feels for a pulse. There is silent confirmation. Anne awakes when she hears Solomon softly cry in his sleep, as he is gently taken from Nikani's side. Fink and Anne are ushered out of Nikani's bed room, and are asked to comfort Solomon while they tend to Nikani. A wash basin and cloths are brought from a closet, and the women prepare Nikani for funerary rites.

Fink and Anne place Solomon in the back seat of the car, with a pillow and a blanket taken from Nikani's bed. Nothing is said to him about his grandfather's passing. Sleep will fall upon him and save him from further pain.

In the early Monday morning sunlight, Fink awakens when a soft knock on his car window is heard. He rolls down the window and accepts two cups of coffee.

"Let the little one sleep, there will be a Holy Man here later, he will talk to Solomon," the woman says softly. Fink looks into the back seat to see Solomon sleeping soundly.

"Last night, I promised Solomon we would have pancakes and eggs in the morning. Is that going to be a problem?" Fink asks.

"Not if you take him to town," says the Indian woman.

"Thank you for the coffee. We'll have him back by nine o'clock," says Fink.

Later in the morning, while Solomon is enjoying pancakes and eggs at Rossi's Cafe, a Holy Man has arrived at the Indian camp. Having traveled all night from the Walker Pass area, he is at the camp to perform a ceremony. A lodge has been constructed at the Indian camp for relatives and close friends. The Indian women of the camp will assist him as he conducts a cleansing of the immediate surrounding area. An inventory of Nikani's belongings will be gathered, in view of the holy man.

At the cafe in town, Fink has finished a breakfast plate of steak and eggs. Anne and Solomon continue to enjoy a much needed breakfast. Solomon sees Sheriff Collins enter the cafe.

"There's Sheriff Collins, and he's headed this way," says Solomon as he begins to get small in his chair.

"Don't worry, the sheriff thought a lot of your grandfather. Enjoy your breakfast Solomon, I'll take care of it," says Fink as he turns to greet the Sheriff.

"Good morning everyone, I'm sorry to interrupt your breakfast," says Collins, looking at Fink with a "we-have-to-talk" look.

"Sheriff Collins. Won't you join us for some breakfast?" Fink asks.

"Thank you, but I already had breakfast. I just came over to say hello to Solomon. It's good to see you again young man," offers the Sheriff.

"Hello Sheriff Collins. Fink brought me back last night to see my grampa," says Solomon, still unaware of his grandfather's passing.

Sheriff Collins begins to offer his condolences, but Fink grabs his attention, heads him off, and changes the subject. "Yes, that's right, we arrived last night. Sheriff, let me introduce you to my bride to be, Miss Anne Porter."

"I'm glad to meet you Miss Porter," says Collins.

"The pleasure is all mine Sheriff. James let me know how instrumental you were in getting notification to the school. It was a very honorable thing to do," says Anne.

"It was something Nikani would have wanted, I know how much he cared for the boy," says Collins.

"Thank you," says Solomon, in a shy voice.

"I just wanted to let you know that you are welcome here, and I hope you have a good visit while you are home," says Collins. "I'll be going now. It was nice meeting you Miss Porter. Be strong young man," Collins nods at Fink then turns to leave.

"I'll tell you what, you two finish up, while I go talk to the sheriff. I'll be right back," says Fink.

Outside, Fink meets the sheriff by his patrol car.

"I was up at the Indian camp before I dropped by the cafe. How could you not tell him?" Collins asks.

"I was going to do just that, but then a relative let me know that a medicine man was going to talk with him. What could I do?" Fink asks.

"The County Coroner is allowing them the funeral ceremony, knowing that the Shoshoni cremate their dead, there's not much for him to do. But that's not why I suggested that you come outside," says Collins.

"What could be more important?" Fink asks.

"Well, it seems that Nikani was somewhat a legend in his own time," says Collins.

"I'm not surprised. What gives?" Fink asks.

"Nikani's passing spread like wild fire here in the valley. Lord only knows how they do that. It appears that a well-to-do family in Bishop are direct descendants of the Jayhawkers that came through Death Valley back in '49," explains Collins.

"Nikani told me the history of that event. Saved a pioneer from certain death," says Fink.

"Must be the one. Anyway, because of what happened back then, that particular pioneer became a very rich man. Made his fortune in LA, and now the family is spread from here to Napa. The family was told of Nikani's death, inadvertently," says Collins.

"The announcement was let known unintentionally?" Fink asks.

"Well, you could put it that way. It turns out that one of their Indian ranch hands; wanting to take a day off for the funeral ceremony," says Collins.

"Sounds right to me. How does this tie in with Nikani's death?"

"The affluent family wants to remain anonymous, but it appears that Nikani is mentioned in the family bible. Because of their good fortune, the family takes the history to heart," says Collins.

"It would be interesting to see how the event was interpreted in the family Bible. As far as I know, the only two that know the story is Solomon and I," says Fink.

"I will mention that to my contact. I'm sure they would be interested in the second account," replies Collins. It was conveyed to me that they want to help in any way they can. I'm thinking with Solomon's education. Am I on the right track with this?" Collins asks.

"One hundred percent," replies Fink.

"Good, because when I talked with school officials, it was apparent that they were impressed with little Solomon's desire to learn," he adds.

"You're absolutely right. To top it off, Solomon is the last link in the Joaquin family blood line. He will need all the help he can get, growing up in this world," says Fink.

"Amen to that. I have to go back to the camp and finish up with the coroner, I'll meet you there," says Collins.

At the Indian camp, while Nikani lay in state inside his bedroom, the coroner is speaking to the three women entrusted with the care and preparation of Nikani's body.

"I have inspected the funeral pyre, and it seems sufficient for the task at hand. In the white man's world, a cremation, or the burning of a corpse, is a thorough funerary procedure. The cremation needs to be complete. That is to say, there is to be nothing but ashes remaining after the procedure," recites the Coroner.

"Are there any questions?" he asks. The women sit calmly in their chairs, arms crossed, each with stern expressions on their faces.

Sheriff Collins appears in the doorway where a Deputy has been posted. Collins observes the moment of awkward silence between the women and the Coroner.

"How are things going," Collins asks.

"So far, everything is going good," replies the Deputy.

"I have to speak with the Shoshoni Holy Man. Where is he?" Collins asks. The deputy points in the direction of the main body of the camp. There, in the midst of a circle, is a single man, speaking to the members of the camp and its visitors.

"I have to get his attention, little Solomon is going to be here any minute now," says Collins as he waves over one of the three women in the Coroner's audience.

"It was my understanding that the holy man was to talk with little Solomon about his grandfather," says Collins. She nods yes.

"If you would, please, get his attention and let him know that Solomon will be here in just a minute," explains Collins. He watches the woman confiding in the medicine man as Fink and Anne come walking into the Indian camp with Solomon. Anne and Fink lead him to the medicine man while the Sheriff looks on. The medicine man kneels to Solomon's eye level. Fink and Anne stand behind him. From where the sheriff stands, he can see Solomon hang his head, his shoulders arch inward, and he begins to weep.

As the sun fades behind the Sierra's, Nikani's body is placed within the funeral pyre and it has been lit. The Cry Dancers, in a manner of respect, have circled the fire and a chant is constantly voiced, and as the fire grows more intense, the chant becomes louder. Fink and Anne observe from a short distance. Solomon is comforted by his relatives. The Shoshone funerary rite of cremation will continue until dawn. Fink has reserved a room for Anne and himself and will be leaving shortly. An Indian woman walks up, and respectfully hands Fink a sage bundle.

"We know it is in Solomon's heart to finish his schooling. We have packed all of the belongings that Nikani wanted Solomon to have. Keep them for him, things get lost at the school. When you leave, we will send him with you. Nikani placed his trust in you, he told us. Now you have the trust of our people. Show Solomon what he needs to know to live in this life. Stand behind him when he needs to know there will be someone there… you, James Fink," says the woman.

"Tell the people of the camp that Nikani's trust in me will remain in my heart, until it's my time," says Fink, holding the sage bundle next to his heart.

CHAPTER TWENTY-ONE
Monday, March 12, 1928, 11:55 pm
Terror In The Night

Through a pouring rain, security lights on top of the dam can be seen flickering in the hard blowing wind. The water level of the dam is just three feet below the spillway gates, and the wind is blowing waves of water over the dam. A low decibel rumbling sporadically can be heard. One of the guards is joined by another. Leaning over the railing at down side. A flashlight beam shows a highly pressurized stream of water spraying outward from new fissures in the dam.

"We have to notify the power plants, tell them to evacuate. This doesn't look good," says the guard.

The guards panic as the footing beneath them becomes violently unstable. They can feel the dam rise upward. When the rumbling settles momentarily, they regain their footing and bolt for the walkway gates. A flashlight is dropped into an opening fissure, and the second guard suddenly leaps to safety, as huge pillars of muddied water begins to shoot upward in a pressured spray. They scramble to the gate, and looking over his shoulder one of the guards sees the lights go out as the dam begins to completely fail, violent enough to knock the guards off their feet. The huge volume of water crashes down and up against the walls of San Francisquito Canyon. It's force pulverizing the rock canyon into mist.

On the parking side of the dam the light poles are shaking and swaying. Other security personnel start for higher ground, running for their lives. Officer James makes his way toward the dam's edge shining his flashlight, trying to see the dam walkway. All he sees is blackness and pressure mist rising from the bottom of the dam. He drops to his knees and begins to cry out for his family who are sleeping in their beds below the collapsing dam.

Down below the dam, the street lights in the little town of Piru continue to glow bright. Inside a store front window, a clock a reads 11:55. Mostly all business in the small town have closed up shop and gone home for the night. Inside a home where a family is sleeping, the head of household is awakened by a deep rumbling, of what can only be described as a freight train. In an instant a thirty foot wall of water crashes into the home, collapsing it like a house of cards.

Outside of an all-night-diner. A Sheriffs Deputy is leaving the cafe. Hearing the crashing water, he looks in the direction of the commotion. What he sees is a wall of water exploding into the town's business district. The Deputy turns towards the diner to warn others, but the water smashes into the cafe with devastating effect. People are swept away, some are pulled under by the tons of debris below the surface. Those who are lucky enough to somehow make it to dry surfaces, manage to pull others from the deluge of tumbling cars, buildings and farm equipment, caught in the torrent flood waters.

In the morning, a cloudless sky welcomes the sunrise in the Owens Valley. Fink and Anne have visited the Indian camp to pick up Solomon and say good-bye. On the way to the cafe, Solomon shows Fink and Anne a shoe box containing some articles. He shows them a small leather pouch, and shakes it up and down.

"Looks like grandpa left some coins," says Anne.

"Yeah, there yellow instead of silver like all the rest of them," says Solomon.

"See?" Solomon says as he pours out some of the gold coins into his hand. Fink slams on his breaks.

"Can I see one?" he asks.

"Sure, but watch out they're heavy," says Solomon.

Fink holds the coin up, then polishes it on his sleeve. "How many is in the pouch?" Fink asks.

"Counting the one you have, twenty," says Solomon.

"Well, what you have here are five dollar gold pieces, made in 1838, minted in Dahlonega, Georgia. It's the first gold coin minted in the United States. Do you know what that means?" Fink asks.

"No, but you can tell me," says Solomon.

"It means you're rich," says Fink, jubilant.

"We'll have to put it in the bank, and save it for you," says Anne.

"I can keep it under my bed," says Solomon.

Inside Rossi's Cafe, it is nearly filled to capacity. Once seated, Solomon places his treasure box on the table, keeping a close eye on it. At the cafe counter, there are several farmers seated, and a conversation can be overheard having to do with water rights. The farmers are alternately looking at Fink's table. Fink is aware but ignores them.

"Solomon, you know that if you want to talk...about anything, Anne and I will be here for you," he offers.

"Maybe I just don't know what to say right now, maybe later I'll talk," says Solomon.

"Okay, just checking," says Fink.

A farmer enters He blurts out headline news of the St. Francis catastrophe.

"Hey! You boys just might want to see this, as he holds up a copy of the Los Angeles Examiner, Tuesday March 13, 1928: 100 BELIEVED DEAD IN L.A. AQUEDUCT DAM BREAK.

"Looks like the Owens River finally made it to the Pacific Ocean," he proclaims.

"Oh my God," is a response from another farmer at the counter.

"I have to find a phone, you two order breakfast I'll be back before you can say pancakes," says Fink, as the waitress takes the breakfast order.

"One order of pigs in a blanket, with strawberry jam, two egg sandwiches, two coffee's and a cup of milk...To go, please," says Anne. "Sorry about that, sweetie," says Anne to Solomon. "Looks like we're eating on the road, today," she adds.

The trip to Riverside becomes a seven hour endurance ride. Prior communication with Ludlow, left Fink with a latest update on the devastation. Their plans to meet in Fillmore added more pressure to the travel time. Fink begins to prepare himself for what he is about to see when he arrives in Fillmore, one of the towns destroyed in the wake of the disaster.

At the Riverside Indian school, Solomon has arrived just in time for the school dinner call. Farewells were given just as they pulled up into the school parking lot. After submitting a favorable news article about the Indian school to the Administrator, Fink and Anne leave for Los Angeles.

"Jimmy, I really wish you would get some rest before going to the flood site," says Anne.

"I wish I could, but I have to cover this story, your understanding would really mean a lot to me. I'll tell you all about it when I get back," pleads Fink.

"Be safe, it's going to be cold tonight, try to get something in your stomach, and dress warmI will be waiting for you," says Anne reassuringly.

CHAPTER TWENTY-ONE
Bodies In The Pacific

Moving through the flood debris in a small boat. Fink, along with a photographer and a boat pilot, are maneuvering through uprooted trees and fragmented houses. A photo is snapped of a child still dressed in her night clothes, being dislodged from the gnarled roots of a tree. Fink slowly sits down in the boat buries his head in his hands and weeps silently. As the outboard continues to move by, horses, cows and pets, that are strewn throughout the disaster site, he and the boat crew are at a loss for words.

Passing rows of military tents, they arrive at a first aid station, a photographer snaps photos of disaster volunteers amidst rows of shrouded bodies. He sees Ludlow, and directs the boat to his location. Once on the bank of the flood waters, makes his way through the crowd to meet up with Ludlow. In a swarm of reporters, the Ventura County Sheriff is about to make a statement concerning the catastrophe.

"I was about to give up on you, I almost didn't make it myself," says Ludlow.

"The things we witnessed upstream. . . I can't begin to describe,"

"You don't have to, I've already had an ear full of sickening accounts," says Ludlow. Fink tries to get closer to the makeshift podium as an officer approaches.

"Just before midnight, the St. Francis dam failed and collapsed sending a one hundred foot wall of water and mud down upon three towns in the Santa Clara Valley. As of tonight, we have recovered 250 bodies, and we expect that number to rise," reports the Sheriff. A barrage of questions suddenly erupt from reporters.

"We have information that ranchers from the Owens Valley may have been involved, is it possible the dam was bombed?" A reporter asks.

"We have no reports or evidence that the dam was bombed, but we will be looking into every aspect of the failure," says the Sheriff.

Fink comes to a realization. The reporter asking the question is also a Times-Tribune reporter.

"Where did they get that scoop?" Ludlow asks. Another reporter in front of them overhears the comment.

"Where've you been? There's no scoop. The farmers and ranchers, they're to blame for this," says the other reporter. Fink and Ludlow leave the conference tent with a mutual feeling that the story line had already been casted.

"It looks like your job got a little easier. Let them hand in their bogus story, keep your name off of it," advises Ludlow.

"Where's your car?" asks Fink.

"Probably a lot closer than yours, need a lift?" Ludlow asks.

"It's about a mile up river. Let me pay the skipper of the outboard. The photographer will probably stay until midnight," says Fink.

The next day, Fink has arrived at Walt's office. After walking through the press room where his coworkers pause to watch him enter Walt's office.

Inside the office, Walt is seated behind his desk as Fink walks in unannounced followed by the an irate secretary.

"It's alright Ariel, I'll handle it," says Walt.

"You dirty bastard! How long did you know about it?" Fink shouts. Walt does not respond instead, he downs a shot of whiskey.

You purposely held back vital information, and for what, a sleazy nod from your superiors on the Water Board! Fink shouts.

"My God Jim, everyone was praying it wouldn't happen. I swear, I was not made aware of the complications until you brought it to my attention. I did everything I possibly could to get the word out. The Water Board was holding out until they could get Mulholland to shut off the flow to the St. Francis.

"I'm cleaning out my desk Walt. The next time you want a story, get it from one of your cub reporters. Better still, get out of that chair, go out to Fillmore, see for yourself what your policy on the politics of modern water and power wreaked on innocents asleep in their beds," shouts Fink as he exits Walt's office.

"I'm sorry, so very sorry," sobs McIntee. At his desk in the newsroom, Fink tosses his work related belongings into boxes and bags. Without a word to his coworkers, Fink leaves the newsroom. Many in the newsroom are sympathetic towards his anger, and like the rest of the city, are in a state of shock brought on by the disaster.

With his box of office files under his arm, he marches straight into the lobby and through the exit doors of the Times-Tribune Building. Outside, Fink trudges towards to his vehicle, as he places a box atop the hood, his attention is drawn to a commotion across the street. Fink sees Mulholland, amid a crowd of reporters. He places the belongings in his vehicle, and starts for the crowd of reporters.

Closing rapidly, he keeps focused on Mulholland as he crosses the boulevard. The crowd of reports are wedged tight into each other, but he pushes his way through. "Hey Jim, take it easy" protests a reporter.

"Take them back to 1926 Willie, when you learned the St. Francis was unstable, and while you're at it, tell them how you paid off the inspectors," shouts Fink. Just then he comes face to face with Mulholland's body guard. Fink recognizes him to be one who assaulted him.

"Hey, LA needs the water," says Fink, as he plants a knee into his groin and gives him a head butt.

"Remember me?" says Fink vengefully. The body guard doubles over in pain. There is a scuffle, but it goes unnoticed as the crowd of news hungry reporters move in unison with Mulholland.

"They died in their sleep you bastard! Men, women and children all dead because of you... you power hungry monster! Fink shouts.

At once, the entire unit of body guards and police quickly overpower Fink and take him down to the ground, in front of Mulholland, who now stands over Fink. Mulholland offers no expression and merely steps over him to continue on.

"Fink, settle down or we'll run you in!" The Police show reluctance in taking any action and they leave Fink laying on the cement walkway. As he rises from the sidewalk, he can see the mob of reporters still trying for any word of the disaster from Mulholland.

CHAPTER TWENTY-TWO
The Legacy: Sky Dancer
1937

Years later, Fink looks back on the days in the trenches of an investigative reporter. Inside a lounge in Los Angeles, a waitress carrying drinks on tray passes. Ella Fitzgerald's "A Tisket, A Tasket" is playing on a juke box. The waitress places drinks before James Fink, now 43 years old, and a potential client to his well established publishing company.

"Look Mr. Jackson the subject matter is just too radical for these uncertain times," says Fink. The advice is not being accepted by Jackson, who restrains his anger.

"As interesting as it may seem to you, it is a different story in other circles of society. The Ku Klux Klan is simply, too controversial. Anything published on those lines, would without a doubt, be misconstrued by the public as being subversive and discriminatory,"

"You mean to tell me that you'll publish anything on Adolf Hitler, but not a great American organization like the Klan. Shoot, Hitler damn sure isn't doing nothing we're not. I thought we're supposed to stick together, as Americans," says Jackson.

Solomon Joaquin, now 25 years old, enters the lounge. Fink sees him and waves him over to his table. Solomon is greeted by Fink, and stands attentively at table side. True to their intentions, the anonymous family of the last Jayhawker of 1849, arranged a full scholarship for Solomon at the University of Southern California Law School. Mr. Jackson looks Solomon up and down.

"Boy, I'm trying to have a private conversation with Mr. Fink, so why don't you just take your brown ass someplace find a blanket to sit on," says Jackson.

"Back home your kind wouldn't have made it past the front door much less be allowed to talk to us white folks," adds Johnson. Solomon is unaffected by the racist remarks.

"Mr. Jackson, I'd like you to meet my Associate Editor, Solomon Joaquin," says Fink. Jackson squirms in his seat and swears under his breath.

"Mr. Jackson here is concerned that we are having doubts about publishing his book about the Klan," says Fink. Solomon smiles at Jackson, in a way that infuriates him further.

"Solomon? That's a Jew name. What the hell are you doing with a Jew name?" Laughs Jackson.

"You know, what the trouble is now days? It's people like you Mr. Fink, who persist in encouraging these people. They get real uppity when they get an education, and that's what is tearing at the moral fabric of this country," says Jackson.

"Mr. Jackson I think this meeting is just about over," insists Fink.

"You got something you want to add to that boy? Or maybe you only speak your tongue," says Jackson.

"Do you know where the term prairie nigger comes from? Johnson asks. Solomon looks down, shakes his head in disbelief.

"The Native American language doesn't contain such a word, or term," says Solomon, looking at Fink.

"However, our language does, contain a word that can mean excrement. Although I've not used that particular word in such a manner, I feel in your case it would be highly appropriate to denote the term as so much brain matter," says Solomon, looking down on Johnson.

Fink quickly stands to move between them just as Jackson quickly gets to his feet.

"You should shave your head, that curly yellow hair of yours looks an awful lot like wool," adds Solomon. Fink holds up a halting hand, and Solomon complies.

"As I said, we will be in touch, Mr. Jackson," says Fink with convicting tone. Jackson gives a hard stare into Solomon's smiling eyes.

"You better watch your back boy," threatens Jackson. Solomon stifles a laugh as Jackson walks towards the door.

"Something I said?" Solomon asks. They remain standing as Jackson exits the cocktail lounge. Solomon mocks a stupid look.

"Fink slash Joaquin Publishing Company. What do you think of that?" Fink asks.

"I like the sound of that. I'll give it some serious thought, after I receive my law degree. Can I edit Mr. Jackson's book? Solomon says jokingly.

"Well of course, but only after you quit going to those Klan meetings," says Fink.

"Go sit on a blanket? Where do these idiots get that stuff?" he asks.

"I don't know, maybe his sister writes the material for him. Come on son, lets go get Anne and celebrate the week end. Fink places money on the table and they start for the door.

Outside and from above the city street, they can be seen on the sidewalk.

"You don't know how happy it makes me feel. Next year you will be graduating from USC, Counselor. It's been an incredible journey. You're going to make your people very proud of you, Solomon," says Fink, into Solomon's smiling eyes.

"After the passing of your grandfather, I was at odds about returning you to the Indian school, and even though you were ten years old, there was determination in your voice, and it was undeniable," says Fink.

"Seems like yesterday, quite a little general wasn't I?" Solomon asks as he hangs his arm over Fink's shoulder. "You want to know something uncle?" Solomon says as they continue to walk.

"I am going to make a difference. Thanks to you and Auntie Ann, I'll be able to make good the promise I gave to my grandfather. I know he wanted me to return to Lone Pine armed with knowledge, truth, and full of life. He is in my heart, keeping alive the vision of a life that awaits us all. On this day they are dancing in the sky, and the dance is for you uncle," says Solomon. *The Sky Dancer*.

THE END

44915852R00166

Made in the USA
Charleston, SC
08 August 2015